THE LAST WITNESS

A D.C.I. Daley Thriller

Denzil Meyrick

First published in Great Britain in 2014 by Polygon, an imprint of Birlinn Ltd.
Birlinn Ltd
West Newington House
10 Newington Road
Edinburgh
EH9 1QS
www.polygonbooks.co.uk

6

ISBN 978 1 84697 288 1
eBook ISBN 978 0 85790 800 1

British Library Cataloguing-in-Publication Data
A catalogue record for this book is available on request from the British Library.

Typeset by Hewer Text (UK) Ltd

*This book is dedicated to the memory of my wife
Fiona's parents, Norman and Illeene MacLeod,
both of whom, sadly, died before its completion.*

'And if you gaze for long into an abyss,
the abyss gazes also into you . . .'

Friedrich Nietzsche

Prologue

He lay back on the trolley as though it was a poolside lounger, cushioned from the motion of the ambulance as it rattled and bumped its way through the Glasgow traffic.

He was aware of the young prison officer, manacled to him by a sturdy pair of handcuffs, stealing furtive looks in his direction. The older officer sitting near the door of the vehicle was chatting to a pretty nurse, his bluff demeanour at odds with her worried face. The woman's nervous laugh at the lame jokes she was forced to listen to bore witness to the fact that she was well outside her comfort zone.

As the journey continued, his young guard offered him a stick of chewing gum, which he refused with an expressionless shake of the head. The older officer stopped what he was saying as the nurse searched in her bag for something – no doubt in order to save herself from further exposure to his coarse humour.

Outside the blackened windows of the vehicle a horn sounded – then another. There was a screeching of brakes, the sounds of a collision. He was flung against his keeper as the ambulance swerved and came to a sudden stop.

There was a scream, and he heard shots being fired. At his feet, the nurse was trying to pick herself off the floor, blood gushing from her nose. The older prison officer was talking hurriedly into a radio as his colleague called out to him in panic, tugging at the rigid handcuffs that bound him tight to his captive.

There was a bang – a deep thud almost too low to hear – as the rear doors of the ambulance splintered inwards in a metallic clash of plastic and steel. He saw a shard of metal imbed itself in the face of the nurse. She looked bewildered, her whole body shaking, as she lifted a trembling hand to her cheek.

Then they appeared: two men squeezing through the ragged hole created by the explosion. Both in black, their faces were masked with balaclavas, and automatic weapons were slung over their shoulders with black webbing straps.

He smiled.

The older prison officer was forcing himself into a corner of the vehicle as though willing himself through its sides and out into the street. One of the gunmen stood over him and released a rapid burst of fire at point-blank range.

He stared at the sliver of grey-haired scalp that now slipped down the darkened window of the ambulance.

The nurse retched at the feet of the other gunman, who kicked her mercilessly in the head. The woman gasped and choked, spitting blood and teeth onto the ambulance floor.

The young officer, still manacled to him, face smeared with his colleague's blood and gore, stared down at her. The first gunman pushed his gun into his stomach and pulled the trigger.

For a split second he thought his arm was going to be pulled from its socket as the handcuffs were jerked by the death throes of his captor.

'Get me out of here!' He could barely hear his own voice; whether his hearing had been affected by panic or his proximity to the gunshots in the confined space, he didn't know.

The first gunman stood over him, then with one hand pulled the balaclava up to reveal most of his face. His smile was strangely familiar, yet entirely foreign.

A terrible fear gripped his heart a split second before his head was blown apart.

1

Five years later, Melbourne, Australia

Wet days in Melbourne were not unusual, but this one, he thought, was particularly miserable.

He looked out over his lush garden as heavy drops of rain splattered onto the jacaranda trees. His grandchildren's toys were scattered on the neat lawn; a riot of dolls' prams, small bicycles and balls of varying size and shape. A climbing frame stood sentinel by a mammoth trampoline, which was in turn faced by a set of swings.

For a moment he recalled his own childhood. The playground in Paisley's Gallowhill was the haunt of bored teenagers drinking tonic wine, drug dealers and the occasional prostitute. The ground was habitually littered with used syringes, broken glass and dog faeces. He shuddered.

Soon the rain would be gone and the warm sun would bring the children of Ringwood East back out to play. That's how the weather went in this country, though the dark clouds looked threatening at the moment. The suburb was really a small distinct town to the east of the city, a magnet for those with ambition and aspiration. With its good schools, safe surroundings and green open spaces, children could be children and adults could seek refuge from an uncertain, dangerous world in their generously proportioned air-conditioned homes, pools and basement gymnasia.

He supposed that at forty-four he was young to have three grandchildren, but he didn't regret it. His daughter – like himself – had been an early starter in the race to parenthood, becoming a proud mother of two before she was out of her teens. His wife had managed to persuade her to join them in Australia when her arsehole of a boyfriend, Andy Lafferty, himself a foot soldier in the Machie clan, had taken up with another poor, impressionable soul, leaving her literally high and dry in a dingy Glasgow multi-storey. It had been a conversation that should not have taken place; however, it had, and the end result pleased him.

In the two years since her arrival, she had fallen in love, got married and had another kid. Her husband was a young civil engineer, neat, sober and kind; a man with prospects, who didn't mind taking the place of a father who lived thousands of miles away. This, of course, assuming he was still alive. Those involved in the seedy side of life in Scotland's largest city often had short, meaningless existences – their bodies ruined by drink, drugs, or both – at the mercy of the deprivation and violence that stalked those on the margins of society.

No great loss.

That could have been his life. He had been sucked into the world of crime when he was still at school. It started with a bit of shoplifting in Woolies and the wee sweetie shop down the road, and was followed by opportunist theft from cars, pockets or broken windows. Dealing and extortion followed, by which time he was part of a sophisticated, organised crime family, built along the lines of a terrorist cell structure to protect those at the top from the police, as well as from those at the bottom. He'd often found himself wondering if the guy in the expensive suit driving the German sports car was the fabled Mr Big to whom they all owed their allegiance, or just another wanker working for a bank. But he hadn't really cared; he had plenty of cash, more than most of the poor sods he had been at school with, even the clever ones. He had that imperceptible quality too, something that couldn't be bought and that brought him fear and respect. He could walk down the street confident in the knowledge that everybody knew his name and what he was capable of. As he rose through the ranks, the names and faces that populated the Faustian inner sanctum became clearer. Soon, he became one of them.

And now? Well, now he was sure that, apart from his family, none of the ten thousand or so citizens of Ringwood East had the slightest idea who he was. That was the way he liked it. A change of identity had helped, but, hey, that was surely the least a grateful nation could have done. The information he had given to the police had seen the conviction of over fifty hardened criminals; some of them the most dangerous men in Europe.

Now he had all of this – the beautiful garden, the pool, the gym, a small business to keep the dosh rolling in – everything he could want. Happy families: apart from, of course, the one left behind in the decaying hinterland of Glasgow.

He awoke on his recliner with a dry mouth and thick head just after four p.m. He must have dozed off. His wife would be home soon, anxious to wash the office off with a dip in the pool and a gin and tonic – a residue of the UK she hadn't managed to shed.

Marna – he could only think of her by that name – dealt with the business. When necessary, he would intervene in any difficult negotiations, or should one of the many delivery drivers they employed become restive. After a contretemps with a rough Queenslander, most of the workers soon learned that their Scottish boss was not to be messed with; visits to their former colleague as he languished in hospital had served as a blunt reminder. As with everything though, there would always be some Jack the Lad ready to try his luck. It was the way of the world, he supposed.

He ambled over to the drinks cabinet, removing the gin for Marna and the Ardbeg for himself. Leaving her bottle on the side, he held his glass under the integrated ice dispenser and, yawning as the cubes clunked into the squat tumbler, popped the cork of the whisky bottle and poured himself a gentleman's measure. He held the single malt to his nose, breathing in the spirit's distinctive iodine aroma.

Here's tae ye, Bonnie Scotland. Stick it up yer arse.

He raised his glass and smiled at the toast that had become a daily mantra. Outside, the clouds were growing darker; it looked like Marna would have to forego her swim and find solace solely in the gin, or perhaps a workout in the basement gym. He sighed and gulped down another mouthful of the whisky at the same moment as the doorbell rang.

'Mair shit fae Amazon,' he muttered, looking at the outline of the tall figure behind the glass-panelled front door. He had to fiddle with the chain and double locks before he was able to turn the large brass handle and swing the door open.

'Good tae see yer keepin' yer door locked, Gerald.'

7

The whisky glass dropped from his hand and onto the thick carpet as he tried to close the door. His visitor, though, was faster, and shouldered his way into the hall, knocking him against the wall.

The pain of the first strike of the machete on his unprotected skull sent flashes through his eyes, his left arm into convulsions, and weakened his knees. The second strike was less painful, his senses dulling as he slid down the wall of his hallway. After the third, he neither thought nor felt any more.

Calmly, his attacker dropped the murder weapon and, leaving the front door open and the dead man in full view of any passing neighbour, bounded down the front steps and along the path to his parked 4x4.

He opened the boot. Inside, Marna lay on her side, trussed in a kneeling position with her wrists tied to her ankles behind her back. The thick duct tape plastered over her mouth prevented her from crying out, allowing only the quietest whimper. Tears flowed from her wide, terrified eyes, mascara running into the mucus from her nose. Roughly, he pulled on the ropes that bound her, letting her fall from the car onto the road. Her scream of pain sounded only faintly behind the plastic tape. The woman's head throbbed and her vision blurred. She could feel the rain on her skin; for some reason her mind scrolled back to a trip to miserably wet Largs when she had been a child – she could clearly see her mother's face.

He bent forward and pulled the sobbing woman up onto her knees, then grabbed her roughly by her long peroxide-blonde hair to make sure she was looking along the pathway and up the three front steps to her home. She breathed heavily through her nose, partly through fear and partly necessity, as mucus was beginning to block her nasal passages.

'There ye are darlin'.' His voice was calm, and strangely unfamiliar now that she had become accustomed to the Aussie twang. 'Just thought I'd gie ye a wee look at yer man. No' at his best the now, eh?' He tugged at her hair again as silent sobs racked her body.

He pulled up his jacket and removed a handgun from the waistband of his trousers.

She thought of her mother again: her hand wiping the rain from her face on the Largs seafront, holding her close to keep her dry.

'Cheerio, ye fuckin' pair o' rats.'

The one shot from the pistol sent its report echoing down the quiet suburban street and a bullet into her temple.

He walked slowly back to the car, pausing to look up and grin at something unseen before jumping into the driver's seat and speeding away, tyres squealing on the wet tarmac.

The dead woman's eyes stared blankly at the ground on which she knelt, face down, all memories gone.

2

His heart thudded against his chest in an alarming way, causing nearly as much discomfort as the tight boots on his feet.

'We're nearly there, darling.' Her voice was clear; she was not in the least out of breath. 'Another ten minutes and we'll get a seat and open the flask.'

'I . . .' His breathing was laboured. 'I . . .'

'Don't try to speak until we stop, love, or you might not get there at all,' she giggled. 'It'll be worth it in the end – you'll see.' She bounded ahead as he stopped yet again to gulp down lungfuls of cold air.

Half an hour later he was beginning to feel just about normal. They were sitting atop a grassy mound at the summit of Ben Saarnie, a modest hill that overlooked Kinloch. The town lay before them in miniature: traffic, buildings and busy-looking people, almost like toys at this remove. He realised what a local he was becoming as he found himself able to recognise some of the cars and vans, picturing their occupants. Never let it be said that Jim Daley is not observant, he thought.

'This was the site of an Iron Age fort, you know.' She was taking photographs with an expensive digital camera. 'Strange to think that hundreds of years ago people stood right here, breathing this air, just being alive. Don't you think, darling?'

At that exact moment, all of his concentration was focused upon removing a Penguin chocolate biscuit from its packaging, his reward for the struggle up the hill. So he employed his habitual reply when he had not quite heard what had been said: something between a grunt and a word, ambiguous enough to be taken as the answer of someone who was actually paying attention.

'I think I'll get my tits out; it's a really liberating feeling at this height.' She smiled as she watched his continued attempt to get at the confectionery.

At last! He had broken into the wrapper and thought he better reply before he set about the contents. 'Absolutely, Liz, aye.' He then devoured half of the biscuit with one bite.

'You've not been listening again,' she said, with an I-told-you-so intonation.

'Eh? Wha' you say?' He spat out a few crumbs as he looked up at her, his mouth full of chocolate.

'Nothing, Jim,' she laughed, putting the viewfinder back to her eye. 'Just you enjoy some more empty calories.'

Suddenly the biscuit tasted sour in his mouth. This little hike was part of the fitness campaign that his wife had so generously devised for him. She reckoned that with regular exercise and an excruciatingly austere dietary regime, he could lose at least four stones before the spring. This was week three, and despite enormous blisters on his feet and a gnawing hunger that never abated, he had managed to shed only a paltry two pounds.

Undeterred, his spouse had shrugged her shoulders at the most recent weigh-in on their newly acquired bathroom scales and declared: 'The first few pounds are always the toughest. After that it's plain sailing.'

He wondered how she was so sure of this. In the many years he had known her she hadn't put on an ounce of weight and had never, *ever*, been on a diet. However, to please her, and to bask in the joy of virtuousness, he continued to suffer the sore feet and rumbling stomach. Yuletide beckoned though, with its temptations of calorific indulgence and general sloth, never mind the immersion in various types of alcohol. He tried not to think about it.

The air was cold and exhilarating as they trudged down the hill. Daley's knees throbbed in time to the rumble of his poorly nourished belly. There seemed to be a kind of blueness in the air, framing everything in a light that could only be that of a Scottish early winter. The still water of the sea loch below appeared more viscous than it should as it reflected the winter landscape; the scene was calm and glorious. Daley hadn't noticed all of this on the way up, concentrating as he had been on reaching the summit without expiring, but he had to admit that his surroundings – and even, to some extent, the experience of hill walking – were stimulating. Was he beginning to fall into step with his wife's pursuits at last?

Well, one step at a time.

Daley's car was parked on a patch of waste ground near the farm gate that led to the hill. The new Toyota RAV4 had come with his new title of Chief Inspector, Sub-Divisional CID, as well as Sub-Divisional Commander (Acting), Kinloch, Y Div.

He had just found the car keys in the depths of his new ski jacket – XXL, very expensive and a present from Liz – when he heard the tinkle of his new iPhone, another trapping of his elevated job status. Strapping himself into the driver's seat with one hand, he took the device from his pocket with the other, squinting at the screen to see that he had an email from his distant superior, Superintendent John Donald.

'Hang on, please, Liz. I better take a swatch at this.' As his wife sighed, he remembered how to retrieve emails and started to read.

From: Supt. J. Donald.
To: Chief Insp. J. Daley
Subject: Killing, Australia
Message: Thoughts – ASAP

Daley clicked on the attachment and the banner of the *Melbourne Star* newspaper burst into view. He slid his finger down the screen until the bold headline was revealed: COUPLE BUTCHERED IN CITY SUBURB. Then the byline: *Husband and wife business team executed in broad daylight.*

Daley scrolled further down, wondering what this distant murder had to do with him. But when two fuzzy, passport-style photographs slid into view, all confusion was immediately banished. His audible gasp attracted a questioning look from his wife, now fidgeting in the passenger seat.

'Fucking hell', was all he could say. 'Fucking hell.'

3

The Semper Vigilo logo flickered on the outsized screen mounted on the wall of Kinloch Police Office's dedicated audiovisual room.

'That's it, sir. The boss should be on in a couple of minutes.' DC Dunn had just connected an internal Skype call to headquarters in Paisley. 'Just give me a shout when you're finished and I'll log off.' She smiled as she stood up, flattening the front of her trousers in the way Daley had become accustomed to in the last few months.

'Thanks. Any chance of a coffee? Or is that a sexist request you're not prepared to comply with?' He smiled at the young policewoman, who made a face at him as she left the room.

There was a faint *ding* from somewhere, and the logo was replaced by the familiar figure of Superintendent John Donald, sitting behind his desk and speaking to someone out of shot, unaware that he was being watched by his long-suffering DCI.

'Where did you pick up these skills, Jackie?' He was smiling unctuously at the unseen figure. 'Buggered if I can get anything out of the damned thing. Don't suppose you fancy giving me a quick tutorial after work? Over a drink or two perhaps?'

Daley coughed diplomatically, making his boss jump in surprise.

'Ah, Jim. Silent but deadly, as always. As you no doubt heard, I'm trying to get to grips with this new technology. I sincerely hope that you're doing your bit in this regard? You got the new phone-i-thing, I take it?'

'Yes, I've got the phone-i-thing, thanks,' was Daley's curt answer. It's not the technology you're trying to get to grips with, you old lech, he thought. 'I'm afraid I haven't worked out how to perform a virtual knock yet,' he said, smiling into the camera.

'Yes, well, no doubt an issue of protocol with which we will have to deal.' Daley could see that his superior was trying to contain his embarrassment. 'Anyhow, to business. My time is precious, as I'm sure yours is, to a certain extent. As big a shock for you as it was for me, I don't doubt?'

Daley raised his eyebrows, adjusting to the sudden change to the real subject of their call. 'You could say that, sir.'

Donald looked at something on his desk. 'Well, I'm afraid that's not the only shock you have in store.' He smiled back from the large screen.

Daley had mixed feelings about this kind of virtual meeting with Donald. On the upside, he didn't have to suffer his close presence, but seeing Donald framed on the massive screen made Daley feel that he was having a conversation with some sort of minor deity.

'As you know,' Donald continued, 'Gerry and Marna Dowie were partly responsible for one of the biggest successes we've ever had against organised crime in this country.' He looked back into the camera, prompting Daley to nod obediently.

'And then they were killed in a car accident on one of the Costas, while in witness protection – or so we were led to believe,' said Daley.

'Yes, apparently their security was compromised in Spain, so this ruse was thought up as a cover. A new life down under.'

'Which clearly didn't work.' Daley sat back in his chair, remembering the pictures from the crime scene that Donald had emailed him. The violence was sickening and brutal; the fact that it had taken place in a suburban street in the middle of the afternoon made it seem even worse.

'Our colleagues in Melbourne are no strangers to gangland violence, but I'm told even they were shocked, not just by the crime, but also the audacity with which it was carried out.' Donald had raised his right eyebrow, indicating to Daley, who had known him for a long time, that he agreed.

'I suppose our connection to all of this is pretty tenuous now though?' Daley was anxious to cut to the chase.

'No. Not at all, I'm afraid to say.'

Daley's heart sank.

'For a start, you and DS Scott were instrumental to the case that brought the Machie family down.'

How could I forget? thought Daley.

'And of course, certain threats were made to you personally, from the dock, if I remember correctly.' Donald smiled again, as though to drive this point home to his DCI.

The trial of the key members of the Machie family and their associates had gone down in history as one of the most successful blows to organised crime ever administered in the UK, one that exposed the tendrils of the family's empire from Aberdeen to Exeter.

The case was mainly predicated on testimony from long-time gang member Gerald Dowie and his mentor, Frank MacDougall, two of Scotland's most notorious criminals. Both men had been part of the Machie clan for many years; it had been their arrest by Daley and Scott, and subsequent deals with the fiscal that had seen them enter the witness protection programme with immunity from prosecution, in return for providing information leading to the capture of senior members of the crime organisation.

Their evidence was spectacular. Top men like Gavin Nash and Danny Whitaker were set to spend most of the rest of their lives behind bars. And, the jewel in the crown, self-styled Godfather James 'JayMac' Machie was sent down to serve no less than five life sentences. Daley could still see him as he vowed vengeance on both himself and Scott, his face a study of absolute, cold hatred, as he was being taken down at Glasgow's High Court.

'Now hang on, Jim, I want you to take a look at this.' Daley could see his boss fumble with something on his desk, then suddenly the ample cleavage of Donald's assistant filled the screen.

'Ah, well done, my dear.' Donald's face was just visible over her shoulder. 'Tell me what you think.' Daley assumed that he was not referring to the plunging neckline, which had now disappeared.

The screen went black momentarily, to be replaced by a black-and-white image of a street filled with large houses. A 4x4 sped up the road and came to a halt. A darkly dressed figure left the vehicle and disappeared from view. Daley noticed the clock on the top right of the image: 16:11, 28 November.

Time ticked by, and Daley was about to protest that nothing was happening, when the dark figure re-emerged from the right-hand side. The man disappeared behind the back of the vehicle and the tailgate was thrust upwards. Daley could see the car rocking slightly, then, to the bottom right of the picture, a blurred image appeared. Daley took a heartbeat to realise that it was a person's head he had seen bounce off the pavement. During the next few seconds, the hardened police officer felt his bile rise and he had to look away.

Despite the blurred quality of the image, the explosion of the victim's head was all too clear; the fact that the body remained in the kneeling position as the shattered head dripped gore onto the roadway made the scene even more grisly.

The dark figure walked towards the driver's side of the car, this time facing the camera. He looked up and smiled. The screen, and Daley's heart, froze in the same instant. 'It can't be, sir. The likeness is startling, but . . . it just can't be.'

'I understand your shock, Jim.' Donald's voice was disembodied; the freeze-frame image still filled the large screen. 'As you can see, the boffins have cleaned it up and the resemblance is uncanny.'

'It can't be, sir,' Daley repeated, staring open mouthed at the image.

Donald's face gave nothing away. 'It gets worse, I'm afraid. There's something else.'

Something else? Daley, suddenly aware his mouth was gaping, shut it with a snap of teeth, making one of his fillings ache in protest.

'Something very sensitive; so much so, it's not something I can risk broadcasting on this . . .' Donald made an airy gesture with his hand towards the camera. 'Foolishly perhaps, I have entrusted vital information to your peripatetic sidekick; he'll bring it to Kinloch tomorrow. Needless to say, this information is highly confidential. Read everything, then we'll talk some more.' He looked to his right. 'I have a meeting in Edinburgh in two hours – this single Scottish police force nonsense – so I have to dash. Good luck, Jim, and let me know when you've digested it all.' He gave a forced smile, then, before Daley could open his mouth, the screen went blank and was replaced once again by the Semper Vigilo logo.

As he watched DC Dunn walk towards him with a mug of coffee Daley experienced a disturbing, out-of-body feeling.

He had never been afraid of ghosts – until now.

4

Daley had been sitting in his glass box within Kinloch's CID room for what seemed like hours. He had resisted the urge to call DS Scott the previous evening, after his virtual meeting with Donald. He would discover the horrible truth soon enough, he thought.

Daley was a man who rarely felt frightened, but his experiences with the Machie family, especially JayMac, had caused him to experience the emotion acutely. It was not unusual for police officers to place themselves in danger's way; in fact, it was an all too regular occurrence. More often than not the violence erupted suddenly, giving the cop little time to fret on personal safety. However, the levels of premeditated violence and downright depravity deployed by the notorious crime family in the running of their empire was, quite rightly, a factor that anyone who had dealings with them had been forced to take into account.

When JayMac and his associates had been at large, the job of every police officer in Glasgow was a much more difficult and dangerous affair. They had worked tirelessly to get a break – some vital piece of information that they could use to unravel the labyrinthine knot of evil over which the gang presided.

In the end it wasn't a member of one of the dedicated squads of detectives who had cracked the case, nor was it a senior officer or member of UK security services. Daley's right-hand man, a humble divisional DS, was responsible for the downfall of the clan.

DS Brian Scott had made the connection between a string of construction companies throughout the UK and the Machie crime organisation. Large plant vehicles such as cranes and diggers had been used to distribute hard drugs, cash and firearms around the country. When was the last time a cop stopped a low-loader bearing a huge piece of construction machinery? The answer was simple: never. More embarrassment was to come when various police forces realised that not only had they failed to detect this scam, they had actually provided officers to escort these 'abnormal loads' all over Britain's motorway network.

Daley recalled JayMac's sneer as this evidence was read out in court. For years, hundreds of the country's boys in blue had inadvertently been making sure that the Machie family's business operated smoothly.

He looked down at the notepad on which he had been absently doodling. Without realising, he had sketched a rough cross on the page. A cross very like the one fashioned in granite that stood sentinel over a grave in a Glasgow cemetery. He quickly banished the thought from his mind.

He was trying to focus on a report he was writing, detailing the evidence against a local farmer who had been distributing illegal tobacco, when the glass of his door was rattled by a knock. Despite the blinds, Daley recognised the formal tap-tap-tap that announced his DS.

'How ye doin', Jim?' Scott stuck his head around the door. 'Sorry,' he said, looking over his shoulder, '*sir*. Not tae worry, it's only thon wee lassie, Dunn, in the office, an' she looks like she's fully occupied on the computer. Lucky her.' Though a talented detective, IT specialist he was not.

'Come in, Brian.' Daley stood up from his large swivel chair. 'How was your trip?'

'How d'ye think? Fuckin' terrible, as per usual. I'm goin' tae ask his majesty if he'll no' think aboot payin' me doon on the plane. That road wid try the patience o' a saint. Ye never think yer goin' tae get here, nae matter how often ye drive it. Ma arse is fair achin'.' He rubbed his backside by way of emphasis.

Daley pulled the guest chair out from the other side of his large desk, and indicated to Scott he was welcome to take a seat. 'I'll get you a coffee, bit early for something stronger. You can get a wee dram down at the County later. Annie will be pleased to see you, no doubt.'

A smile crossed Scott's face. 'I cannae say I'm no' looking forward tae a wee whisky, right enough. That's the reason they drink so much doon here, they're always worried aboot havin' tae drive back up that fuckin' road.'

Daley sat back down. He wasn't sure how much Scott knew. He leaned forward, looking his friend in the eye.

'It's OK, Jim.' Scott spoke before he did. 'I know whit yer aboot tae tell me.'

'You do?' Daley was surprised.

'Aye, of course. You don't think his majesty wiz able tae pull the wool o'er my eyes fir long? Anyhow, wan o' the new DCs fae Springburn heard a' aboot it in the pub.'

'I must say, Brian, you're taking it all very calmly,' said Daley. He wasn't particularly surprised that Glasgow's underworld was already in possession of the information that Donald thought so essentially secret.

'I daresay.' Scott shrugged. 'But at the end o' the day, it's no' as though I wiz wan o' Gerry Dowie's big fans, as I'm sure ye appreciate, Jim.'

Daley looked at his nonchalant DS. His unconventional approach to most problems sometimes made him very hard to fathom, though it was probably part of what made him such an effective police officer.

'And what about our other friend, Brian?'

'She wiz a nice enough lassie,' said Scott. 'I knew her before she got hersel' in tow wi' that arsehole, you know.'

'Who?' Daley was surprised by the reply.

'His wife, och, whit's her name again?' Scott looked to the ceiling for inspiration.

'I wasn't meaning her, Brian. I was talking about the murderer.' It dawned on Daley that Scott's network of informants was not keeping him as well briefed as he thought.

'Oh, so they've got a body a'ready? Quick workers, these Aussies. Well done.'

Daley closed his eyes and sighed. He hadn't been looking forward to this conversation.

'Whit's up, big man? Were ye oot on the batter last night? Yer as pale as a ghost.'

How apt, Daley thought. There was nothing else for it. He opened a drawer in his desk and took a red file from it, handing it across to Scott without comment.

'I hate it when ye dae this tae me, Jim.' Scott took the file and opened it, turning it on its end when he realised that the A4 image within was upside down. He screwed up his eyes and peered down at the picture. 'Wait a minute.' He searched the inside pocket of his jacket and fished out what looked like a brand new glasses case.

'Auld age comes tae us a', Jimmy-boy. It'll no' be long until you get a pair o' these an' a', especially wi' a' that reading ye dae when yer at hame. At least I gie ma eyes a rest when I'm no' workin'.' He donned the glasses, scrutinised the picture and dropped it instantly.

'If this is your idea o' a wee joke, let me tell ye, ye've come away wi' much better.' Scott's face had taken on a pallid hue.

'I know it's hard to take in. I've only just found out yesterday, myself. That is a video still of the murderer of Gerald Dowie and his wife, taken outside their home straight after the killings.' He felt sorry for Scott, who was now visibly shaken.

'It cannae be, just cannae . . .' Scott started to massage his right shoulder with his left hand, wincing slightly. 'Ye know, I've no' felt a peep oot o' this fir mair than three years. Just wan look at that face an' the thing's throbbing like f—' He was stopped by a knock at the door and the emergence of DC Dunn, bearing two steaming mugs of coffee.

'Thought you might like some coffee after your drive, sarge,' she said cheerfully. 'Oh, sorry for interrupting,' she added, noticing the serious expression on her superiors' faces.

'It's OK, lassie.' Scott rarely let anyone leave with a sore heart; unless they deserved to. 'Mebbe this'll keep me fae keelin' o'er. Eh, Jim?'

Dunn made her excuses then left, closing the door quietly behind her.

'Nae sign o' a biscuit, neither,' said Scott, looking down at his coffee.

'Here.' Daley opened another drawer of his desk, removing a bottle of malt whisky. 'I think you need that dram now, Brian.'

'Aye,' he said, taking the bottle and removing the cork with a soft pop, then pouring a measure into his coffee until the mug very nearly overflowed.

'It's no' just the fact that bastard shot me, Jim.' Scott looked up, putting the steaming mug to his lips. Daley noted a slight tremor in his hand, which sent a drip of the whisky coffee down the side of the white mug. After a loud slurp, Scott put the mug down, letting out a long sigh. 'Jim, we went tae his funeral. I saw him trundling doon the conveyor belt at the crematorium. He's deid!'

5

Daley watched as Scott poured another hefty measure of whisky into his mug; there was no need for coffee now, the spirit was all that was required.

They didn't talk for a few minutes; they didn't have to. Both knew what the other was thinking. It had been an unremittingly hard task to break the Machie family: dangerous, frightening, but ultimately successful. How could the spectre from their worst nightmares have cheated the grave and reappeared on a quiet Australian street? The sneer aimed by the murderer at the CCTV camera as he left the scene of horror in Ringwood East was burned onto Daley's memory. Like every murder case he had been involved in: the sight of his mother lying dead in her bed; the face of a child suffocated with a pillow by a drunken father; like – like all too many scenes from Jim Daley's career that played out unbidden before his mind's eye.

'I've got a top secret file fir you fae his majesty, Jim.' Scott jolted Daley from his thoughts.

'Yes, he told me,' the DCI said wearily. 'I don't know what's in it, but it can't be any worse than what we know already. Can it?' Daley looked into Scott's face for the confirmation he knew he wouldn't get.

'Efter the day, I widnae be surprised by anything. Elvis is likely buskin' doon the street.' Scott's weak attempt at humour told Daley how much he had been affected by the revelations. 'Gie me a second. I'll just nip oot tae the car an' get it.'

'I hope this won't be like my promotion. Remember?' Daley recalled how his sergeant had managed to lose a letter informing him that he had been promoted to Chief Inspector. Was that really only a few short months ago? It seemed like years.

'Nah, dinnae worry. I thought he wiz goin' tae make me chain it tae my wrist. He left me in nae doubt how important it wiz. I stuck it under my seat.' Scott left for the car park.

Daley eyed the bottle of whisky, still sitting on his desk. He had never really been a heavy drinker, though there had been times when he had resorted to the bottle in an attempt to anaesthetise himself against life. He supposed that he was lucky not to have the kind of personality that lent itself to addiction. Many of his colleagues, past and present, struggled with alcohol.

'Fuck's sake.' Daley's glass door burst open, revealing a flushed DS Scott. 'Ye'll need tae gie me a hand here, Jim. The bloody file's slipped under the seat an' I cannae reach it. You'll get it wi' they long arms o' yours.'

Scott had driven down in his own divisional CID car, a vehicle that was easy to recognise, adorned as it was with small bumps and scrapes and almost camouflaged by a thick layer of dirt. It was no better inside: overflowing ashtrays added to the stench of stale tobacco smoke, and the floor looked like the object of an ardent recycler's dream, littered with empty crisp and cigarette packets, Styrofoam coffee cups, a half-uneaten pie, and various other objects which remained unidentifiable.

'Right, if ye can just get yer hand in here.' Scott grimaced as he opened the car door and bent down, probing under the driver's seat with an outstretched arm. 'I can get my fingertips tae it, but I cannae get any purchase on the bloody thing.'

'Move over.' Daley ushered his DS out of the way. 'This car just gets worse every time I see it. Have Health and Safety not been on your back?'

'No, but yer man asked fir a lift intae the toon the other day,' said Scott, referring to Superintendent Donald. 'He wiz away tae some reception or other.'

'I'm sure he was chuffed,' said Daley.

'No' really. Anyhow, we got tae Back Sneddon Street, and he telt me tae stop, an' fucked off an' caught the train. Needless tae say, I got a memo aboot it the next day,' Scott declared with a resigned look.

'The contents of which you no doubt took onboard and complied with to the letter?'

'Nah, I flung it in the bin. I've mair tae dae than valet cars – I thought you'd appreciate that mair than anyone, Jim.' Scott looked nonplussed.

Daley raised his eyebrows and smiled involuntarily, kneeling down at the side of the car and reaching under the driver's seat. Sure enough, he could feel the edge of the file, just in reach.

'Nearly got it, Brian,' he said, his face reddening with the strain.

'Gaun yersel, big fella, I knew ye wid be able tae get it wi' they arms o' yours,' he said by way of encouragement. 'Wan last push an' ye'll have it.'

Daley's arm was aching, but he stretched his hand as far forward as possible, managing to catch the edge of the file between his forefinger and thumb. He pulled it out from under the seat and, at the same moment, felt fresh air ventilate his backside as, with a glorious ripping noise straight out of the sound-effects department, his trousers split magnificently.

He stood up, out of breath, then wordlessly handed Scott the file with a flat-lipped expression.

'Well done, Jim. I knew ye wid dae it.' Scott smiled as he took the file, marked 'Highly Confidential', from Daley. 'Another pair o' breeks away. Just as well ye got that promotion – troosers dinnae come cheap these days.'

Daley looked at him through narrowed eyes. 'Don't say another word, Brian.' He turned on his heel and headed back into the office, holding his torn trousers together at the back with his left hand. Scott followed, chuckling to himself.

Daley broke the seal on the file with a penknife that he kept in his drawer. As he was doing this he regretted not putting away the bottle of whisky, as Scott was now helping himself to another large measure. There was no doubt about it, Scott was rattled – more than he cared to show.

The file was reasonably slim, though began with a cover page emphasising its secrecy and how it should be disseminated, as well as the consequences of any revelation, even inadvertent, of the contents therein. There were also instructions detailing how the content should be stored once read, something Daley had never seen before.

'C'mon, Jimmy-boy, gie us the bad news.' Scott's eyes had taken on a bleary look, no doubt caused by nearly a half bottle of single malt. Through his shirt, he was massaging the scar that JayMac's bullet had left in his shoulder.

Daley knew he was in trouble when he saw the first page of the file. Under a banner that read Her Majesty's Home

Office Witness Protection Programme, a black-and-white photograph of a man who looked to be in his mid fifties stared at the camera with a flat, almost disdainful expression.

There was no mistaking Frank MacDougall.

Daley read on, aware that Scott was employing his famous ability to read upside down nearly as quickly as he could normally. Most of the information was familiar; he knew how MacDougall and Dowie had turned on their former partners in crime in return for immunity from prosecution, consequently bringing down the entire organisation. There were details of the trial and the threats that had been made to the witnesses and police officers, including himself and Scott.

He then came to the section he knew nothing about.

After the trials of the major players behind the Machie family were over and the accused – to a man – sent down for various terms not less than twenty-five years, the problem of what to do with MacDougall and Dowie presented itself.

Dowie was keen to get as far away from Scotland as possible, eschewing the offer of a new identity somewhere in the UK. In a way, this suited the authorities, who most certainly did not want what was left of the Machie organisation uniting to find and kill either of their nemeses. Even though Daley now knew his fate, the details of Dowie's placement formed no part of the information Donald wished to make him aware of, so had been redacted.

Frank MacDougall, however, was a very different matter. He had two sons and a daughter, all of whom had been threatened, so needed to be given a new life and identity too. MacDougall had turned down any offer of relocation abroad. Not only did he wish to stay in the UK, he wished to remain living in Scotland. Daley scanned the attempts that had been made to dissuade him from this decision, all to no avail. He had turned down Portugal, Turkey, even relocation to Sweden. Daley, on reading the lengths the British government were willing to go to protect their star witness, wondered – not for the first time – why he was doing the job he was. Would a grateful government resettle him and his entire family in a European destination of his choice with a self-filling bank account for the rest of his life? The answer was instant: no.

Daley merely grunted as Scott informed him that he was going to take a toilet break, and left his glass box.

He read on, to discover that MacDougall's oldest son, Cisco, had quickly tired of the safe house in which the family had been placed – on an ex-army base near London – and jumped the wall one night. He was found with his throat cut in the stairwell of a Glasgow tenement two days later. Daley was mildly surprised that he had heard nothing of this at the time, though reasoned that, because of the circumstances, the revenge killing had probably been covered up. The top men of the Machie family may have been out of the way behind bars, but their legacy lived on.

He turned another page, already feeling the tightness in his throat that presaged bad news.

Then, almost inevitably, there it was. Frank MacDougall's pleas to be relocated somewhere in Scotland had been reluctantly acceded to. He and his family had been given the new identity they had been promised, and sent to an isolated part of the mainland.

Frank MacDougall had been living on a farm only nine miles from Kinloch for the last five years.

Daley pushed the file away, rubbing his temples, trying to take everything in. As he was doing this, the door burst open, revealing his DS, who, not unusually, was swearing under his breath.

'See they fuckin' taps in that toilet,' he said, rubbing at a large dark patch that had spread over the front of his light brown trousers with a paper towel. 'As soon as ye turn the bloody things on, they go aff like a bloody geyser. I look as though I've pished mysel'.' He stopped rubbing when he saw the look on Daley's face and the discarded file lying on the desk before him.

'Sit down, Brian,' Daley said wearily. 'I've got something more to tell you that you're not going to like. Bring me that mug from the top of the filing cabinet, would you? I think I need a drink now.'

Both detectives sat nursing their coffee mugs of malt whisky in silence.

Daley could not believe that he was about to be flung back into what had been the most miserable time of his police career. He looked at Scott from under his brow; his friend was staring into his mug, swirling its contents around, deep in thought. Of all the police officers involved with the fight to bring JayMac and his crew to justice, they had loathed Brian Scott the most, and he had nearly paid the ultimate price for his efforts. Scott had grown up with many of the criminals, so in their minds, using the perverse logic that infused the criminal community, he was as big a rat as Dowie and MacDougall.

The shrill ring of the telephone made them both jump. Daley answered, to be informed by the internal operator that Donald was on the line. He OK'd the call, pressed the conference button on the keypad and held his finger to his lips in an attempt to prevent Scott from muttering his usual oaths while he was on the phone to their superior.

'Ah, Jim.' Donald's voice sounded loud in the glass box. 'I take it that Tweedle-Dum has managed to perform the simple task I placed before him?'

'Yes,' said Daley, winking at his scowling DS. 'In fact, he's sitting opposite me at the moment.'

Not in the slightest put off by this information, Donald continued seamlessly. 'I hope he's not smoking. I had the misfortune of having to travel half a mile in that coup of a car we foolishly let him drive – I very nearly died from a mixture of asphyxiation and botulism,' he said sarcastically, almost inducing Daley to a sudden outburst of laughter as Scott made an obscene gesture at the telephone.

'I've read and digested the contents, sir. Do you wish me to memorise and destroy?' Daley decided to deploy his own brand of sarcasm.

'I wouldn't have thought you'd consider this a laughing matter, Jim, especially since the prime target for the next horror killing is well and truly on your patch.'

Donald never failed to sound like a patronising schoolmaster, which always made Daley bridle. 'I'm beginning to realise why I'm here, sir,' he said, contempt thick in his voice.

'If you think I knew anything of this, Jim, you are mistaken. Fra—' Donald stopped suddenly, changing his mind. 'The subject's whereabouts were as much of a mystery to me as they were to you. In fact, I wish they still were.' Somehow Daley believed his boss's sincere tone. 'If it's any consolation, I have approached the witness protection programme to advise them that, under the current circumstances, he be moved to somewhere we have better resources. I await a reply.'

There was a silence between the men for a few moments before Daley spoke, sounding resigned. 'They won't do that, sir. They'll consider him as safe here with his cover as he's going to get.'

'You always were a pessimist, Jim. Anyhow, I want you to lock that file in the safe in the meantime, out of harm's way, so to speak. I've decided to come down tomorrow – we'll pay a visit to our old friend together.'

'Oh, that's just fuckin' great,' Scott murmured, forgetting that the call was in conference mode.

'And that will be quite enough analysis from you, DS Scott. Better you spend some time cleaning out that car of yours. I'm flying down in the morning, so I'll need the use of a vehicle. Make sure it's shipshape. Do I make myself clear?'

'Eh, aye, sir.' Scott shook his head with a grimace. 'I really meant, that's just whit we're needin', you know, tae gie us a hand an' that.' He smiled encouragingly, as though Donald might be able to see him through the phone.

'Bollocks,' was the rapid reply. 'Just you make sure you're at the airport at ten tomorrow, sharp, with a clean car.' There was a loud click as the phone in Donald's office was slammed down and the conversation with distant Kinloch was over.

'Pit ma foot right intae that, did I no', Jim?'

'Yup,' was Daley's concise but adequate answer. He got up from behind his desk and asked Scott to accompany him along the corridor to the safe. Scott dabbed the front of his trousers with the paper towel as they walked. DC Dunn couldn't hide the look of disgust on her face as they passed her in the corridor.

'Before ye say anything, it's no' whit yer thinking – it's they taps in . . .' Scott stopped as she held up her hand by way of saying that no explanation was necessary and then continued down the corridor, failing to suppress a snigger.

'Brilliant,' Scott lamented. 'That evil bastard back fae the deid, an' everybody thinks I've pissed mysel'.'

'I think you and I will take a wee trip down to the County,' said Daley. 'Something tells me we're not going to have much more opportunity. Well, for the time being anyway.'

'If things go the way they did the last time, we might no' get an opportunity, full stop. How the fuck is this a' possible, Jim? The man's deid an' gone, nae doubt about it.' Scott's face was a mask of concern. 'You saw the back o' that prison ambulance – naebody got oot o' that alive. Fuck me, I even saw him at the mortuary that night – or whit wiz left o' him. They were cuttin' oot his heart, or whitever the fuck they do. I saw it, Jim – an' come tae that, so did you.'

'No, I didn't,' Daley replied vaguely.

'Ye didnae what?' Scott was mystified.

'I saw the back of the ambulance, but I never went to the mortuary. I left that dubious pleasure to you and the gaffer, if you remember?' Daley's weak stomach for forensic pathology was well known.

'Aye, right enough. Ye must hae been the only cop in Scotland that wisnae there. It wisnae a pretty sight, I can tell ye.'

'All the more mystifying how he has apparently managed this resurrection,' Daley mused, with a sigh.

'It cannae be him, Jim. They can dae all sorts these days wi' plastic surgery. Must be some nutter – an obsessive or something. Fuck knows we've seen plenty o' those in oor time,' Scott said grimly as he continued to rub his trousers.

6

The helicopter swayed alarmingly as its pilot tried again to land his aircraft on the helipad of the large container vessel. The wind was reasonably brisk, but his main problem was the swell, which caused the deck of the ship to rise and fall dramatically. He needed all of the experience that his years in the Royal Navy had provided. Not many private pilots, as he was now, would have contemplated landing a chopper in such conditions. He had been reluctant but, for the money that was on offer, he was willing to take the risk.

His wipers were working hard against the flurries of sleet that were being blown off the Atlantic Ocean straight into the windscreen of his aircraft. The point of no return arrived; he had to commit himself to the landing, or pull out and make another attempt. He decided on the former. He was buffeted again by a mixture of the Atlantic gale and the down force of his blades on the undulating deck. He held his breath, then – with a massive jolt – he was down safely.

He did not switch off the engine, as it had been made clear to him that this was an 'up and off' job. A small group of men were standing in the lee of a large shipping container that was chained to the deck. It struck him how little cargo there was on board. He guessed that the vessel was on its way to one of the big English ports to be loaded with thousands of computers, or machine parts, clothes, building materials – anything from a bewilderingly long list of items that formed the bedrock of global trade.

Two of the men ran towards the chopper, hunched down against the force of the blades. He could see the dark slate of the sea appearing in and out of view as the ship lurched in the swell. A lone gull struggled against the wind, indicating that they were not far from land – in fact, about thirty nautical miles from the north coast of Ireland.

He leaned over and opened the passenger door of the aircraft; a slight, swarthy man, wearing what could loosely be described as a naval uniform, stared up at him, tilting his head in a brief nod of recognition. He handed a small sports bag up onto the passenger seat of the craft, which the pilot unzipped, noting with pleasure the large wads of notes held in bundles by thick elastic bands. He had completed a few jobs for the voice over the phone and every one had been lucrative, every one had gone without a hitch: picking up a package here, putting down an unnamed passenger there. He knew it was all probably illegal but he had ceased to care; his attempt to survive in any style on his pittance of a pension was impossible. He had put his life on the line for his nation, and in turn he had received insultingly small recompense. He despised the life of a commercial helicopter pilot; while the remuneration was good, the hours were long and the jobs tedious. He had done enough of that in the Navy. Now it was time for the cream; this payday would see him through the next year, easily. This time next week he would be sailing his small yacht around the Bahamas – the only way to spend a British winter.

He nodded to the man who had handed him the bag of money, zipped it up, and placed it carefully under his seat. A second man, who looked to be in early middle age, with a shaven head and wearing dark aviator-style sunglasses, clambered into the seat beside him. He was wearing dark combat trousers and an expensive-looking dark blue all-weather jacket. He had a large holdall with him, which he placed in the foot well. Though his wiry frame was hidden under his clothing, the pilot could sense the raw power emanating from this individual; he looked dead ahead, straight-backed, as the pilot helped him into his harness.

The passenger placed the headset he had been given onto his head and, after being prompted, grunted in the affirmative to indicate that he could hear what his companion was saying.

The pilot had become used to carrying many different individuals in this way over the last few years; some chattered away nervously, either because they were excited by the prospect of a helicopter flight or nervous because of it. Others kept themselves to themselves; this passenger was firmly of the latter variety.

As he had been taught, so many years ago, he began to run through safety advice for the benefit of his new charge, in much the same way an air steward would on a commercial flight. He was mid flow when the man interrupted him by raising his hand, and for the first time turned to face the pilot.

'Just start this fuckin' thing an' let's get on with it.'

The man's voice was gruff and he spoke quickly. He could have been Welsh, Irish, even a Geordie – it was hard to tell after such a brusque statement. The pilot had a feeling, though, that this man was a Scot – which made sense, as

Scotland, the Ayrshire coast, to be precise, was their destination. He had already programmed the coordinates into his satnav system; they appeared to be heading for the middle of a commercial forest.

He did a last systems check, then slowly raised the helicopter from the deck. The wind buffeted the small aircraft sideways; though he had been ready for this, he still had to act quickly to adjust the trim. This done, they soared into the air and began their short journey.

His thoughts drifted back to the Bahamas. He could already feel the warmth of the sun on his neck.

The passenger looked out over the forbidding sea. He didn't care much for flying and would be glad to be back on the ground. He was pleased that the pilot had taken the hint and shut up. It had been a long haul over the last few days; he had been on planes, boats, trains, fast cars and even another helicopter. But it would be worth it.

On the horizon, he could see a flash of gold through the Stygian gloom; the weather looked to be better ahead. This pleased him, as he hadn't enjoyed watching the pilot's attempts to land the aircraft on the ship.

A few minutes later, a thin line of land was visible under the yellow-gold sky. He was aware that the aircraft was much more stable now, no longer being pushed and pulled in the air by unseen forces. The pilot remained silent; it had been impressed upon him that he was not to announce their arrival in UK airspace. They were now flying low over the waves as the land ahead loomed more distinctly. The noise of the blades could be felt as well as heard, thudding through him, syncopated and repetitive. It reminded him of some of the raves he had frequented in the early nineties. He smiled at the thought.

Maybe encouraged by this change in facial expression, the pilot took his opportunity to speak: 'Another five minutes or so, and we'll be there.' He sounded hesitant, clearly unsure what response this statement would engender.

'Aye, right' was all he said, continuing to look straight ahead. His voice sounded strange in the headphones, tinny and distorted. He moved the holdall with his foot slightly.

After a few more minutes, their forward momentum slowed rapidly, and soon their progress was arrested altogether and they began to hover. He looked down through the semi-glazed floor of the helicopter; amidst a forest of pine trees was a clearing where a bright light was being directed at the aircraft. They began to descend and he felt a bump as the helicopter landed.

He could see the outline of a 4x4 at the edge of the clearing. The rain had stopped and the light diffused through the trees gave the forest scene an ethereal feel.

The pilot leaned across him and opened the passenger door the way someone would for an elderly person or a child in a car.

'Shut this off a minute,' said the passenger. 'I've got something for you.' He saw the glint of avarice in the eye of the airman, who was no doubt well used to receiving large tips for such clandestine work. He nodded, then on flicking a couple of switches, the rotor blades slowed, then stopped.

Released from the harness by the pilot and having taken off the headset, the passenger stepped down from the aircraft, turning to remove his bag from the foot well. The air was cold and the scent of the forest pervasive; the smell of the pines reminded him of Christmas, which in turn induced a thirst for whisky.

The pilot smiled at him as he unzipped the bag, which was now on the seat he had just vacated, no doubt anticipating another bundle of notes.

The semi-automatic pistol was black, well oiled, and the attached silencer ensured that it issued barely perceptible pops as two neat holes appeared in the forehead of the pilot. Blood, bone and brain splattered the window of the helicopter. He put the gun carefully back into the holdall, placed it on the ground, and re-entered the aircraft to lean over the dead pilot. With his left hand, he pulled out the bag from under his seat, feeling the reassuring heft of the bundles of money inside.

'Cheers, buddy,' he said, backing out of the chopper. 'Happy fuckin' landin's tae you an' all.'

The pilot still had the shadow of a smile on his motionless face as a trickle of black blood slid past his eye.

The man stood back, as though admiring his handiwork. He often wondered just when the brain stopped working; even though a bullet had fatally ruined it, was there still a scintilla of consciousness, flickering then failing like a guttering candle?

Somehow, he had managed to cut the tip of his index finger. He looked at it and smiled as he squeezed it between his thumb and middle finger, forcing the blood to flow more freely. He passed his injured finger across the dashboard on the passenger side of the helicopter, leaving a dark stain on the black plastic.

'Hello, boys. I'm back.' He grinned, and strode away from the helicopter and its dead occupant.

7

The two detectives made their way, somewhat unsteadily in Scott's case, down Main Street. The air was cold, and, though it was barely four o'clock, the last rays of the sun turned the loch into burnished copper. The town's Christmas lights were beginning to flicker into life, picked out in a series of glowing orbs in various colours, shapes and sizes that were strung across Main Street, progressing down the road towards the large Norwegian spruce at the centre of the luminous display. People waved to the two police officers from cars, vans and buses; Daley still found this overt friendliness rather claustrophobic, but was beginning to appreciate the general sentiment. One youth, however, shouted an indistinct insult from a half-opened car window, prompting Scott to stop, turn around and squint in an attempt to read the number plate of the offending vehicle.

Daley had decided it was time to get out of the office. He was tired, and his DS was getting drunk. He had a team of uniformed and CID officers heading off to raid a barn, which as a result of careful surveillance was known to contain a significant quantity of illegal cigarettes and tobacco. They had been watching the farmer and his operation for two months, hoping to net bigger fish. This had not happened, so Daley felt it was time to make an example of this particular offender. He knew for sure that there were many more culprits. He had found it strange that in the time they had been keeping an eye on this modern-day smuggler, the man seemed to have taken no deliveries and was simply running down his stock.

He worried about leaks within the office; though he did his best to banish this from his mind, it was always a possibility. In the few months he had been in charge of the sub-division, he had discovered that Inspector MacLeod's legacy was most apparent in a lack of efficiency and obedience of Force Standing Orders. MacLeod, it seemed, had been happy to let everyone take care of their own work, as long as nothing went wrong and he was not shown up in a bad light. As a result, little proper police work had been done, save clearing the town centre of drunks on weekend nights and a perfunctory implementation of road traffic legislation – a mainly pro-forma pursuit requiring little in the way of detection skills. Daley was trying to give some of the younger members of his CID team more experience; the raid on the barn was being overseen by a young cop he had recently promoted to acting DS.

As the pair turned into the doorway of the County under the faux crenulations, Daley remembered his first visit to the establishment and its inquisitive clientele. It was perhaps for this reason that his visits to the hotel had been few and far between in the intervening months. He and Liz had dined there on a couple of occasions at the insistence of the latter, who had struck up a friendship with Annie, the hotel's formidable yet welcoming chatelaine. Every time he entered the premises, he reminded himself that he wasn't an anonymous punter in some city watering hole; rather, he was on display and a possible source of information for the gossip-hungry locals.

Despite having to remain on his toes, Daley couldn't help a sneaking fondness for, in most cases, the guileless population of Kinloch.

The small wood-panelled bar was festive in its own way: various shades of threadbare tinsel meandered along the walls, and a cracked plastic sign proclaimed Happy Christmas in faded red letters. A couple of logs had almost burned themselves out in the fireplace and would soon need replaced lest the fire need mending. On the bar stood a moth-eaten imitation Christmas tree, adorned with a mismatched set of baubles and fairy lights, many of which didn't work and had most certainly seen better days.

'Aye, I can see ye lookin', Mr Daley,' Annie called out as she poured a pint for the only other customer in the bar. 'They expect me tae buy the decorations oot o' my ain pocket – an' I tell you, there'll be green snaw an' yellow hailstanes afore that happens!' Annie's festive spirit had clearly yet to materialise. 'Forbye,' she added, holding her hand out for payment for the pint she had just placed on the bar, 'this crew widna care if it wiz Oxford Street in here, as lang as they can get steamin'. Yer in fir a right treat, wi' this bein' yer first Christmas in the toon, an' nae mistake.' She eyed the change the customer had put in her hand warily. 'An' as fir you, Jocky Sinclair, you can jeest get yer hands back intae they pockets an' dredge oot anither twenty pence. Ye know fine the prices went up last week. It's no' as though it's the first time ye've been in since.'

The man dug deep into his trouser pocket and pulled out a handful of copper coins that he ruefully counted out and handed to Annie. 'Aye, a happy Christmas to you an' all,' she said under her breath as she deposited the coins into the till.

Daley was about to order when she slammed the till shut and turned around. 'Whoot the fuck have ye bin daein' tae him?' She was looking at Scott, who had begun to sway slightly at Daley's side, the full effects of the whisky exaggerated by the short walk and the cold air.

'Never you mind, lady,' Scott slurred with some difficulty. 'Just you get me an' the big man here a couple o' drams – and nane o' that expensive shite he normally drinks, neither. A couple o' low flyers will do nicely. Make them large yins tae, hen.' Scott fumbled inside the pocket of his jacket in an attempt to retrieve his wallet.

'You could say we're having a bad day, Annie,' Daley said by way of an excuse.

'An even worse day fir you, Jim,' Scott hiccupped. 'I've left my wallet up in the motor. I took it oot at Invereray when I stopped fir chips, an' flung it intae wan o' they door pockets. Ye'll have tae dig deep yersel'.' Scott looked at him with a resigned expression that reminded Daley vaguely of Stan Laurel.

He sighed and reached for the back pocket of his trousers, where he habitually kept his wallet. Quickly though, he remembered that he'd had to change into the spare pair that he kept in his locker for emergencies. He had forgotten his wallet, and after searching every other pocket, only managed to produce a couple of pounds in change. He looked at Annie apologetically. 'Sorry. I think we'd better make tracks. We seem to have a cash-flow problem.'

'Indeed ye will not,' declared Annie, placing two small whisky glasses on the table. 'If I wiz tae refuse everybody that had nae money in here a drink, I'd have been oot o' work a long, long time ago, let me assure ye. Yous can owe me. It's no' as if I don't know where to find ye.'

'Well, I've jeest seen it a', said the other customer, Jocky, shaking his head. 'The polis in here steamin' tappin' money fir drink. Aye, I've seen it a', right enough.'

'Just you wait a minute,' Scott said raising his finger to admonish his accuser.

'Fir fuck's sake,' Jocky said, pointing at Scott's trousers. 'This fella's pished his troosers an' a – the polis has gaun tae the dogs, an' nae mistake.' He grimaced, looking at Annie, who looked somewhat surprised herself.

'Hang oan a minute, you. That's no' pish.'

'Best we take a seat, Brian,' interrupted Daley, ushering his colleague to a table at the back of the bar.

'Whit's been happenin' doon here, Annie?' Scott shouted, anxious to stop the whispered conjecture as to the nature of the stain on his trousers that was now taking place between Annie and Jocky.

'Och,' answered Annie, somewhat stiffly, while vigorously polishing a pint glass with a white tea towel, 'jeest the usual. Ye'll mind o' Peter Williamson that used tae come in here?'

'Cannae say I dae,' Scott mumbled as he took the first sip of the drink he didn't really need.

'Aye, ye dae – Peester, nice lad, a right worrier though. Well, he got himsel' caught in his zip – if ye know whoot I mean.' She smiled knowingly in the direction of the policemen.

'You mean?' Daley winced and gestured under the table.

'Aye, exactly, Mr Daley. An' whoot a performance it wiz tae.' The smile had returned to Annie's face, the issue of Scott's trousers seemingly forgotten. 'A' I heard wiz this

46

screamin' comin' fae the toilet. I thought someone wiz bein' murdered.' She looked sheepishly at the detectives. 'Anyhow, I ran in wavin' that rolling pin I keep under the bar – in case o' bother, ye understan' – an' there he wiz, the poor boy, proppin' himself up against the wa' wi' his manhood stuck fast in his flies.' She began to rub the glass with increased vigour, looking into the middle distance, as though bringing this graphic scene back to mind.

'Whit happened tae the boy?' Scott slurred, rubbing the stained area of his trousers as he pictured the episode.

'Well, we'd tae send fir the paramedics,' Annie replied, the smile now broad on her face. 'Wance they'd stopped laughin', they took the boy in hand, so tae speak.' She let out a loud guffaw of laughter, which quickly spread to the other occupants of the bar.

'Yous'll never guess whoot they're callin' him noo in the toon.' Jocky turned, somewhat unsteadily, on his stool in order to face his fellow customers, tears of laughter spilling down his cheeks.

'Zip Up De Do Da,' Annie shouted, stealing the punch line as they all descended into gales of laughter.

'So was he all right?' Daley asked.

'Och aye,' answered Annie. 'Though he wiz walkin' funny fir a couple o' days, mind you. Mair embarrassed than anythin' else, poor lad.'

'We'll get months mair fun fae that,' said Jocky, holding out his glass as a silent request for it to be refilled.

'Aye, so yous might.' Annie replied, 'Though fae whoot I saw, the boy's got nothin' tae be ashamed o'. In fact it's nae wonder he got caught oot, if ye know whoot I mean.' She winked in the direction of the policemen.

'Whoot dae ye mean, Annie?' Jocky swayed on his stool, a look of puzzlement on his face.

'Well, pit it lake this if God had given you whoot he's given Peester, we'd be callin' you Jock the Cock, an' no' wee Wullie Winky.'

Despite the revelations of the last few days, even Daley had to laugh.

Normally, DS Scott resided at the County when his peripatetic duties brought him to Kinloch. On this occasion, though, he decided to take up Daley's offer to stay at his and Liz's home, a well-appointed rented bungalow on the hill above Kinloch.

The two detectives sat on the decking at the front of the house, both wrapped up against the frosty night, while Scott smoked and fretted. After a couple of drinks in the County, Daley had decided it prudent to phone Liz, who arrived in her new Mini Countryman – a gift from her father – to pick them up. She had made lasagne, which, despite their stressful day, the detectives both tucked into heartily.

Daley had noted with concern that his wife was picking at her meal. Her ability to never gain so much as a pound in weight belied a healthy appetite; it was most unusual to see her staring gloomily at a nearly full plate of food.

He thought about this as he watched Scott's cigarette smoke disappear into the starlit night. Below, the loch shimmered silver under an almost full moon; the island which stood sentinel as its mouth loomed black and silent.

'This has a' got tae be wan big scam,' Scott declared, as, much to Daley's chagrin, he flicked his cigarette butt over the garden fence and down the hill. Daley remained silent, watching it splutter out of sight in a momentary shower of sparks. 'Ye know yersel, they can dae a' sorts o' things wi' computers these days. That CCTV film o' him is likely just some kind o' trick photography.' Scott looked hopefully at his boss.

Daley sighed. He spotted Liz's pale face at the kitchen window. 'There's no point trying to fathom this until we can get some more information from his majesty tomorrow. You can guarantee, there'll be something he's conveniently *forgotten* to tell us.'

'Maybe you're right, Jim.' Scott lit another cigarette, puffing clouds of smoke out into the clear night. 'I must admit, I'm pretty knackered. I'll sleep the sleep o' the just the night, for sure.'

'Not something you do very often, Brian,' Daley said, smiling. 'No wonder you're knackered – you've put away a hell of a lot of whisky.' He raised his eyebrows at his DS.

'Och, that's nothin' – the lasagne soaked it up. Don't worry, I'll be tip-top for the royal appointment the morrow. I've got some o' that mouthwash in my bag. Bugger it,' he said, flicking ash across the decking, 'I've left the bloody stuff in the motor, back at the office.'

'I've got a spare toothbrush,' Daley offered as they stood up to go back inside.

'Aye, that'll be fine, but I'm no' sae sure I'll fit intae a pair o' your scants.'

Daley laughed and shut the door with a slam that echoed down the hillside to the loch.

8

Glasgow

The night was still and frosty all over the west coast of Scotland.

The man sat in the battered old Honda with the engine running, keeping the heater on against the chill. He stared down the acetylene-illuminated street, watching as the occasional customer entered or left the bar, wrapped up in scarves and woolly hats. From time to time one or two determined smokers would huddle around a wall-mounted ashtray in order to exercise their habit. He reflected on how much the world had changed. What would his granny have thought about not being able to smoke in a pub? He remembered her clearly, sitting on her favourite seat at the bar, a Capstan Full Strength always drooping from her mouth as she gossiped with her fellow regulars. His face broke out into an impromptu smile at the memory. She had been his touchstone, his anchor in what had been a childhood blighted by drink, drugs and violence.

He remembered the day she died. He had felt as though suddenly and without warning the world had become small, cold and hostile. He stayed in his room for three days, not wishing to see or communicate with anyone. Something in him had changed; he emerged on the fourth day having promised himself he would never be as vulnerable and alone again. Then, and every day thereafter, he had hardened his heart and banished his loneliness; thoughts of his grandmother had receded and had gradually become associated with Scotland's collective nostalgia for sad songs, Hogmanay and times past.

It was nearly one in the morning, and the radio was playing Gerry Rafferty as one particularly booze-laden night owl staggered out into the cold. He briefly heard the dull murmur of drunken conversation and a refrain from the jukebox before the door swung shut. He watched the man fumble in his pockets, take a cigarette from a packet in his hand, and place it between his lips. A lighter flared then guttered, momentarily illuminating his face. The man stood unsteadily, arching his back as he drew deeply on the tobacco. He replaced the cigarettes and the lighter in his pocket and muttered something barely audible to himself, before hunching his shoulders and taking his first faltering steps towards home.

The man in the car smiled as he turned off the radio, released the car's handbrake, then, with the dull clunk of an old gearbox, put the vehicle into first and pulled slowly away from the kerb.

If the pedestrian noticed the car as it idled past him, he didn't falter from his head-down plod. As he progressed down the street, the chunky sole of his boot caught a broken section of the pavement, making him trip and swear.

The driver slowed to a stop thirty yards in front of the staggering figure, switched off the engine and lights and exited the Honda. He stepped onto the pavement, towards the man moving haltingly past a row of empty, boarded-up shops.

They were only a few feet apart when the man from the car, in a darting motion, lunged towards the pedestrian and thrust a broad-bladed hunting knife into the unsuspecting man's belly. A look of horror suffused the dying man's face as he clawed at the knife handle, and a trail of steaming urine threaded from his ankle down his boot and onto the pavement.

The attacker didn't bother to remove the knife from the man's stomach, merely pushed him backwards, turned on his heel, and strolled back to his car before driving sedately away.

Blood bubbled at the mouth of the man lying on the cold dark pavement; the desperate tremble of his hands as they clawed at the handle of the hunting knife, slowed, then stopped.

After what had been a frosty night, Daley had to drive gingerly down the driveway that led from his house to the main road. He made a mental note to call Liz and tell her how slippery the conditions were when he got to the office.

The view across the loch and down to the town was magnificent: the sky was an almost Caribbean blue and the light from the sun glinted off the frosted hillsides and played on the mirror-still surface of the loch. Everything felt clean, fresh and renewed. But bold and bright as it was, Daley still had the heater blasting into the car, keeping the two policemen warm as well as dispelling the ice which slid slowly down the windscreen.

Daley's heart was still heavy, and as he looked across at his DS, slumped gloomily in the passenger seat, he recognised that they were both suffering from the same malady: James Machie.

People waved and nodded as they sat at the traffic lights on Main Street. Scott snorted as the car coming towards them ignored the red signal all together, cruising past them with a hearty wave.

'I take it that Green Cross Code punter never made it here?' Scott spoke for the first time since they left Daley's house.

'These lights have only been up for a couple of months. It takes them a wee while to get used to new traffic management measures,' Daley replied, glad to be talking about something that wasn't James Machie.

'When I wiz a young cop, I'd have been standing there a' day tae get a few bodies.' Scott remembered how young police officers had been encouraged to report as many misdemeanours as they could, learning to construct a proper case, regardless of its nature.

'Brian, if we prosecuted everyone who jumped these lights or committed minor traffic offences here, the court would be a 24/7 job. Have you never listened to your man's "pragmatic policing" speech?'

'Ye know yersel, Jim, I listen tae him as little as possible.' Scott shook his head.

The lights changed, and they drove up the street and turned through the open gate into the car park at the rear of Kinloch police office, situated on the crest of the hill looking down Main Street.

'Well, you'll get the chance to listen to him all day today, my friend,' Daley said as he parked the car in the space reserved for the sub-divisional commander. The detectives exited the vehicle then, after Daley had punched the security code into a wall-mounted keypad, pushed open the heavy security door to the office.

Daley noticed the hush that had pervaded the building, normally a lively, even happy, workplace. This morning everyone seemed subdued. As he passed the bar office, the desk sergeant drew his forefinger across his brow and inclined his head to indicate that a senior officer with a braided cap was present: Donald.

Though Daley was acting divisional commander, he had based himself, quite naturally, within the glass box in the CID room. When Superintendent Donald arrived, he would occupy the boss's office. As expected, he was sitting boldly behind the desk once occupied by Inspector MacLeod.

'Ah, there you are. At last,' Donald murmured, looking pointedly at his watch.

'I'm surprised to see you, sir. I thought you were flying down.'

'I arrived just under an hour ago. I have so much on I decided to drive down early. The roads are so much quieter. I had hoped that your day would have begun long before the time designated to pick me up.' Donald was in an imperious mood, which didn't bode well. 'Things have moved on rather rapidly, I'm afraid to say. Come in here, both of you, and shut the door.'

Daley could hear Scott mutter under his breath as he shut the door firmly. There was only one seat in the room, apart from the one occupied by Donald, so Daley indicated to Scott that he should take it.

'What's wrong with you, DS Scott?' Donald enquired. 'No doubt nursing a gargantuan hangover, judging by the look of your bloodshot eyes. Please do your best not to breathe in my direction.'

Scott opened his mouth but didn't get the chance to interrupt as Donald carried on, barely pausing for breath.

'In the very early hours of this morning, a forty-nine-year-old man was found dead in a street in the East End of Glasgow with a seven-inch blade still lodged in his solar plexus.' Donald looked at the men for a reaction, but gave them no time to comment. 'Two hours earlier, a helicopter was discovered by a night orienteer – whatever the fuck that is – in a clearing in the middle of forestry in South Ayrshire. The pilot had been despatched professionally by two shots to the head.' Donald looked out of the office window, down Kinloch's Main Street.

'Not something that happens every day, sir,' Daley commented, feeling that he had to say something.

'Indeed not, Jim. Most unusual.' Donald was clearly troubled, which worried his subordinates. 'Under normal circumstances these events, as distasteful as they are, would have been viewed as being wholly unconnected; that is, until one looks at the last known movement of the helicopter and the identity of the murdered man in Glasgow.' Donald paused, displaying the skills of the storyteller. 'Peter MacDougall, petty crook, drug dealer and, most pertinently, younger brother of Frank – who needs no introduction.'

'Fuck's sake.' Scott was sitting forward in his chair, looking at the floor.

'I believe the deceased was a friend of yours, DS Scott?' Donald said.

'I widnae say "friend" as such, sir,' Scott replied, clearly affected by this news. 'I wiz at school wi' him. We grew up in the same street, that's all.'

'Well, far be it from me to pry into your tortured personal relationships, Brian. That is, unless something inappropriate has been going on, in which case . . .'

'Sir,' Daley interjected firmly, not bothering to hide his irritation, 'this is not getting us anywhere. Please can we just get on with it?'

'How forceful, Jim. Your new management responsibilities must be suiting you. The CID team from Cumnock have been working on this all night. The helicopter was registered to a Henry Parr, a retired Royal Navy pilot, who passed some of his time by carrying out commercial contracts – ferrying golfers about and so on. However, at first glance it would appear he worked only infrequently, spending much more time at his holiday home in the Bahamas.'

'Which is hard to do when you only have a navy pension to sustain you,' Daley observed.

'Exactly,' Donald affirmed. 'On examination of the aircraft's satnav, it would appear he spent a few minutes at a point somewhere off the North Antrim coast, a specific position he had programmed into the machine. That was prior to landing in Ayrshire – his final flight.'

'And Peter MacDougall – do we have anything more on his murder?' Daley enquired.

'Your colleagues at London Road are working hard on that, but you know the East End, Jim. Nobody saw anything, and the CCTV coverage isn't exactly comprehensive. Most of the street is derelict. All we know is that he left the pub along the road minutes before he was killed.' Donald sat back in his chair. 'Because of the delicate situation concerning his brother, the WPP have asked me to pass on the news about Peter.' He steepled his fingers in front of his face, waiting for a response.

'We've got tae break cover an' tell Frank that his brother has been killed?' Scott was incredulous. 'Can they no' dae that themselves?' he added, shaking his head.

'At last, it speaks,' Donald said. 'The murder of Peter MacDougall has changed things: Witness Protection was reasonably relaxed, as I told you both yesterday, after the murder of the Dowies. That is now no longer the case. The form is that if they believe there is a viable threat to someone on the programme, they liaise with local law enforcement, wherever that may be. In this case, gents, that is us. It's our pleasant duty not only to inform him that his brother has been murdered, but tell him about "you know who" and persuade him that another change of identity and location would be, well, most prudent.'

'Prudent?' said Scott. 'If I wiz him I'd be on my bike quick smart, an' nae mistake, before this ghost, or whitever it is, comes knockin.'

Daley walked over from the window where he had been standing and leaned on Donald's – his – desk. 'I'm still all at sea with this, sir.' He pointed his finger into the desk. 'For a start, if this is JayMac – and surely that is open for debate at the very least – how has this happened? People don't just come back from the dead.' He looked down at Donald, who squirmed in his chair, not enjoying the dynamic.

'Apairt fae the big man,' Scott said, drawing the attention of both of his colleagues.

'The big man?' asked Donald.

'Aye, ye know – JC.' Scott sat back in his chair. 'Jesus, ye know?'

'Perhaps you missed your calling, Brian. Maybe you'd have made Archbishop of Canterbury if you had taken the cloth,' Donald said.

'Aye, well.' Scott was not to be outdone. 'Mebbe we'll need tae gie him a call, see if he can perform wan o' they exorcisms.'

Donald snorted in derision and was about to speak when a knock sounded at the door. After Donald barked a perfunctory 'Yes?', DC Dunn walked in, pausing near the door, where she smoothed some unseen creases in the front of her dark blue skirt.

'Just to let you know, sir, *sirs*,' she began, plainly nervous around Donald, 'the presentation is ready.' She nodded her head obligingly and Daley thought for one awful moment that she might curtsy, but Donald dismissed her in the same offhand manner in which he bade her enter and she left hurriedly.

'I felt it would be beneficial if we were to look back in time,' Donald said, picking up papers from his desk. 'Try and find some way that this – if it is him – could have happened. Come with me.'

They trooped from the office, Donald taking the lead. Behind him, Scott shrugged at Daley and raised a two-fingered salute behind the superintendent's back.

'And you can stop that insubordination immediately, Brian,' Donald said, not bothering to turn around and sweeping open the door of the audiovisual room. 'In fact, I want a word with you, DS Scott – in private.' He looked at Daley, who excused himself, and led Scott into a nearby empty room.

Daley, not trying to hear what was being said, couldn't help being surprised at the bile expressed by the superintendent. It was clear that, despite Scott's careless attitude, he was most certainly not flavour of the month with his boss.

9

DC Dunn was in the room, leaning over the computer that controlled all things audiovisual. Donald placed his arm around her shoulder, speaking to her in hushed tones as though what was about to be revealed was a state secret. Daley was sure he saw the young woman flinch as Donald's hand snaked over her back. How many times had he seen these manoeuvres from his boss?

Donald turned away from Dunn and indicated that his detectives take a seat. 'I think it important that we fully rebrief ourselves with what happened six years ago,' he said grandly, as though addressing a packed auditorium. He looked to Dunn. 'I take it you're finished? Just tell me which button to press, then kindly absent yourself.'

'Press any button to start, and the same to stop,' the flushed DC replied, clearly uncomfortable in her superintendent's presence.

'Great!' Donald exclaimed. 'Off you pop now.' He leaned over the keyboard, glasses perched on the end of his nose, as DC Dunn made a hasty exit.

'Off ye pop,' Scott whispered as she was leaving. 'It's like fuckin' *Downton Abbey.*'

'An excellent programme,' Donald replied. 'But less of

your sarcasm, DS Scott. If I recall, we still have to sort out the little matter of your yearly assessment which, I can assure you, does not make for pleasant reading.' He paused, mind now back on the complexities of the computer. He pressed a button and the huge screen flickered into life. 'I've put this together by way of an aide-memoire, so to speak,' he said and took a seat between Daley and Scott.

The familiar face of a well-known Scottish newsreader appeared on the screen, looking noticeably younger than when Daley had seen her a few nights previously, when he had been watching TV with Liz.

She began to speak: 'Infamous gangland figure James 'JayMac' Machie was sentenced to five life terms in prison at Glasgow High Court earlier today. He and almost fifty members of the Machie organised crime family have been on trial over the last four months in what has been the largest such proceeding in Scottish legal history. The gang, responsible for murder, extortion, the supply of illegal drugs and money laundering, as well as a further seventeen charges, are likely to collectively serve over a thousand notional years in prison.'

The visuals switched from the newsreader to footage of Machie being removed from court by five uncomfortable-looking security guards. Though handcuffed, he was spitting and shouting oaths at the cameramen, journalists and sundry onlookers, some of whom shouted support. His demeanour was at odds with his expensive Italian suit; his screwed-up features spoke only of vitriol and revenge. Daley saw Scott squirm in his seat.

The scene cut out and was replaced with footage of a Glasgow street. The battered white vehicle that had mounted the pavement exposed the horror that had been perpetrated there; the vehicle was riddled with bullet holes, the crumpled doors hanging open to allow a view of the blood-soaked interior. A group of men dressed in white crime scene overalls were doing their best to cover the vehicle with a blue tarpaulin; a police tow truck was positioned to the front of the ruined van. Blue lights flashed from numerous police vehicles at the scene.

'Fuckin' hell, it's a' oor yesterdays,' Scott blurted, unconcerned on this occasion by Donald's presence.

The camera refocused on another reporter, again familiar, though looking younger. 'Behind me are the remains of the prison ambulance in which notorious Glasgow gangster James 'JayMac' Machie died in a hail of bullets just over an hour ago. He was being transported back to his cell in Barlinnie prison after attending the city's Royal Infirmary with a suspected heart attack.

'Though details are sketchy, it is believed that two police outriders, two prison officers and a private security guard were also killed in the attack which involved as many as ten masked men driving a stolen city taxi, heavy goods vehicle and an Audi car. It is thought that the well-planned execution could be the work of rival gangsters who still feared Machie, even though it's highly unlikely that he would have been freed from prison for many years, if ever.'

The camera panned out to reveal a uniformed police officer, replete with gold braided cap; there was no mistaking Donald.

'With me is Superintendent John Donald, deputy divisional commander of the central police division. Superintendent Donald, what is your understanding of these dreadful events?'

Daley watched as Donald raised his brows and, instead of addressing the reporter, looked straight into the camera. 'The events of this morning are tragic in the extreme, especially for the families of my two officers, prison staff and the private security guard who lost their lives trying to protect Mr Machie.' He stopped, disgusted, and turned back to the reporter.

'Do you have anything to say to the Machie family, now that it has been confirmed that James Machie died in the attack, Superintendent Donald?'

Again, Donald chose to turn to the camera with his answer.

'In my job, dealing with the aftermath of violence is, sadly, an almost daily occurrence. Of course the death of any individual in such circumstances is most regrettable; I'm sure your viewers will agree, though, that some deaths are more regrettable than others. I will reiterate that my thoughts are with the families of the dead officers and the murdered security guard. That's all I have to say.'

The camera panned one more time to the wrecked ambulance, then the picture faded out. A re-run of the CCTV footage from Australia played next. Daley glanced at Scott, who was now sitting forward on his seat; this was the first time he had been shown the murders in Ringwood East.

The action played out silently on the big screen. As Marna Dowie's head exploded once more and JayMac made his way to the front of the car, his look to the camera was frozen and enlarged; into place beside it slid another picture – JayMac, looking up into the camera as he was led into incarceration after his trial almost six years previously. Perhaps it was the similar pose that made the likeness so striking.

Donald stood up and turned to face his detectives. 'Well, gentlemen, are either of you in any doubt as to the identity of the man we have just seen?' He inclined his head.

'No,' said Brian Scott. 'It's him; there can be nae doubt. I've known him since I wiz a boy.' He looked down, interlocked the fingers of both hands, and cracked them in a way that always set Daley's teeth on edge.

'Splendid,' said Donald. 'A rare outbreak of consensus between us, DS Scott.' He went to sit behind a desk located under the big screen. 'All three of us are experienced police officers, as well as rational human beings. Well, in the main,' he said, eyeing Scott. 'Employing the processes we have spent our working lives using, it is up to us not to wonder at the apparent resurrection of JayMac, rather to deduce how he did it. Any suggestions?'

Daley leaned back in his chair, staring at the ceiling with his hands behind his head. 'The only possible explanation is that the man who died in the prison van was not Machie.' He craned his head forward, looking at Donald.

'Yes, I had reached a similar conclusion. What about you, Brian?' Donald enquired.

'Aye, all very well, but I saw him – come tae that half o' the force saw him, an' a' the pathologists in Glasgow, the press, his family, every fuckin' body. It wiz him on that slab, I fuckin' swear it.'

'And yet, you also affirm that the man in the Australian footage is him. Make up your mind, DS Scott.' Donald looked down at the desk and sighed. 'Our job is to deal in the here and now, and, as unpalatable as it may be, we have to deal with this second coming, or however you would like to term it.'

'I wid prefer not tae term it anything,' said Scott. 'If ye remember, sir, he nearly killed me, and threatened tae make a better job o' it the next time.'

'I suppose we'll have to go and see Frank MacDougall as soon as possible, sir,' interrupted Daley. 'How much does he know?'

'That's not clear, Jim,' Donald replied. 'He knows about the Dowies, however I'm sure that seeing his old partner in crime returned to life will be as big a shock to him as it's been to us. Let's get a coffee, gentlemen, then we'll make tracks. We have plenty of time to try and work out how JayMac achieved this paranormal feat.' Donald stood, picked up his files from the desk, and left the room.

'And there you have it,' said Daley.

'Aye, simples,' Scott said. 'I'm tellin' ye, Jim, this whole fuckin' thing's a nightmare. It gies me the shivers. I've been in the polis for a long time, an' I've never seen the like.'

'I've no idea how we're going to keep this away from the media. That's one part of his majesty's job I don't envy.' Daley stood, then stretched and yawned. 'I suppose we better get a coffee while we've a chance,' he said to Scott who was rubbing his eyes with both hands.

'It's quite simple, Jimmy-boy – that's just no' goin' tae happen. I'm surprised it's no' oot already.' Scott shook his head grimly. 'Dae me a favour. Can we take your motor tae Frank MacDougall's? I've no' got a clue where it is, an' I just cannae cope wi' any mair memos fae the gaffer.'

10

After consulting the large map on the wall in Donald's temporary office, the three officers set off in Daley's 4x4, much to the relief of his DS, who sat in the back looking idly out at the passing scenery.

'I must say, Jim, you keep a nice car. Pity you can't encourage the gentleman lurking in the back to do likewise,' Donald said, as he glared at a Kinloch pedestrian peering at them as they stopped at the lights on Main Street. 'Have these people never seen a policeman with braid on his cap?' he pondered as they drove off.

'Aye, just no' one that looks like you,' Scott offered from the back of the car, somewhat ill advisedly, in Daley's opinion.

Donald turned around in his seat. 'I beg your pardon, DS Scott?'

'I mean, no' used tae somebody that looks as good as you in uniform, sir.'

'Shut up, Brian,' was Donald's concise reply.

As they drove out of Kinloch, the scenery changed. They were heading north on the west side of the peninsula; the restless Atlantic rolled in white breakers on the rocky coastline. The sea looked cold and grey, despite the blue sky;

distant islands broke the horizon, in front of which a red fishing boat was just visible, dragging nets amidst a cloud of riotous gulls.

The road was quiet despite being the main artery between Kinloch and the rest of Scotland. Daley knew this stretch well, having driven it often when returning home. Home.

In the last few months, he and Liz had become closer than at any other time in their marriage. The easy friendliness of the local people was genuine, as was their collective nosiness; Daley wondered what they really said about Liz and him in private, though he didn't particularly care.

Liz's new career as a wildlife photographer was taking off; already she'd had her work published in a couple of good magazines, eliciting impressive reviews. He'd been surprised at how little she seemed to miss living near the city, with all of its amenities so close at hand. She had recently taken her sister Annie on a shopping trip to Glasgow in the new Mini; they had stayed overnight in the Daleys' home in Howwood, which Annie had admired greatly. On her return, Liz had told him how strange she felt, not being in Kinloch, and that she now considered it her home. He supposed, in a funny way, so did he.

He was distracted by Donald, who was attempting to operate the satnav on his iPhone – a task clearly beyond him.

'These bloody things,' he said. 'Do you have the map, DS Scott?'

Daley saw Scott's surprised look in the mirror.

'No,' he said. 'Naebody telt me tae bring the map.'

'I clearly remember instructing you to pick up a map from the bar officer,' Donald said. 'It's beyond me why bloody satellite navigation has passed this place by.' He looked at his phone with disgust. 'Of course, it doesn't help when one's subordinates can't comply with basic requests.'

Daley could see Scott making a face behind his boss's back.

'If you take a look in the glove compartment, sir, I think there's a map of the area in it,' Daley said, preparing to overtake one of the few cars on the road.

Donald leaned forward, opening the glove box with the satisfying clunk of a well-engineered car. Daley watched him from the corner of his eye as he rummaged about.

'I must say, Jim, it's a veritable sweet shop in here,' Donald said, removing what was left of a packet of biscuits and a chocolate bar.

'Ah, yes.' It was Daley's turn to look flustered. 'Just for emergencies – in case we get stuck in the snow, you know.'

'Some diet, big man,' Scott laughed in the back. 'Lettuce an' grapefruit for tea, then oot tae the car for a poke o' sweets an' a Mars Bar. Nae wonder the weight's no' comin' aff.'

Choosing to ignore the derisory comments on his secret sugar stash, Daley slowed down at a sign pointing to a side road.

'This is the turn-off. He lives in a converted farmhouse along the road. It's a Gaelic name. Can you remember it, Brian?' Daley caught Scott's eye in the rear-view mirror.

'More chance of you giving up chocolate, I would imagine,' Donald snorted.

'Gie me a minute,' Scott said, desperately trying to remember even an approximation of the name, and failing.

A few seconds later, they saw the farm in the distance. A large black Range Rover was parked at the end of the driveway.

'I take it they're being guarded by Witness Protection at the moment, sir?' Daley enquired.

'Yes, until this evening, when we have to take over that unwanted task.'

Without answering, Daley slowed the car and turned into the drive, only for the Range Rover to move across, blocking the way.

Two men got out of the black car; one of them patted his jacket, perhaps to warn the interlopers that he was armed.

Daley pressed the button on his door to lower the window.

'What's your business here?' the man in the suit said abruptly in a London accent, leaning his head into Daley's car and taking note of the passengers.

Daley removed his warrant card from the inside pocket of his jacket. 'Strathclyde Police. Our business is with the occupant of this house – not you – so could you please let us through?'

'Not before I see everyone's ID.' He thrust his hand through the window in expectation of Donald and Scott's identification.

Donald raised his brow and fished his warrant card from a uniform pocket. The man scanned it without comment.

In the mirror, Daley could see Scott frantically searching for his ID; he had gone through his jacket with no result, and was now leaning on one elbow in an attempt to gain access to the back pocket of his trousers.

'Hang on, hang on, I know I've got the bloody thing here somewhere,' he said, now leaning on the opposite elbow to search another trouser pocket.

'Typical,' said Donald, turning around to better witness the struggles of his detective sergeant. 'You know I can have you disciplined for not carrying your appointments.'

The man leaned his head further into Daley's car, glowering at Scott. 'Come on, Jocky-boy,' he said. 'Get a move on. We're out of here in six hours, get our arses back to civilisation.'

Donald released his seatbelt and stepped out of the car, slamming the door behind him. Daley watched as his boss walked calmly in front of the vehicle towards the two men. 'Listen to me, you cocky English bastard.' Donald was clearly in no mood for compromise. 'Get your arse back into that car and move it out the way, before I arrest you both for breach of the peace. And rest assured,' he continued venomously, 'I'll be making a full report to your superior on my return to the office.' He dismissed the Witness Protection officer with a wave of his hand.

'Aye, ye've got tae gie him his due,' Scott observed, calmer now he'd abandoned the search for his warrant card. 'It's nae bother tae him tae get his point across.'

'Ah, but don't think he'll forget you've not got your ID,' replied Daley.

'Oh, I know, Jim,' said Scott. 'I know fine.'

With Donald back in the car, they continued uphill towards the farm, Donald muttering about insubordination and lack of respect.

The landscape was bare; the farmhouse and a couple of small outbuildings, in clear need of care and attention, nestled under the brow of the hill. The area looked barren and windswept, with no sign of trees, bushes or any other type of vegetation.

A mud-splattered 4x4 stood in front of the house, alongside an old pick-up, which was fitted with a caged back, most

69

likely for the transportation of livestock. Daley noted the absence of barking dogs, something he always associated with working farms.

As Donald marched to the front door, Daley turned around; Frank MacDougall might live in humble surroundings, but the view he had over the Atlantic was truly magnificent. The red fishing boat could still be seen, though now a pinprick, against the islands, which appeared somehow closer and more imposing from this elevation. Daley wished he had brought a jacket; he could see his breath cloud in front of him. Scott was stamping his feet to keep warm, his hands thrust deep into his trouser pockets.

'Try and look more like a police officer and less like a travelling salesman, will you, DS Scott?' Donald said as he knocked on the door and straightened his uniform.

Scott was about to protest, when the door cracked open and the face of an elderly woman peered out. Her hair was grey and unkempt, and her bulging eyes stared fearfully at the policemen standing at her door.

'Betty, is that you?' Scott asked, with a look of surprise on his face.

'Aye, an' what if it is?' the woman replied.

'Dae ye no' recognise me? It's me, Brian Scott, Tam's boy. We used tae live two doors doon fae you, remember?'

With a look of panic, the woman slammed the door; Daley could hear her sobbing as she slid the bolts back into place.

'An old neighbour?' Donald enquired. 'Friends reunited, indeed.'

'I cannae believe it,' Scott said, shaking his head. 'Ye widnae think it, but she wiz one o' the best-looking lassies in Glasgow when I wiz a boy. She's a bit older than me, right enough, but I can still see her headin' aff tae the dancin', all dolled up. Total stunner.' He shook his head.

'Well, whatever happened to her in the intervening years, it would appear that she has swapped stunning for stunned,' Donald commented with his habitual acidity. 'Looked to me as though she didn't have a clue what day it was, never mind who we are.' He went to knock again, though hesitated when he heard a loud male voice shout from inside.

'Wait a minute, I'm just coming.' The voice was deep, harsh and straight out of Glasgow's East End. The door opened to reveal a thin-faced young man, who looked to be in his mid twenties. 'Mair filth,' he said, curling his lip at the sight of the police officers.

'Get your father, boy,' Donald instructed.

'Don't ye mean, "Can I please speak with your father, Mr Robertson?"' The young man aped Donald's Kelvinside tones, an arrogant look crossing his gaunt features.

'Just fucking get him, you little bastard. Now!'

The door closed again, and the officers heard the young man shouting for his father as the woman wailed in the background.

'Whit's this Mr Robertson guff?' Scott asked, lighting a cigarette.

'Use some common sense, DS Scott. The whole idea behind having a new identity is that you go somewhere nobody knows you and start a new life. Logic would dictate that a change of name would be rather important, otherwise your enemies need only look up the phone book or the electoral register to find you.' Donald glared at the sergeant. 'And put that bloody fag out,' he added for good measure.

During this exchange of information, Daley was busy taking in his surroundings. The farmyard was covered in crumbling tarmac, broken and rutted in places. Not only were there no dogs, there were no other animals – not even a chicken, or ubiquitous farmyard cat. What looked like a plough lay propped up against one of the outbuildings, its original yellow colour barely visible through a thick coating of rust. In his experience, farms normally exuded a gut-wrenching odour of dung and slurry; it was obvious that whatever Frank MacDougall was doing to sustain the Robertson family, it most certainly did not involve any agrarian toil.

'I wonder what's behind the house?' Daley said.

'Half a ton o' cannabis an' a Sherman tank, likely,' said Scott, reluctantly extinguishing his cigarette on the ground with the toe of his shoe.

'Don't be ridiculous, DS Scott,' said Donald. 'Those on the witness protection scheme are very closely monitored to ensure that no such criminal behaviour takes place.'

'Aye, an' I'm Miss Marple.'

Before Donald had the opportunity to answer, footsteps sounded loudly behind the door and it was flung open to reveal another figure, almost identical in build and height to the previous man, with the same cadaverous face, though this time bearing the evidence of a further thirty years of hard living. Before them was one of Glasgow's legendary criminals: Frank MacDougall.

He looked at the three police officers one by one.

'I must be going up in the world, right enough,' he said and smiled at Donald. 'An inspector comes tae call, eh, John.' Donald winced at the over-familiar greeting. 'An' Jim tae.' He nodded a greeting at Daley. 'I remember when ye were still walking the beat up Toonheid way. By fuck ye've fairly piled on the weight.'

Scott laughed at this, and MacDougall turned next to him. 'Scooty, my man.' MacDougall stepped from the doorway and embraced the detective sergeant. 'How's it goin', buddy?' He seemed genuinely pleased to see Scott, much to the chagrin of Donald, who viewed the scene with obvious distaste.

'Listen, Frankie, we need tae come in, we've got something tae tell ye,' said Scott, a sombre look on his face.

'Fuck me, yer no' comin' tae tell me I've no paid a parking ticket. Come on.' He stood aside to welcome them in. 'Tommy, son,' he shouted, 'make sure you get the instant coffee oot, the polis are here.' He ushered the officers into the hall, at the end of which stood the woman, rubbing her hands together and looking at her visitors with apprehension.

Their host opened a glass-panelled door and led them into a capacious living room, replete with exposed beams, inglenook fireplace, expensive-looking ornaments, tasteful paintings and an enormous television. The ramshackle exterior of the house was certainly not reflected in its interior, which reminded Daley of the houses he'd seen in the lifestyle magazines Liz brought home.

Looking at the woman he now realised was Frank's wife, he found it difficult to imagine that the décor of the room was down to her good taste. She was perched on one of the leather recliners, wringing her hands and looking anxiously at her visitors.

MacDougall noticed Daley looking at his wife. 'On ye go, honey, an' get me an' these gentlemen some coffee,' he said gently, walking over to her and helping her out of the chair. 'Tommy'll gie ye a hand.'

'Are ye gettin' done again, Frankie?' she asked, looking from him to the policemen. 'Are they comin' tae take me hame?'

MacDougall walked her to the door. He spoke softly into her ear, kissed her on the head, and showed her out.

'Whit's wrang wi' Betty?' Scott asked, looking seriously at MacDougall.

'Vascular dementia,' he replied sadly. 'Started when we moved here – you know, just forgetting stuff, birthdays, folks' names – but she gradually got worse. Take a seat, gents, by the way,' he said, sitting in the recliner his wife had just vacated. 'Of course, we had tae take her tae a hospital in London, in case anybody spied her, ye know?' He was addressing Scott solely. 'Normally, this kinda thing doesnae happen until yer auld age. She's just been unlucky.'

'I'm sorry tae hear that, Frankie,' said Scott. 'I wiz just tellin' the boys whit a stunner she wiz.' He smiled at MacDougall.

'Aye, she wiz that.' MacDougall looked away, a glittering tear visible in the corner of his right eye. 'Anyway, fuck this, boys, eh?' His smile returned as he wiped a tear away surreptitiously with the back of his hand. 'If this is a delegation tae tell me mair aboot Gerry Dowie, I'm no' interested. Dinnae get me wrang, I liked the boy, but in oor game – well, ye know yersel, boys, it's an occupational hazard. I'm sorry fir his wife, mind; she didnae deserve that.' He looked regretful, meeting each policeman's eye with a steely gaze.

Donald, who had remained standing, stepped forward, which Daley recognised as a precursor to a lecture.

'I have some bad news for you, Mr Robertson.' Donald spoke formally, using MacDougall's pseudonym.

'Don't worry, big man, I can take it,' MacDougall replied cockily, though with a changed, more concerned expression creeping across his face. 'Just gie it tae me wi' baith barrels.'

'It's my unfortunate duty to inform you that your brother, Peter, was murdered last night in Glasgow,' Donald said, no emotion apparent in either his voice or expression. 'You have my sympathies.'

MacDougall threw his head back and stared up at the ceiling.

It was Scott who spoke, anxious to break the silence. 'I'm sorry tae, Frankie. He wisnae the worst, big Peter.' he said, with genuine sorrow.

'Nah, he wiz just a fuckin' fool.' MacDougall looked back at the policemen. 'I knew somethin' like this wid happen tae him, wi'oot me there tae watch his back, the stupid bastard. I'm surprised it's taken this long.' He stood, brought out a packet of cigarettes from his pocket, opened it, and offered them around. Scott accepted greedily without looking at Donald, who merely raised his eyes to the ceiling.

Scott was just lighting up as the door was flung open to reveal a young woman dressed in designer jeans and a tight-fitting shirt. Her hair was honey-blonde; her face round and pretty, dominated by large blue eyes. She bore none of the signs of addiction or debauchery that addled the complexion of the young man they had seen a few moments ago. She eyed her visitors without expression as she made her way across the floor to her father's side.

'What's wrong, Daddy?' she asked, in tones so well modulated that Scott looked at her with puzzlement.

'Bad news, honey, bad news,' said MacDougall, holding her to his thin frame. 'Yer uncle Peter's been killed.' And, as if she held the key to the floodgates, he started to sob silently into her shoulder.

'Sit down, Daddy,' she implored her father. He took her advice, sitting back on the recliner, head in hands, his shoulders shaking.

'Thanks very much, gentlemen,' she said coolly. 'You've done what you came to do, now just go and leave us in peace.'

'In fact, we haven't,' replied Donald, equally coolly. 'We need to speak more to your father – *in private*.'

'I think that's for my father to decide, don't you?' She answered defiantly, looking at her father, who was trying to compose himself.

Daley pondered the difference between her and her ill-mannered brother; it was clear that something in this girl's upbringing differed entirely from that of her sibling. Donald was insensitively drumming his fingers on the arm of the leather chair on which he was now sitting. Brian Scott, on the other hand, looked upon the scene with what Daley knew was genuine sympathy. His DS had grown up with many of the people it was now his job to bring to justice; in most cases, when their paths crossed professionally, it was treated by both parties like part of the job. He had watched Scott laugh and joke, even sympathise, with people who many others would consider the scum of the earth. Daley also knew that when it came to the crunch and the chase was on, no quarter would be given by either side. The bonds of childhood and community didn't always apply though; JayMac had tried to kill Scott. Now that he appeared to have miraculously cheated the grave, he would likely try again.

'Aye, Sarah, on ye go, honey,' said MacDougall gently. 'Away an' see if ye can calm yer mother doon. That kind o' thing's no' one o' yer brother's talents.'

'What talents?' she replied. 'When you discover anything he's actually good at, be sure to let me know.' She paused, taking her father's hands between her own. 'Are you sure you want me to go?'

'Aye, doll. We're nearly done anyhow. Off ye go.' MacDougall squeezed his daughter's arm and motioned for her to leave the room.

'Your daughter and son are very different,' Donald observed after she had gone.

'Aye, ye could say that,' he replied, his face still tear-stained. 'A' doon tae her granny. Sarah wiz a clever wee lassie; fae the minute she went tae primary school, the teachers wid comment on it. My mother wiz determined she should get oot o' the scheme, get a chance in life . . . And I had plenty dough.' He smiled at Donald, who was more than aware where the dough had come from. 'We sent her tae a private school in Perthshire. As ye can see, the wee Glesga lassie wi' skint knees and a snotty nose came back a young lady. This fuckin' prison is destroying her. She cannae even go tae university, or get a job, because of a' that's happened.' He glared angrily at Donald.

'Aye, but why the fuck did ye no' go abroad when ye had the chance, Frankie?' asked Scott.

'Betty, really' was his resigned reply. 'She never liked being away fae hame, even on holiday. She cried her eyes oot when it a' went mental. There was nothin' I could dae. They suggested the weans go away themselves, but none o' them wanted tae. Oor Cisco paid the price for that.' MacDougall looked as though he carried the world on his shoulders.

'Maybe you should have considered an alternative career, Mr Robertson,' Donald interrupted.

'Fuck off wi' this Robertson shite,' MacDougall shouted. 'Ye know my real fuckin' name – use it. Anyhow, just say whitever it is ye want tae say, an' leave me in peace, will ye? Ma heid's fuckin' burstin' noo.' He stood and walked over to a cabinet, taking out a bottle of whisky. 'Who's for a wee goldie?' he asked, looking around at the policemen.

Scott was about to nod, when Donald replied for all of them. 'We're on duty, Mr *MacDougall*. Anyway, we have something serious to discuss with you.'

'Serious? Yous have just telt me ma brither's been murdered – how much mair serious can it get?'

'We have an idea who is responsible for your brother's death, and the murders of Gerald and Marna Dowie,' Daley said, a look of regret on his face.

'If I wiz you, Frankie, I wid pour masel' a fuckin' bumper,' said Scott. 'Be prepared for a shock.' MacDougall looked at Scott quizzically, though took his advice and returned to the recliner with a small glass filled almost to the brim.

'We have good reason to believe, no matter how fantastic it sounds,' began Daley, 'that all three, and another uncon-nected man, were murdered by James Machie.'

MacDougall sat forward in his seat, looking at the policemen one by one. He took a long gulp of the whisky, then wiped his lips dry with the back of his hand. 'I widnae have thought ye'd be party tae somethin' like this, Scooty,' he said, his anger showing in his narrowed eyes. 'A' these fuckin' mind games mean fuck a' tae me noo. Save it for the kids yous arrest fir shoplifting, cos I'm no' interested. OK?'

'That's just it, Frankie,' Scott replied. 'It's no' mind games. It's true. I've seen the evidence wi' ma ain eyes.'

MacDougall was about to speak when Betty entered with a large tray on which were balanced mugs, spoons, a sugar bowl, a coffee pot and a plate of biscuits. Either from shock at the sudden entrance of his wife, or horror at the resurrection of Machie, MacDougall let the whisky glass slip from his fingers to the polished wood floor.

As her husband retrieved the glass, Betty MacDougall placed the tray on the coffee table and began murmuring in hushed tones. 'There's two sides tae him, constable. Oh, aye, two sides.'

'Sorry?' said Daley.

But Betty just shook her head and left the room.

'What does she mean by that?' said Daley.

'Ach, somethin' just no' connecting right; that's the way she is now.' But, mind, that bastard could be quoting you Shakespeare one minute, then trying tae cut yer fuckin' heid aff the next. We a' used to think he wiz a schizo – ye know? – split personality. Maybe that's whit she's tryin' tae say, the poor soul.' MacDougall stared at the door his wife had just closed.

When each man had helped himself to coffee, and in Scott's case a large quantity of biscuits, they resumed the conversation.

'C'mon, lads,' MacDougall said quietly. 'How can it be? I saw the back o' that van on TV. Yous must've seen the body. Surely ye did a post mortem?'

'Nobody wishes that JayMac still occupied the grave more than me,' replied Donald. 'Please take a look at this, if you require personal assurance.' The superintendent removed a document from the file he had brought with him and handed it to MacDougall.

After a few heartbeats he looked up. 'When wiz this taken?'

'That is an image taken from the CCTV footage of the scene of Gerald and Marna Dowie's murder in Australia a few days ago. It's been enlarged and enhanced, but let me assure you that nothing has been done to alter the detail.'

MacDougall threw the photograph onto the coffee table and downed his coffee. 'This, my friends, is my worst fuckin' nightmare.' He placed the mug on the table with a trembling hand.

'We will be taking over the responsibility for you and your family's personal security this evening,' Donald stated formally. 'In fact, I am detailing DS Scott here as your personal liaison officer. He will be in charge of the officers from the Support Unit who are coming down to do the job. I trust you have no complaints?'

'If I've got tae have cops aboot, better it's Scooty than anybody else,' MacDougall said, forcing a smile.

'I wish ye'd telt me,' said Scott, eyeing his boss with displeasure.

'Logic, DS Scott, logic. As you are every bit as much in the firing line as our friend Mr MacDougall here, surely it's the safest place for you to be, accompanied by a battalion of armed officers? Now let's get back to Kinloch,' he said, standing up. 'Good day, Mr MacDougall.' He turned to walk towards the door.

'Wait a minute.' MacDougall looked troubled. 'How are we goin' tae dae this? I mean, Tommy and Sarah go oot, tae Tarbert an' that. Whit aboot them?'

'The WP officers leave at six tonight. When we take over we'll give you and your family a full briefing,' replied Donald.

Daley nodded a farewell at MacDougall as he followed Donald out of the room. Scott tarried, the two old neighbours embracing before he too turned to go.

'Thanks for the warning,' Scott said, now sitting in the back of Daley's car.

'No need, DS Scott. Or should I call you Scooty?' Donald replied.

As Daley drove out of the farmyard, he looked in the rear-view mirror. Sarah MacDougall was standing in the yard beside the dirty car, watching the policemen go.

11

The man stood at the cliff edge, looking out over the sea. He had a mug of coffee in his hand; the steam rising through the cold air took the chill from his face, just as the beverage warmed his insides. The sea was an iron grey, almost matching the sky. An island shaped like a bread roll rose black from the water: Ailsa Craig. Behind it, a thin strip of land was visible through the gloom: Kintyre. A large bird swooped then dived into the sea not far from the shore, the chill of winter was in the air. Even though it wasn't much later than mid afternoon, the brightness of the day was beginning to leach from the sky. Soon the orange glow of thousands of streetlamps would fill the heavens, obliterating the light from countless stars.

He finished his drink, tipping the dregs onto the barren ground, then walked the short distance back to the cottage, which was perched in splendid isolation near the cliff. Just as he was about to enter, the ringing of the mobile phone in his pocket made him stop. Automatically, he looked at the screen, though the identity of his caller was obvious – only one person had the number of the pay as you go device. He answered with a grunt, sighed at the information being passed to him.

'Just make sure you stand up to your side o' the bargain,' he said. He waited for the brief reply then ended the call.

Inside, the cottage was spartan. The main room housed the living area and kitchen, which could be curtained off if required. A small TV sat on a rickety table, under which piles of DVDs were cluttered. A dusty couch and armchair sat in the middle of the floor at right angles to one another. The fireplace, instead of real flames, housed an aged and rusting electric fire, two bars of which glowed brightly, emanating a faint buzz.

He wasn't good at being on his own, being inactive, left to thoughts of the past, present and future. As he pondered the wisdom of the course he had embarked upon in the last few days, his rising fury confirmed the decision. He remembered once watching a television documentary about sharks; how they had to keep swimming to survive – that's the way he felt. He longed to be on the move, to do the things he had promised himself he would do, before disappearing again to start a new life where, this time, no one would ever find him.

Over the last few years he had been studying to improve his mind. It had been hard at first, until he had become addicted to the acquisition of knowledge. He had always loved books; the ability to absorb things quickly had helped him many times in years gone by. His mother had called it his special gift, though he had many other attributes.

In his new incarnation he had produced essays and even a thesis for distant tutors and lecturers, impressing them so much that they all wanted to meet their star pupil. But distance was what had attracted him to them in the first place; he claimed to be afflicted by everything from agoraphobia to acute depression in order to keep them at bay.

The whisky bottle on the table beckoned. He switched on the TV to keep thoughts of cosy inebriation at bay. A bearded man was attempting to answer a question against a timed, metronomic melody. The man looked at the heavens for the answer. 'It was Adam Smith, ye fuckin' plank,' he shouted at the screen, shaking his head and reaching for the bottle.

The man on the screen answered incorrectly as the golden spirit glugged into the glass. He watched for a few more minutes, getting every question immediately right, unlike the hapless contestant. He wondered why anyone so stupid would consider putting himself up for public ridicule on such a programme.

'Fuckin' arsehole,' he muttered, switching to the BBC news channel. The newsreader was young and pretty, she smiled coquettishly as she delivered so-called news on the public humiliation of yet another D-list celebrity.

'More news now on a murder committed in Glasgow last night,' she announced. He leaned forward and turned up the volume. 'I'm joined by our Scotland correspondent, Gillian Lamont. Gillian, can you give us any more details on what happened earlier?'

They had his full attention.

'Yes, I can, Carol.' The woman was standing in a Glasgow street; a rundown pub provided the backdrop. It was a familiar scene, though it looked different in daylight.

'We have discovered that the man stabbed to death in the street behind me in the early hours of this morning was Peter MacDougall, brother of Glasgow gangster Francis MacDougall, now thought to be in hiding after his evidence brought down the infamous Machie crime family.'

He raised his eyebrows, as the picture flicked back to the girl in the studio.

'Do we have any further details on the incident?' asked the newsreader.

Now, this was interesting.

'Very little; in fact, police here seem reluctant to say much at all about it. All we have is an eyewitness report from some customers from the pub behind me who saw a green vehicle, possibly an Astra car, parked outside in the minutes before the incident took place.'

He picked up the remote and flicked the television off. 'Fuckin' arseholes,' he chuckled to himself. 'Cannae even get the fuckin' car right.' He walked into the small bedroom that was located off the main room and picked up a book by Wittgenstein from the rickety bedside table. Leaving the well-oiled gun beside it behind, he returned to the lounge and started to read.

12

It was late afternoon, and Daley was getting ready to go home. He was tired in the sense of being fatigued mentally – the worst kind of exhaustion, with all of the weariness and none of the buzz that physical effort produced.

When they had arrived back at the office, ten members of the Support Unit were already waiting in the small canteen, armed with semi-automatic weapons, handguns strapped to their belts, and a variety of other paraphernalia, ready to be deployed to guard Frank MacDougall and his family. They were led by Sergeant Tully, who Scott knew from his days as a cop in the Gorbals; the two men had greeted each other warmly before sitting down with Donald to go over the complexities of the situation.

After the meeting, in a gesture somewhat out of character, Donald had instructed this group of officers to go to the County for a meal, to be paid for from divisional funds. The Support Unit personnel were to be billeted there, so Scott decided that he would book in too – partly to show solidarity, and partly to have easy access to the licensed premises.

Donald had then been given a lift to the local airport by a nervous DC Dunn, who had now returned, looking most relieved, and told Daley that she thought him 'quite charming'. As Daley struggled to digest this remark, acting DS Maxwell popped his head around the door.

'Just to let you know, sir,' he said, still ebullient after arresting the farmer selling illegal tobacco on his first operational command, 'we've searched everywhere thoroughly: house, barns, other outbuildings, vehicles, even his tractor. There's a reasonable amount of stuff, mostly eastern European in origin.'

'Eastern European?' Daley's ears perked up. 'The counterfeit tobacco we picked up was mainly from Spain.'

'Aye, sir, that's what was strange. There was very little of the Spanish tobacco left, while this other stuff was lying in boxes: only one opened, with a couple of packets missing. He said he smoked those himself.' The young detective had a puzzled expression.

'OK, where is he now?'

'In cell five, sir,' Maxwell said, with furrowed brows.

'The observation cell?' Daley was curious.

'Aye, sir. On the way here, he burst out crying, wouldn't stop. I thought it appropriate to call the force MD. I was afraid he was having some kind of breakdown. Apparently he's been drinking heavily for quite a while. The doc gave him a sedative and told me to keep an eye on him,' Maxwell said, displaying the qualities of common sense and compassion that Daley had first noted in him.

'OK, Alex,' replied Daley. 'Make sure he's under constant obs overnight. How's he pleading?'

'Guilty, sir, straight away, before I'd even charged him. Guilty,' the younger man repeated. 'I've written a report, if you want it just now, sir?'

'Eh, can you just email it to me, Alex?' said Daley. 'I'll take a look at it tonight. With a bit of luck we'll get him before the Sheriff tomorrow afternoon. Do we have any reason to oppose bail?' he continued, happy to leave the decision to the young detective.

'Not really, sir,' replied Maxwell. 'Unless the FMD thinks otherwise.'

'OK. Thanks. Sounds like he's in the best place for now. I'll see him tomorrow morning, before he goes for pleading.'

Maxwell exited with a nod, leaving Daley to ponder the latest example of a damaged mind he had encountered in his career; he was sure the man in the observation cell wouldn't be the last. He sighed as he got his things together in readiness for going home.

Daley felt drained as he drove out of the car park and down Main Street. The town looked festive, decked out with decorations, the shops' windows brightly lit with various Yuletide displays. People darted to and fro, wrapped up in scarves and warm jackets, clouds of breath freezing in front of them as they chatted.

It was just after four in the afternoon, and not quite dark; the moon and even some stars were just visible through the orange glow of the street lighting. The sky was a deep blue, still illuminated by the last embers of the setting sun, which he could see looking west as he drove around the head of the loch, itself smoothly reflecting the many lights of the town.

He remembered how much his mother had loved Christmas, and felt that peculiar twinge; a tiny pain, a reminder of the eternal absence of family, friends and colleagues who it was sometimes easy to forget he would never see again. It was so strange that people who had occupied your life so utterly, for so long, could just disappear, no longer present to chide, praise, advise, love, cheer, admonish. All that was left behind were fading photographs and memories – both good and bad – and this dull pain that afflicted the bereaved without warning, in the same way dreams of those long gone could spring unbidden into sleep, then linger and fade in the mind over hours or days. Some dreams one could never forget, either because they were so vivid, or they recurred over the course of a lifetime. Daley wondered why the populace of these dreams were so often the dead. Was it purely biology, or were they shadows of the people themselves, echoes of voices from a far distant void? Ghosts, he thought. I'm seeing too many ghosts today.

As Daley approached the turn away from the loch and up the hill towards his home, his eye was drawn to a motionless figure with its hand raised in the air in a static wave. Hamish.

Daley pulled over and got out of the car, walking over to his friend with his hand outstretched. 'How are you, Hamish? Cold night.' He shook the hand of the older man, whose tanned face was crinkled in a smile.

'She's a cauld one, right enough, Mr Daley,' he said, producing his pipe from a pocket in his overalls and filling it from a pouch of tobacco in his other calloused hand.

'I haven't seen you for a while. You should come up to the house for a bite to eat.' Daley issued the impromptu invitation with a smile.

'They tell me ye've arrested Duncan Fearney, fae High Ballochmeaddie farm. Am I right?' Hamish's face had taken on a more serious expression.

'You know I can't speak about that, Hamish, no matter how accurate the gossip is around here,' said Daley, knowing that such an event would have registered in the town within hours, perhaps minutes, of it actually taking place.

'You should know he's a good man,' Hamish observed, as though this was a fact that wouldn't have necessarily occurred to the policeman. 'Aye, an' forbye, that he's had wan hell o' a sad life.'

'You know my game, Hamish. I know good men sometimes do stupid things; but good or not, if they break the law, then it's my job to put them before the courts.'

'Aye, well that's as may be. The fermers have a wile struggle tae make ends meet, these days, especially the wans wi' the wee mixed ferms. Every bugger an' his freens are efter their wee bit money. I'm no' tryin' tae influence ye, mind – jeest letting you know.' He took a long draw of his pipe and puffed the pungent blue smoke back out in clouds.

'Are you busy yourself?' Daley enquired, anxious to change the subject.

'Och, ye know me fine, Mr Daley.' Hamish's smile returned. 'I'm aye busy wi' somethin'. I wiz speakin' tae that bonnie wife o' yours the other day,' he said, winking at Daley.

'Yes, she told me,' Daley replied, tapping Hamish on the arm. 'Listen, we better get out of this cold. Can I give you a lift anywhere?'

'No, yer fine. Besides,' Hamish said with a smile, 'I widnae be sure if I'd end up on remand. Yous polis are arrestin' decent folk left, right and centre, the noo.' He winked again at the detective.

'I'm sure you'd be fine,' Daley said, walking back to his car. 'I mean it about coming up for a meal. I'll ask the boss when it's most suitable.'

'Aye, that'll be great.' Hamish smiled. 'Though she's probably got mair on her mind, what wi' her condition an' a.'

'Right enough,' replied Daley vaguely, employing the same tactic he did with Liz when he hadn't heard or understood something properly.

He got into the car, secured his belt and started the engine. When he looked across the road to wave, Hamish was gone, with sign of him in the rear-view mirror. How does he do that? Daley wondered, not for the first time.

He pulled away from the kerb and headed home, though something new, something he couldn't quite define or grasp, was nagging at his subconscious. He dismissed the fleeting thought, consigning it to the drawer that contained the rest of his worries, and drove on.

Daley parked his car in the driveway and looked across the darkening sea towards the mound at the head of the loch. The ancient causeway that afforded access to the island at low tide snaked across the surface of the water like a sea monster. A nearly full moon shone down on the perfect scene. Nothing moved: no cars on the distant road, birds in flight, vessels at sea. For a brief moment, it was like being alone with the ocean and the heavens, at one with the fabric of time and existence, where dark thoughts are wont to roam.

And roam they did. Daley, staring into the black sky, somehow knew that a human monster resurrected to prey on his worst fears was taking in the same celestial view. It was as if suddenly, and for only an instant, they were two sides of an old, well-handled coin – part of a currency that stretched back and forth across the past, present and future. He and JayMac were merely recent manifestations of the eternal struggle between good and evil.

As quickly as the feeling came, it vanished. He had learned during his time as a detective to trust the subliminal mind: instinct coalesced with procedure, determination and hard work to bring evil to book. As inexplicable as such intuition was, it was to be ignored at one's peril.

He was jolted from this unexpected philosophical reverie by the clunk and squeak of the treble-glazed front door being opened. Liz stood on the decking, a few strands of hair loose across her face, and smiled down at him.

'What are you thinking about, Jim?' she asked, brushing the wayward hair from her eyes.

'Och, nothing, Liz. Just daydreaming, I suppose. What's for dinner? Not bloody pasta again?' He clambered up the steps onto the decking and hugged his wife, drawing the scent of her deeply into his senses. She was warm and soft; he slid his hand up under her loose top onto the smooth skin on the small of her back, making her draw her breath at the touch of his cold hand. Gently, he kissed her.

'Dinner can wait, darling,' she whispered, nibbling at his neck. 'Time for you to work off some more calories.' She took him by the hand into the warmth of their home on the hill. The bright moon spilled its light onto the water and the good people of Kinloch – and beyond.

13

The moon was reflected on the sea far below as he opened the back of the Transit van that had been left for him at the cottage. It was one of four vehicles he'd had the use of. On the surface these were all taxed and insured, completely above board, apart from the fact that their registered keepers were either dead, or in some other way indisposed. On a piece of waste ground in the East End of Glasgow, the burnt-out wreck of an old Honda Civic was being pored over by police forensic teams.

He preferred to travel at night, which was handy, since at this time of the year night seemed all encompassing in Scotland. He'd always liked the dark, even as a child. While his friends shied away from the blackness at the end of the day, the lowering gloom that enveloped the tenements and high-rise flats where they lived, he revelled in its silky anonymity. Even though Glasgow was a city, there were still nooks and crannies the streetlights couldn't penetrate.

One of his favourite haunts had been an old church cemetery, not far from his home. The ancient graves were moss-covered and crumbling, in most parts overgrown, and the lettering that granted the dead their earthly immortality was worn thin by rain, wind and the passage of time. He would trace his fingers along the loops and lines of the words. Soon he taught himself to decipher the names of the dead by touch alone. He remembered each tomb and its eternal occupant; he spoke to them one by one as he made his nightly round of the cemetery.

One gravestone fascinated him more than any other. As he traced his fingers over the gothic lettering, he had discovered a symbol: a skull and crossbones. Underneath, he deciphered the name of a boy. John. He even managed to make out that the first letter of the surname began with an 'M'. The thick briar that curled around the stone tore at his fingers, but he was determined to discover its secret. He knew the name belonged to a child, as he'd been able to uncover the part that confirmed the boy had been three years and four months old at the time of his death. He reckoned that the skull-and-crossbones motif must represent some dire illness or tragedy that had overcome the infant, though as he passed amongst the tombs he realised that dead children were by no means in the minority.

What fascinated him most about this grave though, was what was written further down the stone: another name. This time the script was clearer, less weathered, as the vegetation that had overgrown the base of the monument had protected the inscription. One cold night, when he had been bored, and most of the mysteries of the small graveyard were no longer secrets, he decided to pull away the grass and briars to read what lay underneath, expecting the usual platitudes of sympathy and regret.

It turned out that another child's body lay in the grave. This boy had lived longer, surviving to the ripe old age of seven years and eight months. His name was James. With a shaking hand, which he couldn't explain, he was able to trace the family surname from this undamaged portion of the stone.

As his dirty child's forefinger traced out the letters, a chill penetrated his heart. The 'M' was clear – it was the first letter of the name Machie. His own name. For a long time he had sat on the damp grass over the grave, as though chained to the ground by spirits beneath.

Eventually, he had managed to pull himself free from the invisible bonds cast by the dead boys and return home. For many nights after, his dreams were only those of the dead brothers with his name.

It had taken his young brain some time to work out what the final sentence on the gravestone meant. *Together at birth, united once more in death.*

One night, sometime after, when the screams of the children who had died so long ago awoke him from his sleep in a Glasgow multi-storey, he realised: they were twins.

He never visited the graveyard again, though the ghosts of the Machie twins of so long ago stayed with him always.

14

Donald sipped at a glass of expensive red wine as he stood by the kitchen window in the dark. His wife was at another night class – this time ancient Greek. She had bought into his struggle for self-improvement completely, having already attempted conversational Italian, art history, classical studies and watercolour painting. But Donald wasn't too sure of her heartfelt commitment to this personal renaissance. He knew she was much happier with the glass or two of wine that she and her friends enjoyed in the pub after class than with the journey of cerebral improvement on which they had jointly embarked. So what? They had made new friends, moved in a more elevated circle, and could now both talk with great assurance on a number of diverse topics over dinner – the crucible of his success. Well, that and the old, less refined requisites, necessary for the long climb up the greasy pole.

The moon penetrated his kitchen with its eerie luminescence, making it easy for him to trace the route along the granite worktop towards the bottle of wine and pour himself another glass. He had discovered that he could drink as much as a bottle a night without encountering the baleful effects of a hangover the next day; any more though and the familiar feeling of disconnection would impinge upon the important tasks of the following day. He was too dedicated to success to let this happen, but too stressed to do without the restorative salve of alcohol as part of his nightly relaxation. As a result, he was regimented in his discipline as far as self-medication with the fruits of the vine was concerned.

He had a lot on his mind. The spectral resurrection of JayMac was something he could have done without; he had enough to deal with as it was, especially with the jockeying for position that the introduction of this new 'national' police force was prompting. Many senior officers would be casualties, lured into early retirement by the prospect of enhanced pension deals and golden goodbyes. These incentives though, were not for him. Every problem is the dawn of a new opportunity: this was the mantra he had discovered as he rose through the ranks, part of a code he would never abandon.

As he appreciated the forest berry palate of the Grenache, his mobile phone vibrated in his trouser pocket. He hoped it would be his wife, however, his instinct told him otherwise. He furrowed his brow as the phone's display illuminated his face in the semi-darkness of the room.

'Speak,' was his pre-emptive greeting.

'Our friend has contacted us,' came the brief reply, the voice foreign, the English halting.

'How?'

'By the usual means,' said the voice, nearly as curt with its answers as the questions it was being posed.

'How have you responded?' Donald's voice was edged with a trepidation that his colleagues in the police force would have found most unusual.

'We are arranging a drop. It will be in the next two days. We will inform you when.' The accented voice paused, trying to find the appropriate word. 'It is organised.'

'This is not a good time, not at all,' Donald responded in a shouted whisper.

'Good or bad, what is it mattering?' came the reply. 'In this we have no choice.'

The line went dead. Donald massaged his temples, much in the way he had seen Jim Daley do in an effort to relieve the unremitting stress he always appeared to be under.

'Our friend' had disappeared in a speedboat as the authorities in Kinloch discovered the true extent of the illegal trade in narcotics funnelling through the town and its environs. The part he played in this venal trade was important, and it was essential that he evade capture – but for that he had needed help. Now it was time for Donald to pay the price of assistance.

Donald lifted the wine bottle again, noting with irritation that it was nearly empty.

Maybe it was time for a nightcap of the hard stuff; this was surely a suitable opportunity to break his code of alcohol consumption. He left the kitchen and walked into his large, well-furnished lounge, where he removed a bottle of Ardbeg from the cabinet. As the warm spirit numbed his lips, he angled his head back, eyes closed. Had he gone too far? Was this one calculated risk too many?

15

He looked himself up and down in the long mirror on the inside of the wardrobe door. He remembered a TV programme from his childhood where a cartoon figure donned a new costume every week and did the job that matched the outfit.

He had no intention of doing this job.

The heavy jacket didn't match the clothes underneath. He replaced his woollen hat with a blue baseball cap and transformed his appearance yet again.

He picked up the gun with its silencer from the bedside table, left the bedroom, switching off the ceiling light, then, now in the small lounge, drained the last drops of whisky from the cracked tumbler.

The cottage was isolated enough not to be in the path of many passers-by, but he decided to leave the light in the old standard lamp burning.

'You never know what crooks are on the go.' He smiled at this thought, prompted by the old saying of his mother's, and walked out into the moonlit night.

Scott was standing on the hill behind the farmhouse with Frank MacDougall. A pall of cigarette smoke curled into the night as the two old neighbours looked down the hill and across the river to another rise thickly crowned by commercial forestry. The world was silent, monochrome; the faint tinkle of the burn barely sounded over the distant rumble of the sea as it broke on the rocky shore.

'Dae ye believe a' this shite, Scooty?' MacDougall asked the policeman. 'Oor lassie thinks this is a' part o' the mind games o' the Witness Protection, tryin' tae get me oot the way abroad. I mean, that's the second time Gerald Dowie's died, no' tae mention yer man.' He paused, as though the very mention of his name might conjure him up.

'Well, I'll tell ye this,' replied Scott, drawing at his cigarette, 'they've done a fuckin' good job o' it. Ma heid's well and truly fucked up wi' it an a'.' He flicked the cigarette butt down the hill.

MacDougall hawked and spat copiously. 'If it wisnae for the wife, I'd probably take their advice an' dae one. But ye've seen her – wan mention o' goin' abroad an' she goes mental.' He rubbed his mouth with the back of his hand. 'Who wid've thought that evil bastard wid be able tae cheat death? Fuck knows, he cheated everything else. I suppose we shouldnae be that surprised.'

'It's a shame she's . . . ye know.'

'Aye, it's mair than a pity, a' right. The trouble is I cannae abandon her noo; the docs have a'ready said she'll need tae go intae . . .' Now it was MacDougall's turn to pause. 'Into a place, ye know?' He looked Scott squarely in the face, the moonlight picking out the lines on his forehead in greater relief.

'No' a nice prospect. No' nice at a', Francis,' said Scott, shivering in his borrowed jacket, as an owl piped up from the trees. 'Aye, an' stop ca'ing me Scooty, ya cunt. That bastard Donald's a'ready picked up on it.'

'Nice tae see he hasnae changed much. Still the arrogant swine he wiz six years ago – worse, in fact.'

'Of that, my friend, ye can have nae doubt.' Scott raised his head sharply. 'Did ye see somethin' move there? O'er by that wee boat doon in the river?'

'Whit?' MacDougall whispered, squinting into the distance. 'Aye, there it is again.' He pointed his finger across to the other side of the burn, crouching as he did so.

Scott, who also ducked, grabbed MacDougall by the arm and steered him slowly back down the hill. 'DS Scott tae all stations. Positions over?' One by one the five Support Unit personnel replied, their voices issuing distantly from Scott's radio, which he had turned down to a whisper.

'We've got company,' Scott murmured into the mouthpiece, 'across the river at the back o' the hoose. Who's nearest?'

Scott and MacDougall lay flat on the cold ground, peering over the crest of the hill.

'When the unit boy arrives up here, I want ye tae go back tae the hoose. Make sure everybody's where they should be. OK, Frankie?'

'Gie me a shooter, Scooty. If that's that cunt, it'll be my pleasure tae blast his fuckin' heid aff,' said MacDougall defiantly.

'Aye, I'll just gie ye a gun, an' count the days until I'm banged up in Barlinnie. Just dae as I say. We've won a watch here, he widnae be expecting anybody tae see him.'

A rustling noise from behind startled the two men. They turned to see a figure dressed in black creeping towards them up the hill.

'The house is being secured, gaffer,' he said, no trace of anxiety in his voice. 'Best if you accompany me, Mr Robertson.'

'Ye nearly gied me a fuckin' heart attack,' said Scott, doing his best to sound put out with a whisper. 'Take Frankie back tae the hoose, an' I'll stay here an' keep an eye oot for this bastard. Don't be long, mind. I've no' got a weapon, remember.' Scott's clearance to carry a sidearm had not yet come through from divisional HQ, much to his frustration. 'That bastard Donald couldnae have planned this better; me here on a fuckin' lonely hillside, being stalked by the ghost o' Christmas past, an' only a baton fir company.'

'Best o' luck,' said MacDougall, already sneaking back down the hill with the armed officer.

Scott squinted down the glen. The brightness of the moon had been dulled by a passing cloud, adding to his tension. He reached for his mobile phone, cupping the screen with his hand so that its light would not be visible to the prowling figure somewhere out in the darkness.

The dialling tone sounded in his ear, and the call rang briefly on the other end before it was answered.

'Jim, it's me.'

'Why are you speaking so quietly?' came the breathless reply.

'I'm on the hill behind Frank's hoose. We've spotted something moving. The unit boys are getting the MacDougalls sorted, then we'll try an' find the bastard.' Scott spoke quickly. 'By the way, how come you're so oot o' breath? Has she had ye oot jogging?'

'Something like that, Brian,' Daley said enigmatically. 'Listen, you get back to the house. You're not armed. Leave this to the Support Unit. I'll get over to the hotel and rouse the rest of them. We'll be able to get there in two cars quite quickly. But get yourself back to the house.'

'I cannae hear you . . . Whit did you say, big man? This line's . . . breaking up,' Scott lied before ending the call.

Liz was lying in bed, propped up on one elbow, watching her husband. The livid scrapes down his back were testament to their lovemaking, which had been disturbed by the call her husband had insisted on taking.

'Tell me you're not rushing off, darling,' she said, knowing what the reply would be.

'I've got to, Liz,' Daley panted, struggling into a pair of trousers. 'They've got someone prowling around . . .' He stopped himself. He hadn't told Liz the full extent of the problem they were facing – certainly not anything about the resurrection of JayMac. 'This guy, Robertson, could be in a lot of danger – not to mention Brian.' He pulled in his stomach, wrestling with his waistband.

'I sometimes wonder if I'd get more attention if I changed my name to Brian.'

'Absolutely,' replied Daley, who had clearly not been listening. He had succeeded in fastening his trousers, and was now attempting to tuck his shirt into them, not without difficulty.

'Just as well you're not a fireman, love. By the time you got your kit on, everything would be cinders.'

Dressed, he leaned over the bed and kissed her on the cheek. 'I'll see you when I see you,' he smiled. 'You know how it is.' He left their bedroom and waved goodbye without turning around.

'Be careful,' she shouted. Then, much more quietly, 'We really need to talk, Jim.' She lay back, looked at the ceiling and sighed. We really, really do, she thought, running her hand down her stomach.

Scott felt isolated on top of the hill. The gibbous moon had been restored to its full splendour, the cloud that had briefly plunged the scene into utter darkness having moved on.

He had one of the new-fangled retractable metal batons in his pocket, which didn't add to his feeling of wellbeing. What use would this fuckin' thing be against JayMac? he thought. The feeling of being watched made the hairs on the back of his neck stand to attention; it was as though his whole body was braced for an attack, the nature of which he was desperately trying to discern. His muscles were tense in anticipation of searing pain, his body remembering the gunshot wound to his shoulder inflicted by his quarry long ago.

He jerked as his mobile phone vibrated silently against his leg. Again, he shielded the screen with his cupped hand. He was cheered to discover that it was Daley's name that appeared across the screen in bold letters.

'How's it goin', Jim?' he whispered into the mouthpiece.

'I'm on my way to the hotel to pick up the rest of the unit, Brian. We should be there in twenty minutes or so. Where are you? Who are you with?'

'I'm on my ain, on this fuckin' hill, shittin' mysel', if ye must know,' came Scott's honest reply.

'What do you mean, "on your own"?'

'I'm waiting fir one o' the boys tae get back here. They're securing the perimeter of the hoose.' The stress was apparent, even in Scott's whisper.

'Get yourself back inside, Brian.' Daley's whisper had modulated. 'You're not armed. I'm going to draw weapons, for you too. Fuck Donald.'

'No, thanks,' replied his DS. 'Just get yoursel' up here. Wait!' He stopped whispering and held his breath. Something – somebody – was moving on the low ground in front of the river, only thirty or forty yards from where the detective was crouched. 'Jim, I'll need tae go. Just get here, buddy.' His whisper was barely perceptible, even to himself. He ended the call, placed the phone back into his trouser pocket and removed his baton.

Somehow, the figure he had spotted in the trees had made its way across the burn; it was now crouched but still discernible in the pale moonlight.

Thankfully, the Support Unit members resting in the County Hotel proved much more adept at getting dressed in a hurry than Daley, who pulled up alongside the dark phalanx of policemen waiting in front of the hotel. After a minimal briefing, three of the Support Unit got into Daley's car and the other two, including the sergeant in charge, hurried the short distance to the office to collect another car and the arsenal of weapons that Daley had requested over the phone.

As he was about to pull away from the kerb, he saw the unmarked estate car coming down Main Street from the police office. No big personnel carriers were used in sensitive operations such as this, where discretion was key. Also, as they had arrived in Kinloch in three separate cars, specially equipped with weaponry housing and sophisticated communication equipment, they made three complete and functional units, each operational either as part of a greater whole or individually. The lights of the estate flashed as it passed Daley's 4x4. The cavalry was on its way.

Scott hardly dared breathe; it was at times like this he cursed the fact that he was a heavy smoker. Whenever he was required to remain silent, whether it was in church at a funeral, during one of Donald's endless briefings, or even at the kids' Christmas pantomime at the school, he could feel the tickle in his throat. The desire to cough was fighting with his fear of being discovered. At the moment, fear was winning – just.

Suddenly, just when he thought he could no longer stop himself, he felt someone touch his back. After experiencing the odd sensation of jumping clean off the ground without the use of his arms or legs, he turned to see two darkly clad policemen crouching behind him, moonlight reflected in the automatic weapons they both carried.

Scott shook his fist at them in mock anger and quickly indicated that they should remain silent, then pointed down the hill to where the figure was still huddled, silhouetted against the silvery glimmer of the burn.

Scott, still lying flat against the cold ground, nodded to the two armed officers, one of whom scrambled closer to him. He craned his head toward the DS.

'The rest of the lads are on their way. My orders are to maintain a watching brief until they arrive,' he hissed in Scott's ear.

Scott grabbed him by the lapel, pulling him closer. 'Aye, that's all very well, but the way things are going, he'll be standin' on ma heid in two minutes. We're going tae have tae try and contain him. He'll be at the farmhouse long before they get here.'

The officer pulled his head back from Scott and stared straight at him. He then shuffled back to his colleague, and after another brief head to head, turned to Scott and nodded.

At that second, there was a rustling noise followed by a dull thud and what sounded like a whispered oath.

If this is a ghost, he's no' very sure-footed, thought Scott. He was trying to work out exactly from which direction the noise had come when, without warning, a flash of silver in his peripheral vision made him turn his head to the right. A shadow was now passing the police officers about fifty yards distant.

Daley sped round a corner, sending his mobile phone flying off the dashboard and onto the lap of the policeman in the passenger seat. They were only a mile from the turn-off to the single-track road that led to the farmhouse.

The radio belonging to the officer sitting beside him burst into life. Daley expected that it would be Tully, the unit commander from the other car, but he was wrong: it was one of the armed officers at the farmhouse. They were now in radio range.

'Units engaging suspect, over.' The voice was terse and to the point, no elaboration.

Daley turned to the man next to him. 'Get me Tully. Now!'

Scott jumped again as the two officers beside him leapt into action. Both were wearing powerful head torches, which they now illuminated, spotlighting the intruder, stopping him in his tracks. Two dots played across the man's chest and face like crimson fireflies as he brought up his arm to protect his eyes from the unexpected glare. Scott squinted at the man as his fellow officers shouted instructions to one another. The intruder stretched out his arms and sank to his knees, head bowed.

Scott tried to get a clearer picture of him; he needed to see his face. Slowly, blinking against the harsh light, the figure raised its head and looked straight at Scott.

Whoever it was, it was no ghost. This man was not James Machie. The DS breathed a sigh of relief.

16

He walked quickly along the overgrown path. Three high-rise blocks – the last monuments to the folly of brutalist sixties architecture – reared out of a desolate, unkempt landscape. This brave new world of multi-storey living was about to go the same way as its predecessor, the once ubiquitous Glasgow tenement. He wondered if he was the only person left with any affection for this once thriving neighbourhood.

He entered the building through large red security doors panelled with tough polycarbonate, now rutted by graffiti and burned brown by the cigarettes that had been repeatedly stubbed out on it. The doors had long since been stripped of their electronic locks and transoms; the echo of them banging shut reverberated around the bleak vestibule, which stank strongly of urine. Two of the three lifts were out of order so he stood before the functional one and pressed the button, which would have illuminated green had it not been for the fact that it was shattered, the broken bulb visible through the cracked plastic.

The lift seemed to take an age, but eventually a distant pulse and thud heralded its arrival. It clunked into place and the doors creaked open, hesitantly, as if fretful of revealing was what inside, which in this case was a drunk man, sprawled unconscious in a pool of his own piss on the floor.

He stared down at the unconscious man. The stench of urine, vomit and stale alcohol was overpowering in the enclosed space. The man groaned, and a dribble of saliva migrated down his stubbly chin. He reached into his pocket.

Why she enjoyed documentaries about the war, she couldn't fathom. It had been the most terrifying time of her life. Having grown up in Clydebank, she had witnessed the Blitz virtually wiping out the whole town; thousands had died, including her grandfather who had gone to work on a cold November morning, never to return. He died along with the other occupants of the bus that was carrying him home after his shift at the shipyard was over. The only survivor had been a three-month-old baby, protected from the blast by the body of its dead mother.

However, regardless of the aching loss of friends and family members during the war, she looked back on it now with a kind of nostalgia, a feeling of warmth and familiarity as she remembered everything now absent from her life. Most of her friends were dead, and her family – or what was left of it – had been ravaged by booze, drugs and poverty. She had lost two sons to heroin, and her husband had died nearly forty years ago, the whites of his eyes yellowed as his liver gave up the battle against alcohol.

She got up from her chair stiffly, clicks and pops coming from her knees and ankles. It was time for another cup of tea, then bed, the only opportunity she had now of escaping her loneliness and her aches and pains.

He removed his hand from his pocket and leaned over the man. He put his fingers to his neck and felt for a pulse, pulling the man's collar aside to reveal a red, dirt-encrusted throat.

'There you go, Tony-boy,' he said, sliding a bundle of notes under the collar of the sleeping figure. 'Two hundred quid should see ye aff, ye poor bastard.' He snorted a laugh and looked down at the man. Aye, fir auld times' sake.

The lift juddered to a stop and the doors slid open to reveal the hallway of the sixteenth floor. He pulled the right leg of the unconscious drunk across the piss-soaked floor to the lift entrance; the man was so out of it he barely moved, grunting incomprehensibly as he expelled more dirty brown saliva down his chin. He watched as the doors were stopped by the obstruction.

Worth two hundred quid of anybody's money, Tony-boy, he thought. That's probably the most money ye've made yourself in the last thirty years, and yer no' even awake.

He caught sight of himself in the polished aluminium of the lift door and took the opportunity to straighten the black-and-white checked hat on his head. 'Fuck me, PC Plod,' he chuckled throatily to himself, as he walked along the hallway past welcome mats and little ornaments the occupants of this raised hell had placed outside their front doors in an attempt to make their surroundings more bearable.

He read the nameplate on the door: 16/5. MACDOUGALL.

He knocked loudly. Presently, a light went on in the hall and a small figure came into sight through the frosted glass of the door, moving slowly along the hallway inside.

'Who's there?' The woman sounded frail and elderly.

'Police, Mrs MacDougall. Can I have a word with you?' He saw her reach forward, and heard the rattle of chains and locks as she opened the door.

*

The inside of Kinloch's police office was bright and warm. Scott stood beside a radiator, holding his hands as close to it as he could stand as he tried to warm up after his exposure on the hillside at Frank MacDougall's farm.

'Brass monkeys oot there cryin' their eyes oot, Jim,' he said to Daley, who was busy unbuttoning the waistband of his trousers as he sank into his swivel chair, in the glass box that was his new home from home.

'I'll let that daft kid cool his heels overnight in the cells before we go and interview him,' said Daley, who visibly relaxed as his stomach was released from his loosened trousers, though the buttonholes on his shirt were still stretched to their maximum tolerance.

'Aye, slimmer o' the year, eh? Fuck me, when are ye due?' Scott yawned halfway through this statement, making it only slightly less palatable to his boss, who frowned and pulled his belly in.

'You'll never know how lucky you are, Brian. You can eat and drink anything you want and not put on a pound. I, on the other hand,' he said, rubbing his stomach, 'have to struggle with this, or starve to death.'

'Och, it's a' pent up energy wi' me – my mind's a'ways workin''.' Scott grinned and sat down on the guest's chair, leant back and put his feet up.

'Aye,' said Daley, 'working out when and where you can get your next drink.'

'That's a low blow, right enough, especially since ye're hardly whit I wid call the soul of sobriety,' Scott replied, eyes closed. 'I'll tell ye somethin', I thought that wiz yer man up there on the hill the night. If I'd had a hip flask on me, I wid have drunk the lot.' He smacked his lips together at the thought of the dram he was anticipating.

'That boy got the fright of his life, eh?' Daley said, referring to the young lad who had been waylaid by the Support Unit at gunpoint on the hill, just over an hour before.

'Aye,' Scott chortled. 'No' the kind of assignation he was expecting. Mind you, that Sarah's a bonnie lassie, an' no mistake.' He inclined his head in a way that said, If I were only twenty years younger.

'And before you say it, you'd still be too old.' Daley laughed. 'Anyhow, something's telling me that young Miss MacDougall has her sights set rather higher than a detective sergeant with a glad eye and a fondness for strong liquor.'

'I can hardly believe she's related tae Frank and Betty. She's nothin' like them, or her granny, come to that,' Scott said, now sitting up straight, with his feet on the floor, as though the shock of MacDougall's well-spoken, cultured offspring was too much to get his head around.

'Popular with the young men from Tarbert too,' Daley said, referring to the fact that the young intruder had been on his way to meet Sarah MacDougall.

'Did ye see her faither's face when she said that there wiz nothin' in it, an' she just fancied a shag? I thought Frankie wiz goin' tae blow up an' never come back doon.'

'Well,' replied Daley, 'there's nothing like a night in the cells to cool your ardour.'

'Of that there can be no doubt, James,' Scott said, scratching his head and yawning. He was about to say something more, when Daley's internal phone rang.

'Hello, sir.' Daley made a face at Scott to indicate that Donald was on the line.

'I hear you've had some fun this evening. Who was this clown?' Donald's voice was loud enough for Scott to overhear.

'A local boy, sir. He comes from Tarbert, the village just up the road. Lovesick for MacDougall's daughter, by all accounts.'

'I want you to keep him in custody as long as possible, Jim. Apply for a custody extension if necessary; I'll use my influence if required.' Donald sighed those last few words, as though he was weary of the pressure of command. It was not the attitude Daley associated with his superior.

'What reason will I give the Sheriff, sir?' Daley asked.

'Be creative, Jim. Regardless of the fact that the boy is probably an in-bred halfwit, he's seen too much. It must surely have dawned on him that it's a little unusual that his girlfriend is being guarded by armed police. The last thing we need is for the local gossips to get going and the papers to get a sniff of what's going on.'

'Yes, sir. Surely this is more reason for Witness Protection to move them on, sir?'

'You would think so, Jim, however, our friend MacDougall is digging in his heels. He claims that because of his wife's mental state, her human rights would be infringed if she were to be moved at this time against her will. Mental cruelty, would you credit?'

'Oh yes, sir. Human rights have always been at the forefront of Frank MacDougall's mind,' Daley said. Though MacDougall was not in the same league as JayMac for violence, he had nonetheless committed some crimes of sickening brutality.

'Keep a hold of him as long as you can, Jim. I'll busy myself with trying to get MacDougall and his clan as far away from Kinloch as possible, but rest assured, it will take time.'

There was a brief silence between the two men, a pause that would normally have been filled by some hubristic comment from the superintendent. The resurrection of James Machie appeared to have troubled Donald more than Daley had realised.

Daley ended the call by wishing his boss goodnight.

'Aye, an' I'll come up an' tuck ye in and read ye a story,' Scott added, when he was sure that the receiver was well and truly down.

'Not sounding his usual self, Brian,' Daley observed.

'Nice to know even his magnificence has his off days tae,' said Scott. 'I've had a right hard night, Jim. How about we head doon for a couple o' swift drams as a nightcap, eh?'

Giving the notion only the briefest thought, Daley nodded and stood up. He hauled the waistband of his trousers together, then, not without difficulty, managed to fasten the button.

'Aye, the outdoor life doon here's daein' wonders for your physique, big man,' Scott said with a grin.

'Shut up and get your wallet out. I feel like a large malt.'

'Is that the way of it?' Scott grimaced. 'I wish tae fuck I'd kept my mooth shut.'

'I wonder just how rich you'd be if you had a pound for every time that thought crossed your mind, Brian?' Daley smiled as Scott left his glass office, muttering under his breath.

Marion MacDougall lay on the floor of her living room. It looked really strange from this angle, and she felt confused and cold. The right side of her head throbbed, and she could feel a warm stickiness on her arm. She knew she was only able to see out of one eye, because when she closed her left everything went black, shot through with flashes of red and yellow.

She tried to move her legs, but the pain that shot through her body was excruciating. Even breathing was difficult; the air got stuck in her throat as though her whole chest was blocked by a massive weight.

'More bad news for the economy . . .' The voice belonged to the nice Welshman who read the ten o'clock news. She couldn't work out how it was so late. It was cold – very cold – though somehow it didn't seem to trouble her in the way it normally did.

Out of the corner of her eye, at the very periphery of her vision, she could see something white: yes, a white circle. She tried to steady her breath and focus. The way her remaining vision was blurring, this might be her only chance, her only opportunity to survive, to do something to save her life before her world went black for good.

She managed to move her arm, even though the pain was so acute it made her feel sick. Slowly, she managed to hook her thumb around the chain that held the white disc around her neck. She retched a foul mix of bile and blood, which spilled out over her false teeth and down the side of her face onto the floor. She didn't have much time. Instead of pulling the chain towards herself, she pushed her hand away, feeling the links pass over her thumb, still hooked around it. Though doing this caused her pain, it didn't make her feel so nauseous.

Suddenly, the chain pulled tight, biting at her neck and making her almost pass out in agony. Her breath was short now, but she had managed it; the white disc was under the palm of her hand. She forced it down, hearing the little bleep that indicated it had worked. Soon, very soon, help would be on its way. But would it come soon enough?

17

They went into the County Hotel through the heavy old door, on which someone had scrawled Merry Christmas!!! in fake snow from an aerosol can. A large, artificial tree stood in the vestibule sporting a selection of baubles – not one of which matched the next.

A low murmur of voices issued from the serving hatch to the small bar, indicating that Annie was reasonably busy for this time of night. A large man nearly knocked Scott over as he pushed past the detective, heading down the corridor towards the toilets. Shouts of 'He's got the skitters' and 'Willie's jeest shat himsel'' accompanied the stricken man, as his drinking buddies at the bar speculated as to the state of their friend's health.

As the two policemen appeared at the bar, however, the atmosphere changed. Everyone fell silent.

Unabashed, Scott strode in, removing his wallet from the back pocket of his trousers as he went. He chose a position in between two of the hotel's more regular customers, whom he recognised, and nodded a hello to each in turn.

'Aye, lads, a cold yin the day, is it no'?' Scott rubbed his hands in anticipation of the whisky that would hopefully warm the parts not every spirit could reach. He was slightly surprised by the lack of response from the drinkers but his attention was soon taken up by Annie's appearance through the door behind the bar.

'Whoot can I get ye, sir?' Annie asked stiffly, polishing the bar counter without looking directly at her new customer.

'Two large malts, darlin', an' one for yersel, efter you bein' so kind the last time I wiz in.' Scott's smile elicited little response.

Daley had made his way to the table at the back of the bar, where he usually sat with Liz. She had accused him of purposefully selecting this perch, better to study his fellow drinkers. Maybe he had, though it was also true that this table was furthest from the bar, and the army of those who were not only willing to eavesdrop, but to make comment on conversations that he'd hoped were private. Only a few weeks before, during a discussion with Liz about his interminable diet, an old woman had leaned across from another table and advised Liz that if she expected her sex life to remain active, she better ditch the calorie-controlled regime and feed her man 'a good plate o' mince an' tatties'.

Daley smiled at the old man who sat nearby nursing a small glass of whisky, head turned away, which was unusual for one who was usually so cheery and pleasant.

'I'm thinkin' some bastard must be deid,' Scott announced as he placed two glasses on the table in front of Daley, both brimming with whisky. 'Even yer lassie Annie's no' her usual bubbly self.' He sat down on the chair opposite his boss, and then turned to note that nearly everybody in the room was looking at them.

'Something's up, that's for sure,' said Daley.

Feeling increasingly uncomfortable, the two policemen drank in silence, Scott looking over his shoulder from time to time at the collection of stony faces staring back.

'I'm goin' for a pee, big man,' Scott said to Daley, and made his way out of the bar.

'Aye, I hope Willie Mason shites on ye,' uttered a disembodied voice.

'Right, that'll be enough,' called Annie, though lacking her usual vigour. But it was enough to break the spell, and the murmur of low voices resumed.

As Daley swirled the spirit in his glass, Annie made her way out from behind the bar and towards his table, flicking her cloth at unseen detritus as she progressed.

'Will ye be for another?' she asked coolly, as she lifted Scott's unattended glass from the table, wiped it with her cloth and placed it on a fresh beer mat.

'Yes, if you can be bothered,' replied Daley, slightly irritated by the reception he was getting in what had become his favourite watering hole.

'Listen,' whispered Annie, 'ye cannae expect folks tae welcome yous wi' open erms, when yer giein' poor Duncan Fearney such a hard time. He's a nice man – very popular in the toon. Aye, an' he's had a hard time o' it, since that wife o' hees ran off wi' the AI man.' Point made, Annie turned to go.

'Wait a minute, Annie,' Daley said, looking serious. 'I like coming in here, and you've always made me very welcome, but you must know, I've got to do my job, and no matter if nobody talks to me in Kinloch again, that's what will happen.'

Annie, looking slightly flustered, sat down on the chair that had been vacated by Scott and leaned in towards Daley.

'Aye, I daresay, Mr Daley, but ye've got tae realise how close the folk here are. Hurt wan, an' ye hurt us a'. D'ye know whoot I mean? An' anyhow, the boys appreciated whoot the big fella did for them . . .' Annie stopped abruptly, avoiding any eye contact with the policeman.

'What you mean to say is that they got cheap fags from him,' Daley said, staring at the blushing Annie.

'Noo, I didnae say anythin' o' the sort, Mr Daley. Fuck me, but yous polis are slippery right enough,' she said, regaining some composure. 'I never says anythin' o' the sort.'

'No, of course you didn't,' Daley replied. 'But I hope you understand my position, Annie?'

She rolled her eyes and tutted. 'Aye, I suppose we've a' got oor ain jobs tae dae. We'll say nae mair aboot it. I'll have a word wi' the boys.' She made to leave but Daley had another question.

'Can I ask you what an AI man is?'

'AI?' Annie smiled. 'Artificial insemination, Mr Daley. He's the man who goes roon servicing the coos, if ye know whoot I mean. They ca' him the Bull o' Kintyre.'

Daley watched her leave, trying not to laugh, as he reflected on how it must feel for your wife to run off with the man responsible for impregnating Kintyre's bovine population. When Scott returned from the toilet, he told him the story. The detective sergeant's hearty laugh broke through the drinkers' low chatter as, gradually, the atmosphere in the little hotel bar returned to normal.

DS White was fed up. He hated the nightshift, especially when it meant having to sit at his desk for its entirety, keying reports into his computer, the screen of which flickered at him interminably and worsened the throbbing headache he had suffered since arriving at Police Headquarters in Paisley earlier in the evening.

He was in the midst of typing up an especially complex fraud case, in preparation for a report being sent to the Procurator Fiscal's department. The deputy fiscal he was forced to deal with was as pedantic as he was petty, and not averse to sending back the work of hard-pressed detectives for correction like a scolding headmaster. He and White carried on what could best be described as a silent war of words, each trying to outdo the other with the accuracy of their report or the importance of their perfectionist demands.

White sat back in his chair and rubbed his eyes, yawning at the same time. The lure of the coffee machine was strong. As the words on the screen in front of him began to swirl and blur, he stood, fishing in his trouser pocket for the correct change with which to buy the only beverage that would see him though the long night ahead.

As he left his desk and headed along the corridor to the drinks machine, a group of policemen were queuing patiently outside at the rear door of the office. Their conversation was low and intermittent as one of them punched the security code into the keypad on the wall. The officers were on their meal break; the strong smell of kebabs and Chinese food issued from the various brown paper bundles and white plastic bags they were carrying.

The keypad bleeped, releasing the deadbolts of the heavy steel door, allowing the first in the queue to pull it open. The phalanx of hungry policemen filed in, leaving the freezing cloud of their accumulated breath behind them as they entered the warmth of the inner sanctum of the police office.

The last of their number was about to pull the door closed, when a uniformed cop raced across the car park, carrying a large carrier bag.

'Cheers, mate,' the man said breathlessly. 'I've got an item to be delivered to the office of Superintendent Donald, from the divisional commander at Baird Street. Where is it?'

Anxious to tuck into his kebab, the cop held the door open and directed the newcomer towards a flight of stairs. 'Up to the third floor. You'll get access to the boss's floor via the CID suite. There's always some of those lazy bastards up there at night hiding oot o' the cold.'

'Aye, brand new,' said the visitor. He took the stairs two at a time, the carrier bag swaying to and fro at his side.

'Fuck!' DS White swore as he heard the buzzer at the door of the CID suite. He had just sat down to his coffee, and was about to try and buy his wife's Christmas present online before returning to his dreaded fraud report. He put the coffee down beside his computer terminal, got up stiffly, then threaded his way through the unoccupied work stations towards the door at the end of the long room. The uniformed cop was staring through the security glass, the black-and-white check of his hatband showing brightly in the subdued light.

'Can I help?' White asked, peering at the cop, whom he didn't recognise.

'This is for Superintendent Donald,' the man announced, holding the carrier bag up for inspection. 'Fae the gaffer at Baird Street. Nice wee Christmas present, I'll wager.'

'Just gie me it here,' White demanded, more curtly than he intended. He had enough to get done, without acting as an unofficial Santa for the boss.

'If ye don't mind, my instructions are tae plank it doon on his desk personally. Ye don't know oor boss. He doesnae trust his ain granny.'

White thought for a moment, then decided it would save him a trek up the stairs and allow him to drink his coffee before it was cold. He let the uniformed messenger into the CID office and led him to the lifts that provided exclusive access to the offices of the senior officers. He keyed in the security code and, almost instantly, the lift door sighed smoothly open.

'Just take the lift up, third door on the left, past the pot plants. His name's on the door. And don't worry, the bastards never lock their doors.'

'Right enough,' grinned the cop. 'A' these polis aboot, whit could possibly go wrong? No' a bad lift either. I've been in much worse. No' the slightest stink o' piss.' He laughed as the lift doors closed with a dull thud.

White wandered back to his desk, where his coffee was still steaming in the Styrofoam cup. He sat down, picked up the beverage and stretched his legs out under the desk. As he took his first swallow, he felt a pang of unease he couldn't explain. He took another sip – more than he had intended, burning his tongue – and looked at his watch. The cop had only been on the top floor for a couple of minutes but he knew how nosey his colleagues were. The last thing he wanted was for an officer from another division to get caught poking about in the bosses' domain. He now regretted not delivering the item himself, so he walked to the lift and keyed in the code.

A red arrow blinked at him, indicating that the lift was on its way. With the visitor, he reasoned. He heard the mechanism clunk. Suddenly, the doors slid open; sure enough, the uniformed cop was standing at the back of the lift, not holding the carrier bag this time, but something else, something dark and shiny.

'Right, you,' said White, anxious to be rid of this unexpected visitor.

Before he could say any more, the man raised his arm and pointed a sidearm, with silencer, at the shocked detective.

'What the—' The expletive was never given voice as a neat black hole appeared in White's forehead, forcing his head back with a snap. He swayed on his heels; his last tear was of dark blood that dribbled out of his left eye and down his cheek. Then he dropped backwards to the floor, his head bouncing twice on the thin carpeting like a deflated ball.

The uniformed man bent over White's lifeless body. He removed a mobile phone from the detective's pocket, studied it momentarily, then held it up in front of his face, smiling as the flash went off with the sound of an old-fashioned camera shutter. He placed the phone on the dead man's chest, then walked back through the CID suite, clicking the door open from the inside, then pulling it shut with a clunk as he left.

Daley couldn't sleep. He was plagued by something intangible; a thought he couldn't quite get to grips with, that wouldn't show itself in the clear light of his mind.

Liz's breath was soft on his bare arm, her face illuminated by a shaft of silver moonlight that had found its way through a gap in the curtains. He looked at his watch. Nearly five. He decided that more sleep was going to be elusive so, slowly and gently, he dislodged Liz's head from his shoulder, then slipped out from under the duvet.

Instead of heading for the en suite, he padded along the hall to the master bathroom. Duncan Fearney was due in court that morning, and he wanted to attend, not only to see how the farmer was dealt with but also to have a chat with the Procurator Fiscal – a reasonable man, who was as helpful as he could be, given the difficult job he had. From what Daley knew of Fearney, it seemed most unlikely that he was the mastermind behind the pernicious trade in illegal tobacco, despite being the main source. Someone in this community knew more than they were letting on; Daley was determined to find that person and make sure that the luckless farmer didn't suffer the consequences of his activities alone.

Showered, he brushed his teeth, sprayed on deodorant, slapped aftershave on his face and looked at himself in the bathroom mirror. Parts of his torso that had once looked firm and athletic now looked flabby, pale and somehow arranged in a different way. His hair, which had just been cut, had lost its dark sheen, and was now flecked with grey. He rubbed his hand over his stubbly jaw. He kept an electric razor in the drawer of his desk at the office, so, as was often the case, decided to run that over his face when he was at work.

Holding a towel around his waist, he padded back to the bedroom, sliding back the door of the built-in wardrobe to reveal his suits, shirts and jackets. He pulled a black suit from a hanger – currently his favourite, as it had a roomy waistband – selected a plain white shirt, then removed his underwear, socks and a tie from various small drawers dotted about the bedroom. The last such drawer he came to squealed on metal runners as he opened it. An anxious glance at Liz revealed that she was still sound, albeit muttering something in her sleep. He leaned over her, to try and catch what she was saying so that he could wind her up with it later.

He could see her eyes moving frantically under her lids.

'It's a baby . . .' she slurred, and a smile spread across her face.

Daley shook his head. Knowing his wife's distaste for the whole idea of children, he thought it ironic that she was dreaming about them. Could it be her body clock trying to work on her subconscious? Somehow, knowing his wife, he doubted it.

Dressed, he grabbed his car keys from the table beside the front door and stepped out into the starlit morning. He had parked close to the house, to minimise the walk to the front door in the low winter temperatures. The car had an anti-frost system, so the windscreen was clear. As he approached the vehicle the doors opened automatically, even though the key was in his pocket. He sat in the driver's seat and buckled up, then pressed the ignition button. Nothing. He tried again, this time switching on an interior light to enable him to take a look at the complicated dashboard of the vehicle. Still nothing.

So much for the state-of-the-art keyless ignition, he thought to himself as he got out of the car and slammed the driver's door. Daley stood momentarily beside it, deliberating whether or not to call the nightshift car to pick him up, before remembering his podgy reflection in the bathroom mirror earlier. He opened the door again and removed the thick jacket that he kept in the car for emergencies. He would walk the mile and a half to work; that would help fight the flab. In a temper, he set out down the frosty driveway, trying not to slip on its gleaming surface.

A sudden flash flickered in his peripheral vision, followed by a mind-shatteringly loud explosion, the force of which sent him hurtling to the ground. For countless moments he tried to drag his thoughts into the here and now. Slowly, he pulled himself to his knees, turned stiffly around.

His new divisional car was now a ball of fire, burning so brightly he couldn't see the house beyond.

'Liz!' he cried out, scrambling to his feet, shielding his face from the heat of the flames.

18

He had the presence of mind to remove the phone from his pocket and call Kinloch police. After a short conversation with a shocked constable, he shoved the device back into his jacket and tried to edge nearer to the blazing car. The driveway was narrow at this point, and he was afraid that the fuel tank had yet to explode, but his only thought was for his wife. He decided to risk it.

As he edged past the vehicle, he came within a few feet of the fire; the heat seared at his skin and took his breath away. He could hear, feel and smell his eyebrows and hair singeing in the intensity of flame, and he very nearly slipped on the grass, now slick and wet, the fire having already melted the night frost. He stumbled on. In seconds that seemed more like hours, he was beyond what was left of his vehicle and running towards the house. Twisting shadows danced over the front wall of his home. The large front window was gone, and Daley now stumbled over part of the wooden decking that had been damaged in the blast.

Liz . . . He felt throat-clenching fear – visceral and debilitating. He tried to swallow back a sob as he searched in his pockets for the key to the front door that, miraculously, remained solid and intact. In the distance, he could hear the wail of sirens as he finally managed to fumble the key from his pocket and into the lock.

'Liz!' he called out, now standing in their lounge, which was transformed by the light from the leaping flames outside, the crackle of fire, and the smell of burning fuel, plastic and upholstery that was beginning to make him choke.

He ran through the hallway and flung open the door to their bedroom. Away from the dazzle of the fire he could see nothing. He ran to the bed, searching frantically with arms outstretched, like a child looking for a favourite toy in amongst the sheets. But the bed was empty.

He raced into the kitchen. The pale light of a distant moon fought for supremacy with the blaze cast into the sky on the other side of the house.

There, halfway up the small hill at the end of the garden, he could see a pale shimmer. *Liz!*

He flung the back door open and jumped down the short flight of four steps onto the path; his right knee buckled agonisingly under his weight and sent him tumbling to the ground. He pulled himself up, his hands grazed and stinging from his attempt to break his fall on the frozen pathway.

'Jim!' Liz shouted, her voice strained. She was standing bent over, both hands clutching her stomach, wearing only her nightdress. 'Please, get an ambulance. Please.'

DS Scott found it hard to force open his eyes. He had opted to stay in the hotel that evening rather than accept the invite to his boss's home. His experience on the hill above Frank MacDougall's farm had somehow eased his mind; he was sure mistakes had been made and the dreaded JayMac remained the ashes he had seen him returned to at the crematorium in Glasgow, all those years before. This was all an elaborate hoax: a deadly effective one, but a hoax nonetheless. These thoughts rushed through his mind like draining water, as the loud knocking on the door of his hotel room roused him from the deep pit of a whisky-fuelled slumber.

'Aye, aye, I'm just comin'. Is there a fuckin' fire or somethin'?' he shouted, immediately regretting all that he had drunk the previous night after Daley had returned home. In all honesty, that was part of the reason he had decided to stay at the hotel – to have a good bevy and try and forget James Machie had ever existed, never mind been resurrected.

He turned the key in the door, easing it open to reveal a whey-faced constable, standing tall in the hotel corridor.

'You'll need tae get dressed, Sarge. There's been an explosion at DCI Daley's house.'

'A whit?' Scott could barely talk; his tongue seemed to be welded to the roof of his mouth. 'If this is some wind-up, son, I'll kick yer arse frae here tae Paisley.' But the look on the young policeman's face was enough to send Scott in a frenzied search for his clothes.

Daley had removed his jacket, which he draped over Liz's shoulders. He didn't want to go back into the house, as he wasn't sure if a further, more catastrophic explosion would take place when the car's fuel tank caught. For the same reason, he didn't want to go to the front of the property, as they were at least now being shielded from any possible blast by the bulk of the house. The only other way out was up the steep little hill upon which they were now sitting.

'Liz, we'll need to climb up the hill, then go across the fields to get out of here. There's no way we'll make it past the car, and I don't want to risk it.' He tried to sound as encouraging and calm as possible, and mentally thanked God for his police training. He was worried about Liz, who was now sitting on the cold ground, hunched over in his jacket and in obvious pain, the source of which she refused to discuss. He assumed that she was in shock, however, he realised that she needed urgent medical attention.

'I don't think I can, Jim,' she gasped. 'Please, please, do something.' She began to sob.

His throat constricted as he searched his mind for some solution. He pulled the phone from his jacket pocket once more, noticing that the screen was cracked, probably a result of the tumble he had taken on the back garden path. Thankfully, it looked as though it was still operational.

'Good morning, Kinloch Police Office.' The voice was calm, yet the strain was apparent to anyone who knew DC Dunn.

'Listen, it's me, Jim,' said Daley. 'Liz and I are at the back of the house, in the garden. We can't get round the front because of the fire, and Liz is too . . .' He searched for the right words. 'She's in pain and she won't make it up the hill. Someone's going to have to get back here. She needs medical attention now!' Daley was now shouting, and regretted it almost immediately as he felt Liz flinch in his embrace, then wail in pain.

'Yes, sir,' replied Dunn, herself sounding close to tears. 'I'll . . . I'll get a hold of the officers at the locus. The fire brigade and ambulance are on their way, and so is DS Scott.'

'Please do your best. Please.' Daley ended the call, as Liz seemed to go into spasm, her whole body bracing. He tried to comfort her, stroking her hair and whispering in her ear. He held her close, trying to make sure that her bare legs were covered with as much of his jacket as possible. It was then he felt something slick on her thigh. It was clearly blood.

He redialled the phone and clutched it to his ear. 'Brian, please get someone round here, to the back of the house. Liz is . . . She's in agony. No visible injuries I can see, but she's bleeding. We're trapped.' At his side, Liz seemed to be drifting into unconsciousness. 'For fuck's sake help me, Brian.'

'Hang on, big man, hang on!' Scott was now exiting the police car at the entrance to Daley's driveway. He heard the line bleep dead as he rushed to the small huddle of people standing some distance away from the burning car.

'Whit the fuck's happenin'?' he shouted to two young policemen and a senior fire officer who stood shielded from the flames by a police car.

'We have to wait for my appliance to arrive. They'll be here soon. We can't risk trying to enter the property past the car in case of further explosion.'

'Whit's keepin' them?'

'They're retained units. They have to form up at the fire station before they can leave. Let me assure you . . .' He wasn't given time to finish his sentence, as Scott pushed his way past him and the two cops.

'Sergeant, I must insist that you stay clear of that vehicle,' the fire officer called, as Scott edged up the hill towards the car, which appeared now to be blazing less furiously than when he had driven across the town, where it had been visible for most of the way.

'You can insist whatever the fuck you like,' Scott yelled, as he broke into a run.

Daley's mind was racing. Every time he tried to move Liz, she begged him to stop. The pain she was feeling seemed to be getting steadily worse. He had decided to give it two more minutes, then, despite her pleas and the agony of his injured leg, he was going to have to take her to the front of the house and past the car. He tried to keep the thought of the explosion at the back of his mind.

Just as he was about to try and haul her up in his arms, he saw a figure appear around the side of the house.

'Brian!' Daley exclaimed. 'Fuck, I'm glad to see you.'

It took Scott only seconds to work out what was going on. Liz's face was deathly pale, and his boss and friend looked desperate and dishevelled, panic in his eyes.

'Quick,' said Scott, taking control of the situation, 'grab her under her arms, Jim. I'll take her legs.'

Liz groaned as the two detectives lifted her on the count of three. Daley was holding her under the arms as her head lolled on his chest.

'Right, Jim, we'll have tae risk it roon past the motor.'

'OK,' said Daley. 'But I've hurt my leg, so don't go sprinting off.'

'Just you keep up, big yin,' answered Scott. 'Here goes.'

The two men bore Liz around the corner of the house, and into the light of the burning car. Daley was panting, sometimes moaning in pain, but he kept going, urged on by Scott. Even though the fire had died back considerably, a sickening stench of fuel filled the air.

'I think it's going to go up, Brian,' Daley shouted.

'Just keep goin', Jamie,' shouted Scott over his shoulder. 'If the fuckin' thing goes before we get her past it, fuck knows when we'll be able tae get her help.'

They carried on, skirting the car by as great a distance as possible. They were just a few yards past the flaming wreck when there was a loud crack, accompanied by a blinding flash. Daley saw Scott fly forwards, still holding onto Liz's legs, which dragged him down too.

Liz Daley screamed out in pain.

Donald was pulling into the car park at the back of Paisley HQ. He hated being roused from his sleep, especially by such news. An officer had died. There could be no worse scenario.

He was irritated to spot an ambulance filling his private parking space, so decided to leave his car in the next bay, belonging to a chief inspector he didn't like.

Despite the urgency of the call, and the seriousness of the situation, he had needed a shower to help clear his head. He was aware that he had consumed too much alcohol the night before, well over his self-imposed limit. He felt for the little canister of breath spray in his pocket, mentally cursing the fact that he had forgotten to squirt some into his mouth before he left the car. He thought about surreptitiously doing this as he made his way to the security door, however this plan was scuppered as the two-shift inspector appeared in the doorway, looking pale and drawn.

'Good morning, sir,' he called, somewhat uncertainly. 'Thank goodness you're here.'

'I hardly think "good morning" is appropriate under the circumstances, do you, Inspector Ray?' Donald was on the offensive. The death of an officer was regrettable, most regrettable, however, his job was not to wallow in the misery of it all. His role was to take the situation forward, console grieving relatives, identify what had gone wrong – who had made mistakes, and why? – and kick arses, while at the same time ensuring his was not on the line.

'I want a full briefing, in my office, in five minutes,' he growled, as he made his way through the bar office and towards the lifts.

'Eh, well, that's the thing, sir.'

'Spit it out, man!' Donald swung around like a guardsman on drill, looking at the harassed Ray under beetling brows. 'What is *the thing*?' Spittle bubbled at the corner of his mouth.

'Sir, your office – the whole top floor, as well as the CID suite – it's, well, it's the crime scene.' Beads of sweat were now visible on the man's brow.

'It's *what*?' said Donald, his eyes bulging from their sockets. 'Is this what you couldn't tell me over the phone?'

'We've set up a temporary office in the shift sergeants' room – I'll show you along.'

'I know where it is, Ray. Be there in five minutes, and bring me a fucking black coffee as well as a full and detailed report,' Donald barked over his shoulder, as he stomped off to his new domain.

Daley sat in the waiting room of Kinloch's hospital. The early morning sun shone through the window, sparkling off the leaves of the tree outside, which remained locked in the cold embrace of frost.

Both hands were now dressed in neat bandages, covering the sharp grazes he had sustained on the garden path. Had they not been so covered, he would have been wringing them together in worry. Liz was still with the doctors, who were reluctant to say anything of any consequence or help to the stricken detective, who was left to fret, blinking in the early sunshine.

The waiting-room door was flung open, and Daley turned his head quickly, hoping to see one of the medical staff bearing good news. Instead, the figure of DS Scott was framed in the doorway, his tongue sticking out in concentration as he tried to manoeuvre himself and two coffee cups through the swing door without spilling anything.

'I swear tae fuck, these places are designed tae make life mair difficult than it a'ready fuckin' is. Two quid each for a cup o' shite coffee? Blind robbery, man,' he said, handing Daley one of the cups, which the latter grasped gingerly in his bandaged hand.

'Did you manage to find out anything, Brian?' Daley enquired anxiously.

'Nah, no' a fuckin' dickie bird. These bastards are tighter than a whippet's arse. Just buy a nurse a cup o' coffee up in the city and ye can get the whole medical history o' anybody you want. No' here, Jim. Sorry, buddy.' He noticed Daley's expression change from hope to despair.

'She was in so much pain, Brian. I can't work out why – it's not as if she could have been affected by the blast. I mean, she was in the bedroom at the back, and it was virtually untouched.' Daley's voice tailed off as he looked back out of the window at the frozen tree and the sharp peak of Ben Airich behind.

They remained in silence for a few minutes, apart from the intermittent slurping of Scott drinking his coffee.

Suddenly the door swung open again, sending Daley to his feet as he saw a white-coated doctor stride into the room, a clipboard clutched in his right hand. Scott, just about to take another gulp at his coffee and startled by the sudden arrival, contrived to spill half of the beverage down his shirt and tie, though he kept the oaths that followed at a barely audible level.

'Any news, doctor?' Daley's face was ashen; his right hand trembled as he held the coffee cup.

'Mr Daley.' The doctor looked at him over a pair of small-framed glasses that gave the impression that he was older than his actual years. 'Could we speak in private?' He cast a glance at Scott, who was still wiping coffee from his tie while mouthing obscenities to the floor.

'Sorry?' Daley was momentarily confused. 'No, it's fine. Anything you have to say can be said in front of my friend here. Anything.'

'OK, your choice,' said the young man as he consulted the clipboard, squinting through his spectacles. He flipped over a page, which he took a few moments to scan.

'Say whit ye have tae say, buddy.' Scott was anxious to see his friend put out of his misery, a sentiment that Daley echoed, along with a silent prayer.

'Well, as you know, Mrs Daley fell heavily, causing her a great deal of pain; something that, considering her condition, is highly dangerous, both for her and . . .'

'Her condition?' Daley sat down with a thud, as more coffee splashed onto the floor of the waiting room. 'She's not been right for weeks – no appetite, being sick, really pale. What is it she has? Please say it's not cancer.' He looked imploringly at the doctor, a facial expression that was somehow at odds with his bulky, lived-in appearance.

'Cancer?' It was the doctor's turn to look confused. 'No, no, nothing of the kind. Though it is fair to say that your wife has had quite an ordeal. She's relatively young and fit, so, somewhat miraculously, given the shock as well as a small loss of blood, both she and the baby are absolutely fine.'

Daley tried to speak, but only a croaked whisper would issue from his mouth. He looked at Scott wide-eyed.

'Ahem,' Scott cleared his throat noisily. 'I think whit Jim's tryin' tae say is: whit baby are ye on aboot?'

'Oh,' muttered the clinician, now grasping the situation. 'Your wife is almost four months' pregnant, Mr Daley. Not the most traditional way of finding out, I grant you, but still, the secret's out now. Congratulations are in order.' He smiled awkwardly at Daley, who was looking utterly bemused.

'Aye,' said Scott, smiling, 'as my auld mother used tae say: ye never know just whit a day will bring.' He walked over to Daley and slapped his back. 'You're tae be the proud faither – an' no' a pair o' breeks tae yer name, hardly.' He looked down at what remained of Daley's trousers, both knees of which had been ripped to shreds.

19

Donald looked round the shift sergeants' room absentmindedly; he reflected that he was now spending as much time in Kinloch as here, in Paisley HQ.

He decided to have the largest desk – the one he had chosen to use – moved to the far wall, in an attempt to recreate the gravitas of his own office. He pulled a girlie calendar from the top of a filing cabinet and threw it deftly into a metal wastepaper basket, a curl of distaste playing across his lips. He gathered various dirty coffee mugs, old newspapers, sweet wrappers and other detritus together and left them on the desk nearest the door. He was about to make a call for someone to come and clear them away when the phone rang.

Donald, used to seeing the caller ID displayed on his own telephone, picked the handset up and answered hesitantly. The tone of voice on the other end was enough to set Donald's teeth on edge. The patrician timbre could only belong to Sir Charles Hastings, the Chief Constable.

'Good morning, sir,' Donald gushed down the phone. 'A most miserable day.' As soon as he had spoken the words, he regretted them; they seemed much too banal considering what had happened to one of his fellow officers during the night.

'And set to get a great deal more miserable, John,' Hastings bellowed in reply. 'I'll be with you in about an hour. In the meantime, I want you to lock down the office, transfer all divisional operations to the sub-division. These incidents could well turn out to be the worst and most damaging points in our careers . . .' The rest of his words were lost to the superintendent, whose analytical mind had latched onto the word 'incidents'.

'Incidents plural, sir?'

'Yes, *incidents*, man! Don't tell me you haven't been informed about events in Kinloch?'

At the mention of Kinloch, Donald's stomach began to churn and he felt his legs weaken. He dropped into his swivel chair, off which he nearly skidded such was the force with which he had sat down. 'No, sir. What with the murder of an officer in this office during the night, I'm afraid I have been rather preoccupied . . .' God, was this it?

'You better get a grip there, John,' Hastings roared.

'Well, it is over a hundred miles away, sir,' Donald said, floundering, and feeling more like a condemned man than he had hitherto in the whole of his career.

'Not in Kinloch! In your own bloody office! I found out over an hour ago. What the hell are your people doing? You should have been briefed with developments long before now. Not like you to run a slack ship, Superintendent Donald, not like you at all.'

'Yes, sir . . .'

'DCI Daley's car has been blown up by some device or other. Bloody lucky he and his wife weren't killed, by all accounts.'

'Really, sir? How awful. I can't believe I wasn't informed,' Donald replied, already feeling his pulse slow, and the panic in his chest subside. Jim bloody Daley, he thought. Thank fuck, I thought it was all over for a moment.

Back in Kinloch, Daley was sitting beside his wife's bed, holding her hand as she slept, a look of serenity on her face. A monitor flickered and bleeped at her side, though he was oblivious to it.

Two very distinct thoughts were competing for centre-stage in his mind: who had tried to kill him, and nearly succeeded in killing his wife, and how long had she known she was pregnant? The questions chased each other around his head like a dog after its own tail, and no answers came.

He felt her hand twitch in his. He looked at her face. Her eyelids were flickering. She had been given a very mild sedative in order to help her get over the trauma of the last few hours. This was the first chance he'd had to talk to her; if she woke properly, that was.

Her head turned on the pillow, and she began to move her lips, so dry they made a faint sound. He reached for the glass of water on the bedside cabinet, and brushed the hair gently from her eyes.

'You're OK, darling. I'm here. We're going to be all right, all three of us.' The last words were said quietly, almost a whisper; in fact he hadn't meant to say them at all.

She opened her eyes, their cornflower blue starkly contrasted against her pale face.

'You know then.' Her voice was quiet; her expression spoke only of anxiety.

He smiled at her. 'Yes, I know. Why didn't you tell me?'

She closed her eyes, and Daley thought momentarily she had gone back to sleep, however, she began to smile herself.

'It just never seemed to be the right time,' she said hesitantly, looking up at him. 'I . . .' She began to cough, so Daley put his hand behind her head and lifted it gently off the pillow, putting the glass to her lips. She took a few sips, then he let her head gently back down.

'All that morning sickness, being off my food . . . Didn't you even notice I've not been drinking?'

'Yes, well, no, actually,' he replied, with a stage grimace.

'Some bloody detective you are,' she said, and her smile broke into weak laughter. Her husband laughed softly back.

When Daley arrived back at the Kinloch CID suite, he was surprised to see DS Scott, DC Dunn and another young DC busy sticking pictures onto a clearboard. There, in the centre, was his face – the image taken from his official warrant card picture – looking careworn and jowly. It crossed his mind that his hair didn't look too good either, however, the site of his burnt-out car alongside a photograph of Liz brought him back to reality with a bump.

Many of his days in Kinloch were low-key affairs, involving the type of crime it was the CID's bread and butter to solve: petty theft, assaults, the odd case of shoplifting or minor drugs offences. Today it was only ten thirty in the morning, and already someone had tried to kill him, nearly succeeded in killing his wife, and he had found out that he was going to be a father.

'Whit are ye doing here, Jamie' Scott said. 'Ye should be back hame taking it easy, or beside that wife o' yours. How is she, by the way?' The DS winked. 'Everything still hunky dory, you know . . .' He pointed towards his belly, his brows raised in anticipation of news.

'Everything's fine, thanks,' Daley replied, sitting down stiffly on a chair behind one of the work stations. 'Please,' he said, gesturing to the officers, 'carry on. Don't let me stop you.'

Scott returned his attention to the task in hand, somewhat put out. 'Aye, well, there ye have it. Despite the latest attempt tae kill oor boss, he's still hail 'n' hearty, though he'll be needin' tae buy another pair o' troosers.'

DC Dunn tried to conceal a smile. 'So glad you're OK, sir, and Mrs Daley too.'

'Right,' said Scott. 'Looks like yous two have plenty tae keep yiz goin', so better get on wi' it, eh?' He smiled at DC Dunn, and turned to Daley with a more serious look on his face. 'Better take a wee trip intae yer box, Jim,' he said, pointing a thumb over his shoulder, as though Daley might not be sure where his own office was located.

Once inside, Daley closed the blinds on his glass world. He had got used to the office, but hated sitting on display, like a dyspeptic goldfish. He lowered himself carefully into his own comfortable chair; his knees were still painful, and felt as if they were now stiffening up. He remembered his grandfather complaining about his painful joints.

'What's the problem, Brian?' he asked, sure that nothing could be as bad as almost being blown up, then nearly losing his wife.

'Och,' said Scott, sitting opposite him and leaning forward on his chair, 'yer man's on his way doon. Aye, an' no' in guid trim neither, I can tell ye.'

'Not with any faux sympathy for me,' Daley replied with a snort.

'No. Well, that's no' tae say he's no' worried aboot whit happened tae you an' the missus, but he's got other problems tae sort oot tae.' Scott looked upset, head down, staring blankly at a spot on Daley's desk.

'Spit it out, Brian.' Daley's eventful morning was starting to catch up with him, and he was brusquer than he intended.

'Rab White's been murdered – shot deid – in the CID office in Paisley last night.'

'Rab? You mean DS Rab White?'

'Aye, Jim, oor Rab White. Fuck me, I just had a few pints wi' him the other day . . .'

Daley's mind was racing. A murder and an attempted murder of two police officers with close connections, from the same division, on the same night. What were the chances? He leaned back in his chair and looked at the ceiling.

'The boss was being pretty mysterious on the phone,' said Scott. 'Tells us there's details he can only discuss face to face.'

Daley looked at Scott. 'Are you thinking what I'm thinking, Brian?'

'Aye. JayMac.'

He made his way carefully down the steep, narrow pathway that wound down the side of the cliff. Beneath, the sea washed restlessly against the iron shore. Sharp black rocks and crags punctuated the waves at random intervals, standing out angrily against the grey of the ocean which was only a slightly darker shade than the sky above.

He shivered involuntarily. He had never been comfortable at sea, having lived his life almost exclusively in land-locked domains. The concept of an endless expanse of water brought a twinge of fear to his chest, which he banished with his habitual resolve. All his efforts were for the greater good, to satisfy the cloying need for revenge. He strengthened his resolve. Nothing, nobody would stand in his way. He placed his fears in the back of his mind, where they would stay.

He stopped for a while on the path; the descent was making his knees ache. He looked out over the sea. Where only yesterday a grey-green strip of land had been visible, there was now nothing. Waves and sky met at the horizon, giving the impression of a much more closed, less vast entity. He realised that this was merely illusion, and that his destination was in the same place as when he had last squinted at it through the small window of the cottage. Still, the notion of sailing off to the unseen was not a comforting one.

He looked along the rest of the path, which zigzagged down towards the shore like a pale scar. Many of the men he had known carried such a disfigurement like a badge of honour. He strode on. The wind was keen on his face, flecked with water carried up from the sea below. He could taste as well as smell the briny air. Above him, gulls wheeled and squawked, wings held out straight and still as they soared heavenward on the breeze.

As he progressed, he could feel the hard rock of the cliff path give way to a softer footing. The gradient grew dramatically steeper, and he found himself slithering down the remaining few feet of the path onto the rough shore, a mixture of rocks, sand and pebbles. He had to jump the last couple of feet onto the shingle, as the wind and waves had eroded the bottom of the path, taking what looked like a big bite out of the hillside.

About two hundred yards down the beach he could see waves crashing against a dark arm of stone that jutted out into the sea. The structure looked more natural than man-made, though he knew it to have been constructed many hundreds of years ago by smugglers who had plied a lucrative trade all along the rocky west coast of Scotland. His time in the little cottage had been put to good use; he had filled his brain with more information, the assimilation of which had become his drug of choice. He smiled to himself at the thought of these men – men just like him – struggling barrels of whisky, rum or tobacco from the little quay, along the beach, and up the narrow cliff path. Crime paid, but it always came at a price.

At the end of the little pier bobbed a small boat, white bodied, with a blue cabin. He crunched his way forward, stepping gingerly onto the ancient structure, slick with seawater and weed. As he edged along, he nearly slipped, cursing as he regained his balance. The boat bobbed against the pier, buffered against damage by two old tyres hung from its side.

He sat down and thrust his feet into the boat in order to steady it, pulling the vessel tight to the little jetty with his legs, then slithered on board, dragging his heavy bag with him, which landed at his feet with a hollow thud. He made his way along the narrow deck and ducked inside the cabin, dragging the bag with him.

After pulling the door shut, he surveyed his surroundings, surprised by the spaciousness of the cabin. Two chairs stood proud on metal plinths in front of a battered console upon which sat a polythene folder and a device that looked not unlike an unwieldy mobile phone from the early nineties. He unzipped the folder, removed its contents, and started to read.

Basically, the task in hand was simple: the gadget was not

a phone, but a satellite navigational instrument already programmed with his destination. He read the accompanying documents, which described how to use the technology and also included a mobile phone number. He pulled his own from his pocket and dialled.

After four rings, the phone was answered. 'Aye, it's me,' he said to the voice on the other end. 'I'm on this fuckin' boat. I've got the kit.' He paused, listening to the reply. 'Aye, whitever,' he said testily. 'Just make fuckin' sure yer there before I am.' He ended the call, and put his phone in his pocket. Picking up the satnav device, he switched it on with the red LED button. Slowly, a map, with numbers and directions, appeared on the screen. He pressed another button and waited. In a matter of seconds, the device emitted a chiming noise, the screen changed, and a large arrow hovered around a point above which the word 'destination' was picked out in green script. Slowly, more writing scrolled up the screen: *Make sure the arrow continues to point at the destination. Based on a constant speed of 15 knots, you will reach destination in 2hrs 5mins.* Then the screen flickered and changed: *Your final destination is McDonnall's Bay, Kintyre.*

'Aye,' he said. 'Follow the yellow brick road, eh, Frankie-boy?'

20

Daley sat in the public gallery in Kinloch Sheriff Court. The room was Victorian, with wooden panelling and benches, and a vaulted ceiling. Ornate carving adorned the Sheriff's bench and the dock, where a miserable Duncan Fearney looked out over the courtroom, nervously twisting his fingers together. The usual aroma of disinfectant, age and muted fear permeated the air.

Daley had taken an interest in the Fearney case for a number of reasons – not least of all because he felt some sympathy for the man – but his internal alarm was sounding, telling him there was more, much more, to this than met the eye. The detective had checked Fearney's records and had found a solitary conviction for speeding in the late eighties. Taking advantage of local knowledge gleaned from some of the long-serving cops in Kinloch, it appeared as though this foray into organised crime was entirely at odds with the man's character. As Daley eyed the forlorn figure in the dock, he reminded himself that the farmer would not be the first, or the last, individual lured by the beckoning finger of easy money. Though his head remained down, Fearney occasionally looked up from under his brow, his eyes fleetingly connecting with those of the detective. Gone was the sullen resentment at being caught; he now bore a look of utter hopelessness.

The Sheriff was in heated discussion with the Procurator Fiscal, which was delaying the start to this preliminary hearing and giving the local populace the chance to enter the public benches to support their fellow Kinlochian; something, Daley knew, that was not unusual.

His mind was jumping between the death of Rab White, his wife's pregnancy and their narrow escape from death when he felt a tap on his shoulder. He turned to find Hamish's slanted eyes staring at him from his parchment-coloured face.

'Aye, Mr Daley, how are ye the day? I hear ye had a wee bit o' excitement earlier on.'

'Hello, Hamish.' Daley smiled, pleased to see a friendly face. 'We had a narrow escape, but Liz is OK. She'll be in hospital over the next couple of days – just for observation.'

Hamish looked at him for a few moments, said nothing. 'And how about the wean?' His tone was conversational, as though there was nothing remarkable about his question.

'How the f—' Daley stopped himself, remembering where he was. 'How do you know about . . . I've only found out myself . . .' He was yet again astonished by the older man's apparent ability to read his mind. 'Did Liz tell you?' he asked in an angry whisper, annoyed that his wife might have chosen to discuss her pregnancy with this old man before her husband.

'No' she did not. An' don't you be giein' her a hard time o' it, for she didnae say wan word tae me on the subject.' Hamish was adamant. 'When ye've seen as many new lives brought intae the world as I have, ye get used tae a' the signs.' He smiled, pleased with his own sagacity.

'Was that what you were trying to tell me when I offered you a lift?' Daley was calmer now, as he recalled his most recent conversation with Hamish.

'Jeest you keep yer han' on yer ha'penny, inspector. It's no' guid for a man at your time o' life tae be gettin' intae such a stooshie. No' noo yer goin' tae be a faither, at any rate.'

Daley was about to reply when a head appeared between him and Hamish, as another member of the public gallery chose his moment to join their conversation. Daley knew this man from the bar at the County Hotel; he was always friendly enough, though somewhat lacking in social graces. 'Aye, congratulations tae ye, Mr Daley. Well done indeed,' he grinned, pushing his arm forward to shake Daley's hand. 'Lead in the auld pencil, right enough. Mind you, that cannae be difficult wi' a lassie as bonnie as yer wife,' he continued, dropping his voice.

'Thank you,' replied a flustered Daley, wondering who else knew more than he did about his wife's condition.

'An' how are you daein', Hamish?' the man enquired of the old fisherman, who was now chewing at his unlit pipe. 'Nae wonder yer pipe's gaun oot. I've had tae cut right back on the fags noo, tae, ever since poor Du—' He didn't finish the sentence; instead he cleared his throat exaggeratedly and looked at Daley. 'Oh aye . . . Eh, I wiz goin' tae anyway since the wife telt me I needed tae stop. Bad cough, ye know.' He sat back in his seat sheepishly.

'I'd have thought the good people of this town would be more interested in the fact I nearly got blown sky-high this morning,' Daley remarked with a sigh.

'Och, don't be sayin' that, Mr Daley.' Hamish took the pipe from his mouth. 'Naebody in Kinloch wid be as rude as tae mention such personal issues tae a man in your position. That would be hoor o' a rude.'

'But it's OK to ask me about my wife's pregnancy, about which you all seem remarkably well informed?' Daley said.

'Ye still havenae quite got yer heid roon' the wee toon yet, Mr Daley.' Hamish smiled. 'There's no' wan business in the place – or hospital, come tae that – that doesnae have someone's cousin, or sister, or mother, or auntie working in it. Dinnae look so pit oot,' he continued, in response to the look of concern on Daley's face. 'Doctors, nurses, even policemen; they're a' good at their jobs, an' keep their ain council, in the main. But ye must remember, there's a'ways a body fae the toon sitting on their shooder, havin' a wee listen, or a wee look. No' wi' any kind o' malice aforethought, mind.' He winked at Daley in self-congratulation at the use of the legal term. 'Nah, rather jeest so we're a' up tae date wi' whoot's goin' on in oor ain community. Aye, jeest the way of it,' he concluded, taking another smokeless draw of his pipe.

'To what end?' Daley asked, mentally calculating just how many locals were employed at the local police office.

'Och, jeest so we don't appear rude, ye understand. For example, how wid ye have felt if ye'd had a' this great news aboot a new wean bottled up in yer heart, an' no' a soul tae share it wi'? Ye'd have been fair scunnered, an' that's a fact.'

As Fearney fidgeted in the dock, the court officer took a seat at his desk, then shuffled through a pile of papers and opened up a laptop. Proceedings were about to begin.

Hamish leaned in towards Daley and nodded towards Fearney. 'That's a man on the edge. I've known Duncan noo fir a guid many years, an' I tell ye, he's damn near lost a' reason.' Hamish shook his head in sympathy for the farmer. 'No' a bad man, Mr Daley, jeest a foolish wan. But dae ye no' think there's something else?'

'Else? What do you . . .' But Daley had to stop mid sentence, as the clerk was now calling the court to order.

The hearing hadn't taken long. As expected, Duncan Fearney had pleaded guilty to the sale of contraband tobacco and cigarettes. In most circumstances, such was the gravity of his crime, he would have been remanded in custody, but Daley had earlier called the Procurator Fiscal, asking him not to oppose the inevitable bail request from Fearney's solicitor. He sensed there was much more to this crime, and to have Fearney fretting away in the remand wing of Barlinnie Prison in Glasgow would do nothing to further the investigation. He would learn much more from observing Fearney's actions while he was out on bail. Tobacco smuggling was now as big a business as illegal drugs; Fearney was just a hapless team player, so who was the captain?

Fearney stood on the pavement looking lost. One of his fellow Kinloch residents slapped him on the back and offered him somewhat resigned good wishes. The farmer had looked genuinely surprised when he had been granted bail; no doubt his solicitor had prepared him for jail. Indeed, the solicitor himself – a youngish man with a nervous twitch and thick glasses – looked mystified by events. As he lisped a few words to his client in the dock, Daley got the impression that here was a solicitor unused to many successful outcomes for those whom he defended.

'Mr Fearney,' Daley hailed the farmer.

'These are duty paid, inspector,' Fearney replied, holding up a packet of cigarettes as proof, a look of fear spreading across his face.

'I'm glad to hear it,' Daley said, trying not to intimidate the man. 'Just wondered if you needed a lift back home, I know it's a bit out of the way.' He smiled, with all the enthusiasm that he could muster.

Fearney looked about. 'It's true tae say I huvnae arranged a lift back. I never expected tae be goin' back hame the day, inspector. The lawyer picked me up.' He looked down at a small suitcase beside him on the pavement, shrugged his shoulders, and picked it up. 'I daresay I'll need tae take ye up on yer kind offer.' he continued, with the resignation of a man whose life presented him with diminishing choices.

Daley motioned for him to follow him to the pool car – a replacement for the 4x4 destroyed in the explosion earlier – which was parked not far from the court building. He fished in his pocket for the unfamiliar key fob, taking it out, then pointing it in the general direction of the car, setting the lights flashing briefly and a small tone sounding from the horn.

As the pair drove through Kinloch, heading for the back road where Fearney's farm was situated, the passenger said nothing. Daley noted how jumpy Fearney became as the road led them out of the town and into the countryside. He would frequently jerk his head, as if to shake out some thought trapped inside, and his hands were constantly moving. He rubbed his chin, cracked his knuckles, and dug his nails into his thighs.

'I'm sorry fir being rude a wee while ago, Mr Daley,' he burst out. 'It's been a bugger o' a time fir me, I can tell you that without fear or favour.' The strain of the last few days could be heard in his voice.

'Yes, I know you haven't been in trouble before, Mr Fearney. It's always harder for those who aren't used to the criminal justice system. Many of the people I deal with on a regular basis couldn't care less what happens to them; they're as used to being in jail as in their own living room.'

'Aye,' said Fearney, letting out a deep sigh. 'I've met some o' them.' He turned to look out of the car window. The fields, trees and bushes all bore a thin film of frost, reluctant to thaw; not something that normally happened in the relatively balmy environs of Kintyre. Daley looked at the temperature reading on the dashboard, noting that it was only one degree above freezing, and decided to take the edge off his speed.

'Whit dae ye think will happen tae me?' Fearney asked.

'Hard to say,' said Daley. 'Your good record will go in your favour, though make no mistake, this is a very serious crime.' He looked sidelong at his passenger, who was fighting back tears.

'An' if I wiz tae help ye oot – ye know, gie ye a wee bit mair information, like?' Fearney enquired in a hopeful tone.

'It's not like the TV, Duncan,' said Daley. 'We don't do deals. But I won't lie to you; if you help us bring your suppliers to justice, it won't do you any harm at all.' He stole another quick look at his passenger, who had leaned his head back against the headrest.

'I'll need tae think aboot it a', Mr Daley. These are no' the kind o' folk ye want tae be messin' wi', let me tell you.' Suddenly he looked desperate.

Daley nodded sympathetically, recalling that Fearney had said hardly anything to the officers who had interviewed him since his arrest, only answering to direct questions about his name, age, address and his acceptance of guilt.

'If you give me a couple of days, I can try to help you, Duncan. Protect you from whoever it is that has been using you.' Daley spoke quietly; he had decided to give Fearney enough time to make a move, however unlikely that seemed from the broken man in the passenger seat. He slowed the car down and turned onto the track that led to the farm. The road surface was pitted with deep potholes in which dirty brown water had gathered.

As they neared the place, he heard Fearney sharply draw in his breath and sit upright. Up ahead, in the muddy entrance to the yard, stood a man wearing a camouflage jacket, a shotgun split open in the crook of his arm. He stared blankly at the car as Daley drove past him to park in the untidy yard.

'Friend of yours?' he enquired of his passenger.

'Aye, sort o'. He has the wee croft up on the hill, helps me oot noo and again,' Fearney replied. 'Jeest for bags o' potatoes an' the like,' he added hurriedly. 'Nae money changes hands.' Daley noticed that, despite the chill of the day, beads of sweat were visible on his brow.

As the farmer left the car, Daley decided to do likewise; his instincts told him that, whoever the man at the gate was, his intentions towards Fearney were less than friendly. He ducked out of the door, leaving it open, and walked around the vehicle to where Fearney was standing, looking between Daley and his neighbour in an agitated manner.

'Aye, well, thanks for the lift, Mr Daley,' Fearney announced loudly and deliberately. 'But like I telt yer men, ye'll get nae mair fae me, nae matter whoot ur the consequences.' He smiled – nervously, Daley thought – at the man with the shotgun, who had now taken an aggressive stance, his hitherto disarticulated shotgun now in its firing position, held across his chest in his large hands.

Daley walked towards him, his hand outstretched. 'Jim Daley,' he said. 'I'm the local chief inspector. How are you?' He smiled at Fearney's neighbour, who pointedly did not take up his offer of a handshake.

'I'm careful whose hand I shake, mate,' the man replied, with an arrogant look on his face, chin up. Stocky, of middle height, he wore filthy black wellington boots, into which his dark green waterproof trousers were tucked. His hair was shaved close to his head, and his face was just beginning to take on the jowly appearance of middle age. He looked as though he had once been powerfully built; fit, now running to fat, Daley knew all about that.

'Mr Fearney tells me you help him out on the farm?' said Daley. He stood three feet away from his camouflaged interlocutor, towering over the man.

'Yeah, I do as it goes,' he replied. 'Is that a police matter, now?'

'What's your name?'

'You mean Dunky-boy here hasn't told you?' He turned to Fearney. 'You ashamed of me, Dunky?' He sneered at Fearney, who shuffled uncomfortably, looking as though he wished the ground would swallow him up.

'Your name, sir,' Daley repeated, this time more forcefully.

'Paul. Paul Bentham, to be precise. Happy now?' His accent was from somewhere in the south-east of England – not cockney, but not far off. 'Nice of you to give me mate here a lift, but we've got a lot of work to do, especially since you've had 'im rotting in your cells at Kinlock,' he snorted, mispronouncing the town's name in an anglicised fashion.

'What have you been doing with the gun, Mr Bentham?' Daley looked at him coolly; already, he had developed a dislike for the man.

'Oh, you know, Mr Daley,' Bentham said, moving forward until he and the police officer were almost toe to toe. 'Lot of vermin about right now – especially today, as it goes.' His sneer transformed into a lop-sided grin as he stared up at Daley.

The chief inspector was beginning to feel increasingly irritated by Bentham, but rather than lose his temper, he forced himself to speak to the man quietly, leaning his head forward, so close that he could smell stale alcohol on the other man's breath.

'Have you got a licence for that, Mr Bentham?' It was Daley's turn to smile.

Bentham looked at the policeman for a few heartbeats, then answered: 'Yeah, what d'you fink?'

'Good, so you won't object to producing it at Kinloch Police Office within the next forty-eight hours, then,' he said.

Despite his best efforts, the smile on Bentham's face faded slightly. 'No problem. What time's best for you, Mr Dalcy?'

Daley leaned his head back, rubbing his chin as though he was considering some intractable problem. 'What about nine tomorrow morning?' He smiled back down at Bentham, taking full advantage of his taller, heftier build.

The man was about to answer when Daley held up his hand. 'Wait a minute,' he said with a smile. 'I know you and Mr Fearney here have a lot to be getting on with, and I don't want to keep you back.'

Fearney gave a nervous snort, clouds of cold breath issuing from his nostrils into the cold air.

'I'll have my officers attend your property instead. You know, check your firearm storage facilities and that your records are up to scratch – much easier than you having to trek all the way into the town.' And with that, Daley turned on his heel and walked back to the car.

He opened the driver's door and looked at Bentham again. His stance hadn't changed, but he looked much less pleased with himself. 'Were you a military man, Mr Bentham?'

'Seventeen years in the Royal Marines, Mr Daley,' he replied, the arrogant smile back on his face.

Daley merely raised his brows, and then nodded a farewell to Duncan Fearney, who muttered a muted thanks to the police officer.

As the car churned down the rutted farm track, Daley looked in his rear-view mirror. Bentham was gesticulating at Fearney with a pointed finger, his face contorted in aggression. You're not as smart as you think you are, Mr Bentham, Daley thought. His attention was dragged back to his driving as the offside front wheel disappeared down one of the deeper potholes with a spine-jarring thud. The policeman decided to proceed more cautiously.

21

The land in front of the small boat presented a looming, red-grey edifice. Seabirds soared skyward from their nests only to plunge back into the sea like small missiles, their wings tight to their bodies. After a few seconds, they would bob back to the surface with, if they were lucky, a writhing fish clasped in their yellow beaks. He wondered idly about the many things he didn't know about the world – would never know – reasoning that even the greatest minds the planet had ever produced could only know a fraction of such a complex existence.

The satnav device was silent, showing only 'Proceed on present heading' on the luminous screen. He looked ahead through the window, trying to work out where he would be able to berth the boat. There seemed to be no break in the cliffs, which towered over the scene with an almost palpable, terrifying intensity. The fresh briny smell of the sea was gradually being replaced by something earthier – the taint of guano deposited over hundreds, perhaps thousands of years on the rocks before him, mixed with the sulphurous odour of rotting seaweed. The land also seemed to impart a kind of chill; not the same as the bracing wind on the sea, but a dank unseen hand whose clammy fingers grasped at the soul.

He shook himself from this torpor. For most of his life,

such thoughts had played no part in his world; life was there to be lived, to grip onto and enjoy in an explosion of the senses. Drink, drugs, money, sex, power: all of these combined to create a boost to the ego that was hard to resist. However, as time rolled on, the drugs had to get stronger, the drink more plentiful, the sex increasingly perverse, the lust for power never-ending, only to stand still; the same joy, warmth, ecstasy, thrill – the feeling of invincibility – faded and turned in on itself in a voracious orgy of self-consumption.

He had only realised why this had happened when he started to read. The many quiet days had led to a thirst for something new: not a search for the next high, or submissive flesh, nor the lust for wealth and vengeance; the real power, the real thrill, came from knowledge, from understanding, from the ability to analyse and understand life itself. He had consumed philosophy and history with the same intensity he had once snorted cocaine; it had, in its own way, become just as addictive.

Would he have been able to feel the very soul of these silent rocks had he not read Kant, Wittgenstein or Nietzsche? Would he ever have felt this alive?

Like everything else in life, knowledge came at a price; as cocaine and drink ruined the body, thought and philosophy ate away at joy. The world was every bit as hard and unforgiving as he had suspected when he was a small child; only now, well, now he knew it to be infinitely more terrifying.

As the small boat ploughed slowly towards the red cliffs he reasoned, as he had so many times before, that to face the real challenge, the existential question that was posed to every living thing, he had to be free from the past – and that meant revisiting it.

He jumped as the satnav sprang into life.

22

Daley couldn't remember when he had last seen Donald looking so careworn, and it was most unusual to see him out of uniform. He was wearing a dark grey suit, with a crisp white shirt – all well and good – but the pale grey tie was squint, hanging from the open neck of his shirt, and there was a tinge of salt-and-pepper stubble on his chin. Daley saw the ghost of the overweight, untidy shift sergeant of many years ago manifest itself on the immaculately dressed man he had grown used to.

Daley himself felt shaken up by the events of the previous few days. Since his home was now a crime scene and lacking windows, he had spent an uncomfortable night in the County Hotel. The peeling wallpaper and dirty net curtains had brought on melancholy, and he'd found himself being assailed by memories of the blood, gore and horror he had been forced to confront during his career. This was a sure sign that he was becoming stressed by this case.

'At last,' Donald declared, as DS Scott entered his temporary office, once occupied by the unfortunate Inspector MacLeod. Officially, as acting sub-divisional commander, the office should have been Daley's preserve, but he preferred the low-key glass box within the CID office.

'Sorry, boss,' said Scott. 'Had to organise a squad to conduct a firearms check.'

'What?' Donald looked exasperated. 'Police officers lying dead and you're checking people have a padlock on their gun cupboard? His face turned bright red, in stark contrast to the whiteness of his shirt. 'And stop calling me boss. It's sir or superintendent, you disrespectful prick.'

'DS Scott was carrying out my instructions, sir,' said Daley, in defence of his friend. 'And this is not just a normal firearms check. I've a feeling we could be on the way to uncovering more levels of the tobacco smuggling operation.' He continued in a flat tone that spoke more of his desire to assert his authority than it did the sharing of information.

'In light of recent events, and bearing in mind that guns are involved, I hope you have insured that the proper safeguards are in place?' Donald said. 'The last thing I need is another dead policeman.'

'Nae worries there, *sir*,' said Scott. 'I've sent two o' the off-duty firearms boys off wi' the team, an' the DS in charge is armed, tae, so they've got plenty o' firepower if things go wrang.' He sounded rather pleased with himself.

'Whatever, whatever.' Donald waved one hand in the air, as he used the other to massage his brows. 'I have some more bad news – well, more detail about the bad news you already know.'

'We're all ears, sir,' said Daley.

Donald looked at him angrily. 'So that's it, is it? Senior officers in my division spreading fucking gossip and confidential information to each other, while I'm left in the dark like an arsehole.' Donald slammed his fist into the desk, sending a tartan paperweight crashing to the floor.

'Sorry, sir?' said Daley, a mystified expression on his face. 'It may have escaped your notice, but I've had more on my mind today than "fucking gossip", as you put it.' He was trying hard to keep the irritation from his voice but, as usual with Donald, he was finding it an onerous task.

Flopping back in his chair like a deflating balloon, Donald held up his hand in a conciliatory gesture that was as close to an apology as he was ever likely to make, and stared grimly at the ceiling. 'This morning I had a visit from the Chief Constable. When Rab White was shot, the killer decided to leave his mark at the scene.' He picked up a file from the desk and opened it carefully, eyeing its contents as though they still shocked him, though it was clearly not the first time he had viewed them.

'Sir?' Daley looked perplexed.

Donald removed a large photograph from the file and handed it across the desk to Daley, who looked at it steadily. Scott looked over his shoulder. Daley let out a long sigh, while his DS let out a groan.

'Taken with White's own phone camera, then left at the scene,' said Donald.

'Well, sir – let's be honest – even though this is the last thing any of us wanted, are you really surprised?'

'Shocked, surprised, baffled: who the fuck knows what to think, Jim?' replied Donald. 'It's one thing seeing a CCTV image from twelve thousand miles away, but looking at that man's face as he gloats over the body of one of my men, in the corridor of my own police office – well, to say it's disconcerting is putting it mildly.'

'Disconcertin'!' exclaimed Scott. 'Fuck me, I'm disconcerted by the cost o' a pint, or my gas bill. This isnae disconcerting – it's fucking terrifying.'

Donald sat forward in his seat, laid his elbows on the desk. 'Look,' he said, 'I think we're facing the biggest and most dangerous challenge of our careers here.' He looked in turn at his two subordinates. 'What happened to you in the early hours, Jim, is just the beginning. Here we are, fish in a barrel, so to speak; all the people JayMac hates the most gathered together in Kinloch. Sitting ducks.'

'Ye'll need tae make up yer mind, sir. Are we fish or ducks?' Scott replied, seemingly in all sincerity.

Donald stared at the DS, his face expressionless. Daley waited for the inevitable explosion, but when it happened, it took both he and Scott completely by surprise.

The superintendent threw his head back and began laughing, quietly at first, then a full belly laugh, his shoulders quivering as his face reddened and tears came to his eyes. 'You really are a prize prick, Brian,' Donald wheezed. 'A real arsehole.'

It didn't take long before Daley felt his face break into a smile, and then he too began to laugh.

Scott looked at them both, shaking his head. 'I must admit, that's no' the response I wiz expectin'.'

'Hysteria, Brian, pure hysteria,' replied Donald through a series of coughs. 'Nothing more, I assure you.'

It took a few moments for the laughter to dissipate. There followed a silence, as though each of them were coming to terms with what had happened and what was likely to happen.

'How did you find out about the ear, Jim?' Donald asked, in an almost friendly way.

'What ear?' replied Daley.

'"All ears", is that not what you said?'

'An expression, nothing more, I can assure you, sir,' said Daley.

'An inspired and most prescient one,' said Donald. 'Our midnight murderer left a package on my office desk before he killed DS White. Of course, they had to get the bomb squad to give the place the once over, so I've only just discovered its contents, and who those contents are likely to belong to.'

'Sir?' said Daley.

'The box contained a severed ear. It had been hacked off only hours before delivery,' said Donald. 'As you know, the Chief Constable is all over this now, as are the Serious Crime Squad, and would you believe, in what can only be described as a miracle of detection, they have managed to locate its owner.'

'Fuck me,' said Scott, a look of disgust on his face.

'Marion MacDougall, an eighty-two-year-old widow, who lives alone in the Springburn area of the city,' said Donald. 'No doubt an old acquaintance of yours,' he added, looking directly at Scott.

'Dae ye mean Frank's auntie, by any chance, sir?'

'The very woman, DS Scott. She was found by her carer yesterday, beaten half to death and missing her right ear.'

'First his brother, now his aunt,' stated Daley. 'One thing puzzles me though, sir.'

'Just one thing, Jim? You surprise me.' Donald's return to sarcasm hadn't taken long.

'If JayMac knows Frank's whereabouts, why doesn't he just come after him, rather than work his way through his family?'

'Why does the cat play with the mouse before biting it in two?'

'Or maybe he doesn't know where Frank is, an' he's just tryin' tae flush him oot,' Scott said, a hopeful note in his voice.

'If that is the case, DS Scott, how do we explain what happened to your colleague's car yesterday, right here in Kinloch?'

'Sir,' said Daley, 'at what time was DS White killed?'

'Two in the morning, Jim. His assailant was identified leaving the office on CCTV camera at 0206 hours.'

'In that case, it couldn't have been this ghost of JayMac who planted the bomb under my car. It must have been done between nine, when I got home, and five in the morning when I was about to leave – unless he has a helicopter, which I'm sure someone would've heard or seen. There's no way he could've been responsible for the assault on Mrs MacDougall and the murder of DS White, and still had time to plant explosives under my car. We're a hundred and fifty miles away. It's impossible.'

'Indeed, DCI Daley,' smiled Donald. 'Something I had already deduced, of course. There are only two possible answers to this particular conundrum . . .'

'He's got help. The bastard's no' only back fae the died, he's got the band back together!' interrupted Scott.

'That, or whoever tried to kill me has nothing to do with JayMac, and it's an unhappy coincidence,' Daley reasoned.

'Unhappy indeed, Jim,' Donald agreed. 'But who else would want to blow you up?'

Daley shrugged. 'Apart from the recent tobacco case, I've not exactly been putting myself about in Kinloch over the last few months.'

'We're still on the trail o' they drug smugglers,' Scott said enthusiastically. 'Still no' a hint o' getting' tae the bottom o' it, mind you.'

'Mmm.' Donald tidied up his files and closed the laptop on his desk. 'I think that will have to go on the back burner for now. It would appear we have a much more deadly problem on our hands.'

'Dae ye want me tae get oot an' gie Frankie the bad news, boss,' said Scott. 'I mean, sir.'

'No,' said Donald. 'You keep your eyes on what's happening with this firearms operation. Jim, go and break the news to Mr Robertson, if you would. I'd like you to report on how he takes it. And get him to keep those bloody children of his under control. The Protection Unit tell me they're coming and going as though there was nothing wrong.'

'Yes, sir,' replied Daley. 'I'll get out there now.'

'Oh, don't look so crestfallen, DS Scott,' Donald mocked. 'I'm quite sure you'll be able to get a dram or two later – in your own time.'

Brian Scott opened his mouth to speak, then thought the better of it and decided to smile sweetly instead.

He was a passenger in the front seat of the 4x4 as it churned its way up the muddy hill track.

He hadn't uttered a word of greeting to the driver. He didn't feel like speaking. Somehow being here, on this jut of land, had brought a stillness to his soul, the same kind of peace felt by the desperate once they know their decision to take their own life is irreversible: the serenity of inevitability.

He scanned his memory, wondering if he could bring to mind who had first identified these thoughts: Nietzsche,

Freud, Jung? *And if you gaze for long into an abyss, the abyss gazes also into you.*

A wave of tiredness lapped behind his eyes. He removed his holdall from the foot well as the vehicle skidded to a stop before the front door of a run-down cottage, not dissimilar to the one he had recently used as his base in Ayrshire.

'Wait here,' he ordered, as he ducked out of the door and went to open the tailgate. He removed his things, then, instead of entering his new abode, went to the driver's door, standing still as the window hummed open.

'Don't forget,' he said. 'From now on it's the reverse of what we've been doin'. I want tae keep these bastards guessing, so I'll be keeping a low profile for the next few days. Understood?'

The driver nodded, so he carried on. 'I want you to deliver our little package here, not tonight, later tomorrow sometime.' Then, without any kind of farewell, he walked away, opened the front door of the cottage with a kick and disappeared inside.

23

Daley saw the reaction as soon as Frank MacDougall opened the door; the man seemed to crumple in front of him, as though he knew more bad news was imminent.

'Ye better come in, Inspector Daley,' said MacDougall, and showed him into the lounge where they had last met. 'If this is aboot the kids, Mr Daley, there's fuck a' I can dae aboot it.'

Daley shook his head and spoke quietly, in the official voice that he – and every other police officer – used at times such as these. 'No, Frank, it's not about the kids. I'm sorry to say that I have more bad news for you.'

'Gie it tae me straight,' MacDougall said, rubbing his forehead. His face seemed more gaunt, and he looked as though he'd aged in the short time since Daley had last seen him.

'Your aunt Marion is quite seriously ill in hospital, Frank.'

'And no' of natural causes, I take it.'

'No,' said Daley. 'She was attacked in her home by a man dressed as a police officer. Later, the suspect delivered her severed ear to our HQ and murdered one of my colleagues in the process.' Under normal circumstances, he wouldn't have been so blunt, but Frank MacDougall was no stranger to extreme violence.

'So there's no doubt then?' he said, looking straight into the policeman's face for the first time since his arrival.

'We have photographic evidence that seems to confirm that this is, in fact, James Machie. I don't know how it's possible, but it would appear that he's back, large as life.'

'This is just the kinda shit that sick bastard thrives on, tae,' MacDougall said shaking his head. 'Will she be OK? I mean, she's no' goin' tae die?'

'It's too early to say,' Daley replied. 'She's in a pretty bad way, Frank.' His reply was as honest and accurate as possible, given the information he had to hand.

MacDougall walked over to the large window which looked down the hill and the open sea beyond.

'You know me, Mr Daley, never scared o' anythin' in ma life. Nothing. But this . . . this is something entirely different. I'm no' ashamed tae say, I'm oot o' my depth here. What can I dae tae help my family? Is that bastard just goin' tae pick them off wan efter the other?'

'You could start by making sure that your children stay put in this house while we try and sort this all out, Frank. The protection squad tell me they both refuse to remain on the farm here.'

'They're both adults. What the fuck can I dae tae keep them here? They've both got new names. Fuck me, there's no way JayMac would even recognise them, even if he knew where we were.' MacDougall looked almost hopeful. 'Remember, he's no' seen them for years.' He lit a cigarette and drew on it deeply. 'They hate each other, ye know.'

'Who does?'

'My kids. They can't stand the sight of each other. Not since . . . well, not since we lost oor Cisco.' He took another long draw on his cigarette. 'Tommy knew whit he was up tae, gettin' involved in that scene, but he never let on. Sarah'll no' forgive him.'

'It can't be easy for them, all this forced togetherness.'

'Aye,' said MacDougall, not really listening to what Daley was saying. 'He should never have risked goin' back tae Glasgow. I warned him. Ach, he wiz a'ways a hothead. I'll never know whit the fuck he thought he wiz goin' tae achieve.'

'I'm sorry,' said Daley.

'We're a' fae different worlds, Jim. Me, I'm gettin' tae be an auld man noo. Betty doesnae know if it's New Year or New York. And Tommy . . . fuck me, we a' know where Tommy wid be if he wisnae here – in the slammer, or shootin' up in some close somewhere.'

Daley had been listening to this familial introspection with the detached mind of the detective. Slowly, however, it dawned on him that fatherhood was a chancy business; the man before him bore witness to that. It would soon be his worry too.

'Sarah deserves better than this,' MacDougall said, picking up a silver-framed photograph of himself and his daughter. 'She's got it a': beauty, brains, the lot. It's her that suffers maist here. Smart as a tack. She'd gie Jamie Machie a run fir his money.'

'She might have to if you don't keep her here – just until this blows over, Frank.'

'Blows over?' MacDougall was incredulous. 'He's no' a wee storm that'll blow oot like the yins across the bay there. That bastard's a fucking hurricane!'

'Still,' Daley said. 'Better safe than sorry. Machie seems to be quite adept at achieving the impossible.'

'How's he done it, Jim?' MacDougall looked suddenly desperate. 'How the fuck has he done it?'

'There's only one explanation, Frank.' It was Daley's turn to look out to sea. 'The man who was killed in the back of the prison ambulance wasn't James Machie. However impossible that sounds.'

'Aye,' MacDougall agreed, looking suddenly thoughtful. 'When I heard the bastard was dead, I suppose it lifted a hell o' a weight aff my shoulders.'

'We never did get to the bottom of who was responsible for his, well, assassination, in the first place, did we, Frank?' said Daley, one eyebrow raised.

'Bit o' a mystery that one,' said MacDougall. 'Listen, I'll try ma best tae get the kids intae line, but ye've got to remember, they've got a right tae a life. It's bad enough they've been cooped up here in the fuckin' sticks, without telling them where they can go and whit they can dae. The Witness Protection mob are a'ready wantin' us tae go intae hiding in a mair secure unit – some mothballed army base, or something. No way!' MacDougall stubbed out his cigarette angrily.

'I don't need to tell you what danger you and your family are in,' Daley said. 'We just can't call this one, Frank – can't call it at all. I'll never understand why you didn't take the chance to go abroad.' He scrutinised MacDougall. 'All expenses paid.' Something wasn't right; his instincts told him so.

'Fat lot o' good it did Gerry Dowie,' MacDougall replied, without a flicker of emotion.

Daley couldn't disagree.

'Don't worry,' MacDougall said. 'I know what Machie is capable of, make no mistake aboot that. I've also no intention of joining my brother,' he said picking up a crystal decanter filled with whisky. 'A wee dram, before you go? I think we both need it.'

Daley nodded.

As the amber nectar burned its way down his throat, MacDougall's home telephone rang. He answered, replying to the caller with only a grunt, and handed the cordless handset to Daley. 'Looks like I'm yer new secretary.'

'DC Dunn, sir.' Daley could hear Donald's voice booming in the background. 'Couldn't get your mobile.'

'I can hear all is not well,' said Daley.

'There's a problem at the firearms search, sir.' Dunn sounded rattled. 'DS Scott went to check it out, something to do with explosives, sir.' She paused, and Daley could hear a fresh verbal onslaught in the background. 'It's OK, sir, nobody's hurt, but the boss thinks you should attend . . . just in case.'

'I'll head over there now.' Daley hung up and handed the phone to MacDougall.

'Aye, it's true whit they say, Mr Daley.' MacDougall smiled. 'A policeman's lot is no' a happy one.'

Even though it was just after three in the afternoon, the daylight was beginning to fade as DS Brian Scott and a local DC drove past the Fearney farm, then up a dilapidated track to Bentham's cottage.

His mobile rang. 'Hi, Jim,' Scott answered. 'How did Frankie take the news?' He listened for a few moments. 'When you get tae Fearney's farm, gie me a bell. I'll get one o' the boys tae come and pick ye up in a Land Rover. Ye'll never make it up this hill in a normal motor.' He was jolted by yet another deep pothole, as though to confirm the statement. 'They've found somethin' up here. No' sure what yet, but I'm just aboot tae find oot.'

Scott ended the call and replaced the phone in his trouser pocket; he normally kept his phone in his jacket, however Donald had insisted that he and his driver wear flak jackets. Already, he was beginning to feel constricted by the tight body armour; he tried to wriggle it into a more comfortable position.

A member of the Firearms Unit was waiting at the front door of the cottage, an automatic weapon slung over his shoulder.

'What's goin' on here, and why a' the mystery?' asked Scott as he alighted from the Land Rover.

'Take a look fir yersel, gaffer.'

The cottage, which looked rundown from the outside, was remarkably tidy inside. Similar to Frank MacDougall's property. What was it with these people who lived in the middle of nowhere?

Tidiness was where the comparison with the MacDougall residence ended. No designer furniture here. The front door led straight into a small living area, off which was situated a curtained-off kitchenette and a wooden staircase. Underneath the latter a door lay open to reveal a small bathroom. In the hearth, the remains of a log fire glowed feebly, yet it felt more chilly inside the dwelling than out.

Scott took in the scene with a professional eye, but nothing untoward presented itself. The carpet was a dark red colour, worn in places, but clean; there was no dust on the table in the middle of the room, and on a threadbare couch a collection of magazines was neatly piled. All was tidy and ordered, though the lack of pictures or decoration gave the distinct impression that no woman shared this space.

He could hear footsteps and voices above, so he and the young DC ascended the creaky, uncarpeted staircase. Now upstairs, Scott, who at five feet ten wasn't particularly tall, had to crouch to avoid hitting his head on the low ceiling. The small landing was narrow with two doors leading off it, through one of which he could see a couple of people. An armed firearms officer loomed in the doorway, stooped and awkward.

'A'right, Stephen?' Scott recognised the armed officer as one of the men who had shared his recent scare at MacDougall's property. 'Whit's goin' on?'

'Take a look,' said the policeman, crouching back further into the room and giving them space to enter.

Scott ducked through the low doorway, and instantly his breath was taken away by the arsenal of weaponry piled along one side of the small room. The face of the young cop from Kinloch who was acting DS was pale and serious.

'What should we do, Sergeant?' he asked, looking bewildered.

'First of a',' said Scott, 'I want everybody oot, apart from Stephen fae the unit. One of ye get down tae Fearney's farm and wait for DCI Daley.'

There followed pushing, shoving and muttered apologies as five grown men attempted to move in the cramped space. Eventually, only Scott and the firearms officer remained in the room, as the others creaked their way down the rickety staircase.

Scott looked at Stephen, who was now kneeling over the stash of weapons. 'What d'ye reckon, big man?'

'I reckon we'll need more bodies,' the cop answered. 'Aye, an' no' the local plod either. This little lot will need to be checked over for possible booby traps, unsafe weapons, explosives. That looks like Semtex.' He pointed to a pile of metal boxes. 'And I recognise this too.' He pointed to a stainless-steel box the size of a large matchbox, with red, yellow and green wires protruding from one end.

'Spill the beans, fir fuck's sake.'

'It's a motion sensor detonator,' he said, looking over his shoulder at Scott, who was squinting at the device in the poor light. 'The kind terrorists use to blow up cars. Old style – from the seventies, or early eighties, by the looks of it. It's primitive, but it'll still kill you.'

All of a sudden, Brian Scott felt very cold, and very unsafe.

Daley took in the hoard with a shake of his head. His first impression of Paul Bentham had not been a good one, but he hadn't suspected that the man packed this amount of firepower.

'Aye, some haul, Jim,' said Scott, unable to peel his eyes from the collection of automatic and semi-automatic weapons, metal ammunition boxes, explosives, loose grenades and other deadly military paraphernalia.

Daley had just spoken to Donald, who had ordered the property shut down and guarded until a specialist team could come down from Glasgow. The inspector from the Firearms Unit had arrived just after Daley, and declared that he could see nothing of imminent danger.

'Worth a few bob if sold to the right people, Brian,' said Daley. 'Come on, nothing more we can do here. I want to check in on Duncan Fearney on the way back. If anyone knows where Bentham could have disappeared to, he's the man.'

The detectives got into a marked Land Rover, leaving two detectives and two armed firearms officers behind to guard the scene.

'Don't yous get lonely now,' Scott shouted from the driver's window, as he revved the engine and pulled slowly away from the cottage.

After a short but uncomfortable journey, they drove into the farmyard.

'No sign o' life,' said Scott as they exited the vehicle.

The freshly painted yellow door stood out in the gloom. Daley knocked loudly, while Scott cupped his hands and peered in through a dirty window. From a large shed across the muddy yard, cattle lowed pitifully. Scott, having seen nothing through the window, walked towards the cowshed, screwing up his nose at the smell of manure.

'I'm no expert, Jim,' he shouted, 'but these poor beasts need milking, don't you think?'

Daley walked to the entrance to the shed. A dozen or so cows were penned into separate compartments were lowing agitatedly. He could see by their distended udders that they hadn't been attended to recently.

'You check inside the barn, Brian. I'll see if there's another way into the house,' said Daley. His instinct told him all was not well. The image of Bentham threatening Fearney, viewed from the rear mirror of his car the day before, replayed in his mind.

Scott's muttered oaths as he entered the cowshed were soon drowned out by the noise from the animals, as Daley hurried towards the farmhouse. Down a muddy track, he could see a large circular structure, painted blue. It looked a bit like a massive paddling pool, the like of which children cooled off in on hot summer days.

He cursed as filth splattered onto his trousers, and he wished he had remembered to bring a pair of wellies.

The slurry tank was higher than it looked, well over head height, so he looked around for some way to gain access to the top, to allow him to see inside. He had nearly given up when he discovered a metal ladder attached to the far side.

The rungs of the ladder were slippery with dirt and dung; his foot slipped on the second rung, nearly sending him tumbling. The stench was truly appalling.

Daley craned his neck over the side, and almost fell backwards again as the putrid odour hit his nostrils. The slurry was a greenish brown colour; a layer of pungent steam hung over the tank. The movement of a shiny beetle caught his eye as it meandered across the crusted surface, making Daley's heart lurch.

'Jim! Quick, o'er here!'

Daley half scrambled, half fell down the slick ladder, hurrying to respond to the urgency in Scott's tone. He had assumed Bentham had done a runner – maybe he'd been wrong.

Scott was standing at the entrance to the cowshed. 'Look, Jim. It's not good.'

The noise from the cattle and the stench of dung was an assault on the senses, as Daley followed Scott deeper into the shed. The distressed beasts observed the two men with large rheumy eyes, steam from their breath billowing up into the cold air. A faint yellow glow came from a single lightbulb.

Daley's eye was drawn to the whitewashed wall at the far end of the building. Amidst the smears of cow dung another, darker stain was slathered across the wall: blood. Beneath it, a crumpled body lay on the floor. Half of his face was missing, sprayed across the byre.

'Poor bastard,' said Scott. 'This Fearney character hasn't had much luck. But at least we know who we're after now – that Bentham guy.'

'No, we don't,' said Daley, desperately trying to swallow back the bile he could feel stinging at his throat. 'That is Paul Bentham.'

24

Tommy MacDougall revved the engine of the car and gunned it down the farm track. The bright headlights picked out two armed police officers, trying their best to remain inconspicuous, loitering inside a lean-to shed attached to a barn that backed onto the narrow roadway. Their breath was fleetingly illuminated in the halogen light.

Fuckin' arseholes, he thought as the vehicle fishtailed over a slick patch of dirt. He hated the police. He hated everything, and especially his family: his father, his poor mother, but most of all, his sister. He despised the way she patronised him – laughed at him openly. He hated the way she spoke, looked, walked; he hated her opinion of him, his life, what he liked to do and who with. It made his blood boil. He often fantasised about hitting her, over and over again, ruining her pretty face and silencing her forever.

He was on the main road when his mobile phone, which he'd flung onto the passenger seat, rang.

'I'm on my way. Whit d'ye want?' he said, mouth twisting in distaste. 'What! Are you sure? That gear should've been safe as houses up there. The fuckin' shop is empty, for fuck's sake.' He listened to the reply with growing irritation. 'Nah, it's no' ma fuckin' fault we had tae change plans, is it? Listen, dinnae say anythin' aboot this, right? There's a lot o' shit happenin', so I'll deal wi' a' this. Dinnae bother gettin' a hauld o' anyone else, OK?'

Conversation over, he threw the phone back onto the passenger seat. 'Bastard!' he shouted, banging his fist against the steering wheel.

He glanced at the digital clock on his dashboard; he was going to be late. He pushed his right foot firmly down on the throttle as the BMW's headlights briefly flashed across a sign: A83 Kinloch 7 miles.

The three police officers sat round a table in the empty dining room of the County Hotel. Two of them were eating heartily, while the third eyed his fish and chips with obvious distaste.

'You no' hungry, sir?' enquired DS Scott through a mouthful of chicken curry.

'What do you think, Brian?' said Donald, lifting a glass of white wine to his mouth.

'If ye don't want yer chips,' said Scott, 'I'll happily take them off yer hands.' He was about to pass comment on the shrivelled fish, but was silenced by a look from Daley.

'So you're here for the duration, sir?' Daley asked.

'Yes,' said Donald. 'Though I can assure you, it gives me no pleasure whatsoever. The Chief Constable is of the opinion that the seriousness of this case demands the presence of a senior officer.' He drained his glass. 'Unfortunately, it would appear as though I'm destined to be drawn to this bloody awful place. Where the hell is that useless waitress?' He turned in his seat in order to locate the missing member of the hotel staff. 'We had to wait half a bloody hour for this crap to be thrust before us, now the wretched girl has disappeared.'

'I'll hoof it up to the bar mysel', Scott declared, getting to his feet while removing the napkin which he'd thrust into his shirt collar. 'Anyone fir a top-up?'

'Yes,' said Donald. 'Get me another half carafe of this gnat's piss.'

'Just a pint for me, Brian, please,' Daley said with a smile. He had been keeping a close eye on Donald. They had gone straight into the dining room on their arrival, as the superintendent had made it clear that he had no intention of sitting in the bar for an aperitif amongst 'the yokels'. He had already had two glasses of wine, plus a half carafe when his meal had arrived. Daley remembered how much Donald used to drink in the past, and could see echoes of it in his superior's current behaviour. Back then, beer and whisky had been his tipples of choice. Not for the first time in the last few days, Daley noticed the ghost of the gruff and boorish man of so many years ago breach the acquired confidence of Donald's new personality. It made him uneasy.

'So, you're to be a father, Jim,' said Donald.

'Yes, sir. I don't think it's really sunk in yet.'

'Well, it's been rather a fraught few days, to say the least,' said Donald. He abandoned his attempt to snare the remaining peas, thrust his cutlery noisily onto the plate, then pushed it away. 'But everything is . . . as it should be, on that front, then?'

Daley wasn't sure whether it was the tone of the question or the question itself that annoyed him more. He felt the familiar sensation of his temper straining at an invisible leash. 'Meaning what, exactly?'

Donald held his gaze for a moment, and then shrugged. 'Congratulations, I'm sure. Mrs Donald and I have never been blessed in that department. I suppose I rather assumed you and Liz would be the same.'

'What was it you used to say, sir? To "assume" is to make an "ass" of "you" and "me"', Daley said, his face like thunder.

'Just a polite enquiry from a concerned friend, Jim, nothing else.'

'You and I have never been friends, John. I would prefer to keep it that way.'

'Really, Jim, I'd hoped you'd be able to divest yourself of that temper as you matured – I can see now that hasn't been the case.'

'Well, sir, we can't all start out as one thing and become something entirely different, can we?' It was Daley's turn to be condescending.

Donald was about to reply when Scott appeared back in the dining room, unbuttoning his shirt collar and loosening his tie with one hand.

'It's a' right. Annie's bringing the drinks in two ticks,' he announced. 'Right,' he said, now back in his seat and looking at his colleagues, 'whit have I missed?'

'Nothing,' said Daley. 'Nothing at all.'

'Instead of all of this chit-chat, gentlemen,' Donald announced, 'let's try and assess – as best we can – exactly where we are with this horror.'

'No' really anywhere, as far as I can see, sir,' answered Scott.

'It does feel as though we're standing by, waiting for Machie to make his next move,' Daley said. 'It's not as though division or the crime squad have turned anything up, is it?'

As Daley spoke, Donald's phone bleeped, vibrating loudly

on the table. He picked it up and scrolled through the email he had just received.

'Not true, Jim,' he said. After one of his dramatic pauses, he continued: 'Cumnock CID lifted DNA from the helicopter. Our worst nightmares have come true.'

'A match with Machie?' asked Daley.

'Not quite,' said Donald. 'You will remember that, since his death, all physical records of Machie have been expunged.'

'Yes,' said Daley, bridling at Donald's tone.

'But you will of course remember JayMac's sister – the lovely Ina?'

'Aye, how could ye forget?' said Scott.

'She was arrested for shoplifting last year, stole an outsized bikini.' Donald couldn't help smiling at the thought of the grossly obese Ina Machie squeezing herself into the garment. 'Anyhow, there is no doubt; the unknown person present at the scene of the helicopter murder is Ina's sibling. Taking into account the visual evidence, combined with the fact we know who her only sibling is, well . . .'

Daley remained silent, staring ahead in disbelief.

'Is DNA infallible? I mean, surely there's an element o' doubt.' DS Scott's voice bore traces of despair.

'There is an element of doubt in just about everything,' Donald barked back. 'This, plus the evidence of our own eyes, as well as this person's actions, surely minimise that doubt. We must now consider this madman to be James Machie and concern ourselves more with how to stop him from doing any more damage rather than worrying how he has managed this resurrection.'

'We still have no idea if he knows where MacDougall is,' declared Daley. 'That's what's strange. MacDougall's aunt says Machie never said anything to her during the attack. Didn't even ask where Frank was – poor soul.'

'How did MacDougall react to your lecture on keeping his brood out of trouble, Jim?' asked Donald.

'Not well, sir. He seems to feel powerless as far as keeping them to heel is concerned.'

'I might have known he would prove inadequate when it came to raising a family. Mind you, a task no man takes on lightly, eh, Jim?'

Daley realised that the superintendent was, at the very least, half cut. Before he could make further comment, Scott greeted the arrival of Annie with a full drinks tray. 'Ah, there she is – an angel o' mercy. Whit took ye so long? It's no' exactly busy, the night – where're a' the punters?'

Annie cleared a space on the table and began placing the drinks in front of the men. 'Lager for you, Brian. And a pint for you, Jim. I mean, Mr Daley.' She smiled nervously at Donald. It was clear that the formidable chatelaine was uneasy around the superintendent. 'And a half carafe of the house white for you, sir.'

'My dear woman,' Donald gushed. 'Please, call me John – no need for all of these formalities. After all, I'm a guest in your fine establishment, and could be for some time. Tell me, Angela, why are you so quiet?'

'Annie, sir. I mean, John.'

'Oh, who is she, and what has she done to have spirited away all of your customers?'

'I'm Annie,' she continued, nodding and smiling to soften the blow for Donald, who had made the mistake.

'Sorry?' The inebriated police officer was now completely befuddled.

Seeing that the conversation was going nowhere, Annie decided to change tack. 'It's the big switch-on tonight. You know, the Christmas lights.'

'But they're a'ready on,' said Scott, looking mystified.

'Aye, that's jeest cos the celebrity coudnae make it last week,' she told them. 'It's a' go the night: float parade, the pipe band, and a' the wee shops are open wi' mulled wine an' mince pies. It's a right community event. The weans jeest love it.'

'Right,' said Scott, relieved that his concerns about an empty bar had been put to rest. 'When's the fun start?'

'In aboot an 'oor,' said Annie, looking at her watch.

'Surprised you didn't know about this, Jim,' Donald chided. 'Clearly a concern in terms of crowd control, if what Angela here says is right.' He stared at Daley down his long nose.

'All sorted,' Daley answered. 'I'm not the only policeman in Kinloch, sir.'

'Quite,' said Donald, pouring more wine into his glass. 'Though you're supposed to be in charge.'

'Och, nothin' for you boys tae be worried aboot,' assured Annie. 'It's wan o' they times when there' no nonsense. Yous should take a wee wander outside – it's a lovely night.' She stopped for a moment, as though reconsidering. 'Well, apart fae the time Peter Wilson an' Hoggie McIntosh had that fight and went through Broon's windae.'

'Oh?' said Donald, raising his eyebrows.

'Aye, an' a couple o' years ago when Dougie McMillan an' his daughter had that argument aboot the length o' her skirt, an' she tried tae run him doon . . . Oh, an' when Bessie Gilchrist got steamin' and fell in front o' the parade, an' the

Pipe Major near took her heid aff wi' his mace thing, or whootever it's called. Aye an' there was the time . . .'

'I'm sure everything will be fine,' interrupted Daley, not wishing to hear any more stories about the disasters that were likely to occur during the switch-on of the town's Christmas lights – occurrences he had been told nothing about. He consoled himself that the ever-reliable Sergeant Shaw was in charge, a uniformed officer steeped in the traditions of Kinloch, having spent over twenty years in the community.

'At least this will give them something to keep their minds off the goings-on this afternoon,' Donald declared, watching Annie pad back to the bar with an empty tray.

'Any word fae the forensic boys yet, sir?' Scott asked.

'The explosives team at the cottage are going through everything with great care, for obvious reasons. As for Mr Bentham, well, forensics have only one question to answer.'

'Aye, I think we can rule oot suicide,' said Scott. 'I think we a' know the answer tae that, wi'oot havin' tae wear a white coat tae find oot.'

25

Tommy MacDougall waited, shivering, at the rear of the building, the front of which faced onto Kinloch's Main Street. He clutched a cigarette in one hand; the other was thrust deep into the front pocket of his hooded top.

The building had belonged to a large retail chain, forced into bankruptcy after the global financial crash. It was a flat-roofed construction of three storeys, with grey pebble-dashed walls and large, boarded-up windows. A goods entrance was secured by a padlocked roller door, adorned with graffiti, which he squinted to read in the dim light of the security lamp. He snorted a laugh at the more risqué remarks, recognising the names of some of the individuals mentioned. A few feet above his head, the bottom rungs of the external fire escape hung in mid air. Though the citizens of Kinloch had objected to the building's construction in the sixties, the shop had become a cornerstone of Main Street. Tommy illuminated the dial of his watch, his hand trembling with anticipation as well as the cold. He needn't have worried about being late; the person he had come to meet was late too. Or so he thought. Movement overhead made him crane his neck towards the fire escape.

'You, how did you get here so quickly?' he said, unsettled by the appearance of the man above him. 'Fuckin' typical. We've got tae move a' the shit on the busiest night o' the year. Whit aboot this pair on the roof ye told me aboot?'

The man said nothing, just gestured to Tommy to follow him up onto the fire escape.

'Whit the fuck's wrong wi' you?' said Tommy, as he placed his right foot on the first rung of the rusting ladder.

Daley had been surprised when Donald expressed a desire to join the throng of people and watch the parade of floats leading up to the official switch-on of the Christmas lights. Had his boss not consumed so much alcohol, he would more likely have spent the evening in his hotel room, or back at the police office weaving his interminable webs.

Daley's thoughts drifted to the visit he had paid Liz at the hospital earlier that day. He was worried by how pale and tired she had looked, but the doctor assured him that it was merely an after-effect of the trauma she had suffered, combined with her condition. She dozed as he held her hand. He tried to picture what their child would look like, hoping earnestly that it would resemble his wife and not him.

Once he had been assured that she was in no immediate danger, he had rather welcomed the break, the chance for some space amidst the turmoil of the last few days. He kissed her on the forehead before taking his leave. Only as he walked down the long corridor of the hospital did the darkness again encroach on his mind.

Thoughts of Liz were banished by Scott, who beckoned him and Donald through the crowd to a better vantage point. He was surprised how busy the street was, and reckoned that the great majority of the town had turned out to witness the spectacle. Beside him, Donald was huddled into a heavy, and no doubt expensive, overcoat. Daley could hear him swear under his breath as they made their way through the throng, Scott on point.

'Just here, boys,' Scott called over his shoulder, gesturing to the doorway of a shop. Inside, visible through the large windows, people were drinking from plastic cups and helping themselves to mince pies.

'I might have known we'd end up at a bookie's,' Donald moaned as they took their position in the large doorway. 'I hope they're not consuming alcohol in there. Free or otherwise – an absolute contravention of their licence under the Betting, Gaming and Lotteries Act.'

'Aye, well, since we've been consuming alcohol ourselves, an' we're off duty, I dinnae think we should attempt an intervention the noo, sir,' Scott joked, winking at Daley.

'I'm sure your bookies' *interventions* are very frequent, Brian,' Donald replied, turning his attention to a woman with a large furry hat who had positioned herself in front of him and was obscuring his view of the pageant route on the road beyond. 'Excuse me,' he said, tapping her on the shoulder, 'we are police officers and require a clear view of the proceedings. Please move along.'

'Whoot?' said the woman, frowning at Donald. 'Who died an' made you king o' the world? Piss off!' She turned her attention to a small child fussing at her feet.

The look on Donald's face sent Scott into paroxysms of silent mirth. The superintendent was about to speak when a voice issued forth from an incredibly loud public address system.

'Noo, how are yiz a' daein'?' was the first question, accompanied by a blast of jaunty accordion music. This prompted a less than enthusiastic response from the crowd, ranging from pleasant hellos to more profane utterances. One shout of 'Fuck off, Dan!' could be heard above the rest, which caused a ripple of laughter amongst the citizens of Kinloch.

Unabashed, and with a brief clearing of the throat, the announcer continued. 'Noo, in whoot's a first for us a' at Kinloch FM, we're proud tae be covering tonight's entertainment live, broadcast tae ye all wi' oor PA, for which we can thank the good people at Rankin Motors! Gie it up for Rankin Motors!' This was greeted by a ragged cheer. 'Can ye hear me?' he roared, after which cries of 'Turn it doon, for any sake' or 'Shut that fuckin' thing up' were heard.

'I'm no' giein' away the identity o' oor special guest, but a' I'll say is yous should a' look up,' he announced.

Suddenly, from somewhere above their heads on the four-storey tenement behind the policemen, a powerful spotlight illuminated the flat roof of the building across Main Street. Daley could hear the strangled whine of bagpipes being inflated, then the roll of snare drums before the pipes sounded, in readiness for a tune. Then, without warning they burst into life. The crowd applauded, and to his left Daley spotted the flash of silver buttons and tartan as the pipe band rounded the corner of the esplanade and began their march up Main Street.

'Pit yer hands the'gither for the Kinloch Pipe Band!' bellowed Dan, clearly audible above the skirl of the pipes and the cheers of the crowd.

Daley looked side on at Donald, who looked less than impressed by the commencement of the festivities, possibly because the woman in front of him had been joined by some of her friends and their offspring, one of whom – a small boy with a runny nose – was tugging at the hem of the superintendent's coat, while looking up at him with big eyes.

Behind the band, flat-backed lorries made up the procession, each decorated according to different themes. A group of hairy-chested, bikini-clad men, all wearing long platinum-blonde wigs, gyrated under artificial palm trees on what looked like half a ton of sand. They held cans of beer and were obviously a little worse for wear, staggering as the vehicle chugged up Main Street, waving and shouting to the crowd.

'They must be freezin', Scott shouted in Daley's ear, as he watched Donald give the little boy a nudge to try and make him let go of his coat. The women in front were busy throwing coins into charity buckets carried by men dressed as Santa Claus.

'Credit where credit's due, mind you,' said Scott. 'They're a right community doon here – the way it used tae be.'

Each float was accompanied by its own music, which blared out of speakers on the back of every lorry, making the din truly deafening.

'A big hand fir the lassies fae the Douglas Arms,' shouted Dan, as a float done up to look like a Restoration inn passed slowly by, populated by half a dozen women dressed in low-cut, lace-up bodices, who laughed merrily as they threw small toys into the crowd, sending the children of Kinloch into a frantic scramble. Daley could smell fried onions and burgers being cooked in a van further up Main Street; it would be doing a roaring trade. Despite his meal at the County, his stomach began to rumble. To his right, he could see Donald wiping furtively at a trail of snot left slathered across his coat by the little boy, who was now deep in the scrum of children trying to get their hands on one of the precious toys which were still being sent spinning into the crowd.

'A big cheer for Santa!' Dan announced, as the star of the parade rounded the corner. A large man dressed as Father Christmas sat in an elaborate grotto, replete with elves dressed in exceptionally short green skirts and matching hats.

'This is practically pornography,' declared Donald, as one of the elves raised her skirt even higher, to reveal suspenders holding up green fishnet stockings. She was rewarded with a lascivious jeer from the men in the crowd.

'Aye, you'd know,' said Scott under his breath. 'There's no' enough o' this type o' thing noo'adays,' he continued more audibly. 'It's great tae see the kids oot an' aboot, an' no' wi' their heids stuck intae some computer.'

'Very laudable, I'm sure,' the superintendent replied, again examining the hem of his coat with a look of disgust on his face.

The women in front of them were making the most of the event by passing a bottle of sparkling wine around; they had come prepared with plastic glasses and two large bags of crisps. They chatted merrily, shrieking with laughter at the sights and sounds of the evening while their children played happily with their new toys, salvaged from the scramble.

Daley took it all in with a burgeoning feeling of warmth and contentedness. Maybe it was down to the goodwill of the season, or perhaps the alcohol he had consumed, but more likely, he reasoned, it was the feeling of being part of something bigger than yourself. He had become used to being a reluctant witness to all that was wrong with humanity; it was easy to become the jaundiced observer, with the expectation that things could only get worse, never better. But here and now, as part of this little community, he felt a surge of hope.

Across the road, now that the procession had passed by, he spotted a man holding the hand of a toddler. The little boy was muffled against the cold with a blue bobble hat and a thick jacket. He stared up wide-eyed at the lights and the people as the man kneeled at his side, whispering in his ear and pointing to everything around them – helping this tiny, new mind make sense of it all. A broad smile was spread across the man's face.

Daley realised that he would soon be that man; he was about to jump onto the merry-go-round of fatherhood, with all of its attendant highs and lows. His heart began to beat more quickly as the responsibility of it all brought emotion welling up in his chest. One thing was certain: there were many worse places to bring up a child than Kinloch. This unique town appeared to have retained something lost by many other communities in the modern, complex world; a sense of belonging and home, of being part of something more. He beamed with pleasure.

As Daley bathed in the glow of impending fatherhood, he didn't notice that someone had appeared silently at his side. He turned to the figure and was pleased to find Hamish, puffing clouds of blue pipe smoke into the night air.

'A fine sight, Mr Daley,' he said. 'Aye, fine, indeed.'

'Yes, Hamish,' Daley replied, still smiling at the little boy across the street who was now pointing excitedly at Santa.

'No' so nice fir Duncan Fearney, mind you, eh?' Hamish turned his slanted gaze to the detective.

'How do you know about that, Hamish?' Daley hissed into the old man's ear. 'Don't answer that,' he said after a moment's consideration. 'Just don't let the boss hear you. He'll have you up in the office being questioned as a possible accomplice before you know it.'

'Aye, weel, he'll need tae get past this lot first,' commented Hamish, gesturing to the crowds with his pipe. 'I remember in 1952, young Erchie Dougall went AWOL fae his National Service – jeest at this exact time o' year.' He smiled at Daley. 'In them days, a' we had wiz a big tree wi' a few lights on it, doon at the cross – nane o' this extravagance. Mind you, the folk turned oot jeest the same tae see the lights go on, an' the star pit on top o' the tree.'

Daley listened patiently, knowing that Hamish would eventually reach some point pertinent to what they had been talking about.

'So there wiz half the toon, gathered roon' the tree – drink havin' been taken, mind you. These two redcaps appeared; apparently they'd known aboot poor Erchie's movements an' had decided the time was ripe tae catch him, oot in the open, so tae speak.' He had to raise his voice, as the pipe band was now blowing a particularly strident reel nearby. 'So yer two men made their move. They grabbed oor Erchie an' tried tae drag him intae custody an' back tae the army, where nae doubt he wid have been fair badly treated fir his indiscretion.'

'Being absent without leave is a bit more than an indiscretion, Hamish,' said Daley with a smile. 'What happened?'

'Och, tae cut a lang story short, before they could get tae Erchie, they got mobbed by the crowd an' flung intae the loch. Aye, they wirnae fae the toon, ye understan'. As ye know fine, we may fight like fury amongst oorsels, but woe betide any strangers that pick on one o' oor ain.' He smiled at Daley as he took another long draw of his pipe.

'Very clever, Hamish. But I'm warning you, whatever you know about recent events, say nothing.' Daley raised his brows at the old man.

'Did I no' tell ye: Duncan Fearney is a desperate man, Mr Daley, an' as ye know fine yersel, desperate men dae desperate things.'

'I would like to talk to you tomorrow, Jim,' Donald slurred in Daley's other ear. The effect of the quantity of wine the superintendent had consumed had now well and truly kicked in, no doubt accentuated by the cold evening. 'Most important . . . Most sensitive. I . . .'

'Let tomorrow deal with itself, sir,' Daley interrupted, the feeling of contentment draining from him at the mere sound of Donald's voice.

'Tomorrow it is then,' replied the superintendent with a small hiccough. The look of disdain reappeared on his face as the group of women in front, who had now donned party hats, burst into song.

'Noo, ladies and gentlemen, can I have yer attention please!' Dan's voice boomed from the loudspeaker. 'As yiz a' know, the lights went on last week.' This elicited a jeer from the crowd. 'Noo, come on – it's nae use blaming big Hughie. He just pulled the switch when he should ha' kept his hand on his ha'penny.' The crowd continued to grumble. 'Well, when we switched them off again, everybody complained, so they were jeest left on.'

To a background of 'Get on wi' it', 'That's a load a' shite!' and 'Away an' bile yer heid!', Dan, a determined performer if nothing else, pressed on. 'Since the lights are on a'ready, the community council have managed a wee surprise.'

'Are they sober?' shouted someone.

Dan ignored this. 'Tonight,' he continued, 'oor special guest comes a' the way fae darkest Africa . . . Ladies an' gentlemen, Tarzan!' He roared into the microphone, and the PA system whined in protest. 'Tarzan will descend via the wire, fae the top o' Woolies – or whoot wiz Woolies – an' land jeest here, where he will press the switch that will set off a fireworks display!'

'Fuck me,' Scott said in Daley's ear. 'I hope they health an' safety boys have checked a' this oot. The last thing we need is Tarzan splattered a' over the boss's good shoes.'

'Are yous ready?' Dan encouraged his audience. 'Ten! Nine! Eight!' The crowd joined in the countdown as a spot-light whirled to the top of the building across the street. 'Seven! Six! Five! Four!' Only then did Daley spot the thin wire, which angled down from the top of the building to the pavement below.

'Three! Two! Wan!' All eyes were on the roof. 'Ur ye up there, Tarzan?' Dan shouted.

Daley could see movement; Tarzan being strapped belat-edly into his harness, he reasoned.

'We'll dae the countdoon again. Tarzan's obviously been busy wi' Jane,' Dan quipped, to groans from the audience. 'Ten! Nine! Eight!'

Daley watched as a figure appeared at the edge of the roof. He squinted, as the crowd bayed for Tarzan to descend the wire. 'Seven! Six! Five!' Daley could make out a second person on the top of the building, though less obviously than the first as they were both dressed in black.

'Four! Three! Two! Wan! Tarzan, come on doon!' called Dan.

After a short pause, the crowd began to clap, as with a shove from the figure behind, Tarzan began a slow descent. Something was wrong. As the bright spotlight picked out the detail, it was clear that the individual on the wire was limp, and not wearing a costume loincloth, but jeans and a hooded top that was pulled up over his face.

Scott looked at Daley with a bemused expression. It was then, from the section of the crowd underneath the wire, that screams began to issue. Daley tugged at Scott's sleeve, pulling him past the group of women, who were silent now, staring up at the descending figure. A girl ran towards Daley, screaming, holding her hands out; under the orange glow of the acetylene light her face appeared to be stained with black spots.

'Help me,' she shouted. The crowd started to surge away from where the wire terminated. Screams and shouts rent the cold evening air.

Panic erupted as Daley and Scott fought their way towards the spot where the wire was anchored. Daley could see uniformed officers trying to calm the stampeding crowd, to little effect.

Amidst the tumult, the detectives reached the hooded man, now slumped on the pavement, illuminated by a pool of light. Scott bent down and gently removed the hood, then immediately recoiled.

'Jim, fucking hell. Fucking hell.'

Daley looked down at the dead face of Tommy MacDougall, a neat slash in his throat. Livid black blood oozed from the wound, creating a dark puddle beneath his body.

*

As his phone rang in his pocket, Daley wondered why it sounded so loud. When he answered it, he realised why: the throng of onlookers on Kinloch's Main Street had fallen silent. He looked at the faces in the crowd; all looked sad and shocked, and a number of people were crying. He looked up and was almost blinded by a fierce light; the corpse was now bathed in a white glow. He gestured to Scott to get whoever was operating the spotlight to switch it off. The detective sergeant hurried off, as more uniformed officers appeared and struggled to usher the townsfolk back home, while others rushed towards the building where Tommy MacDougall had been killed.

Daley could hear the stress in his own voice as he answered the call.

'Constable Ingram of the Protection Unit, sir.'

'Can I get back to you? We have a bit of an ongoing situation here,' Daley replied, as he spotted Superintendent Donald, flanked by two uniformed officers, trying to force his way through the crowds in pursuit of MacDougall's killer.

'Not really, sir. It's urgent. The gaffer asked me to call you personally.'

'OK, but be quick,' Daley said.

'Our subject has been contacted by a third party, sir. He says he's holding the subject's daughter captive.'

Daley swore. 'Fuck. When did this happen?'

'About five minutes ago, sir.'

If they had questioned whether Machie knew MacDougall's whereabouts, there could be no doubt now.

As Sergeant Shaw and a constable covered the body of Tommy MacDougall with a tarpaulin from one of the floats,

Daley hurried across the road and tapped Donald on the shoulder.

'What is it?' snapped Donald. His expression softened, slightly, when he realised he was addressing his DCI.

'We need to get to the office right now, sir.'

'But we've got a murderer to catch, fir fuck's sake.' Again, Donald sounded like the man Daley had first known more than twenty years before. A mixture of alcohol and murder had rubbed the polished edges from his new accent.

'Frank MacDougall's daughter has been abducted, sir.'

The look on Donald's face was one of mounting despair.

26

It was pitch-black outside. She looked around the dank and dreary room. A small table lamp illuminated the tiny kitchen where she sat; damp streaked the whitewashed brick walls of the room above an old cooking range, which was dirty and rusting. A cracked Belfast sink was piled high with unwashed plates and pots. She watched a spider, its web spread across one corner of the ceiling, as it progressed steadily along a silken thread to where a wretched fly struggled for its life.

'No' whit yer used tae, I daresay.'

'No,' she answered, 'but it's good to see how the other half live.'

'Ye really are up yer ain arse, aren't ye?' he said. 'Who would've thought Frankie-boy could have produced a stuck-up wee lassie like yourself?' He laughed at the thought.

'Who would've thought someone like you would be reading Wittgenstein?' She nodded at the well-thumbed paperback on the table.

'Everything that can be said, can be said clearly,' he answered, his expression unreadable.

'How clever,' she said. 'You must be *so* proud of yourself.'

He stood up, looming over her, and she noticed an old scar on his neck, red and puckered with marks left by poorly executed stitching.

'See, where me and yer faither came fae, reading a book wiz only marginally better than bein' a poofter, know what I mean?'

'My father prefers Jeremy Kyle and football. He's not much of a reader. I very much doubt if he knows what mathematical philosophy is, never mind Wittgenstein.'

'Oh, ye've a lot tae learn, darlin'. Never be surprised by anything your faither can dae.' He ran his hand over the dark stubble on his head. 'That wiz wan o' ma big mistakes.'

'Only one? Are you sure?' She smiled. She supposed she had never thought of her father in those terms; as someone cold, calculating and callous, like the man who stood before her now.

He leaned in close. 'I've made some. Who's no'? Ye never know, ye might have made wan yersel.'

'I read a paper recently,' she declared.

'Oh aye. Whit wan – *The Sun* or the *Racing Post*?'

'The paper was part of my OU Sociology course, actually.' He laughed mockingly.

'People like you could've done it all, been what they wanted to be: business, politics, anything. You would've thrived and been successful.'

'People like me?'

'Yes, sociopaths.'

'Aye, did ye not know I used tae own wan o' the most successful construction companies in Scotland, darlin'?' he replied, removing a cigarette from a packet and lighting it with a Zippo.

'So why didn't you go straight? You could've been rich now – rich and free – never having to look behind your back.'

'Aye, very good.' He exhaled a trail of smoke. 'Have ye any idea how fuckin' borin' that wid've been – not tae mention poorly rewarded? Can ye see me sitting behind a desk wi' a computer an' some wee whore secretary on ma lap?'

'Actually, I can. Right up your street, I would imagine,' she said smiling.

'Ye see wrang, then,' he said.

'No one can think a thought for me, in the same way no one can don my hat for me,' she answered.

'Aye, smart, right enough. Well done, darlin'. Let's hope ye manage tae keep that clever wee head intact,' he said, then left the room.

As she watched him go, her smile faded.

Frank MacDougall paced around the family room at Kinloch Police Office. His tears had dried, leaving his eyes red and puffy. He had raged, screamed and even started punching a wall, which had left raw gashes on the knuckles of his right hand.

Donald, acting on instructions from on high, had moved quickly to have MacDougall and his wife rushed in an armed convoy to the police office, where they were to remain for the time being.

'Two o' ma weans deid and another missing,' he moaned, rubbing his face with both hands. 'I don't give a fuck whit anyone says, Scooty, I'm no' moving oot o' this toon until ma wee lassie's found, even if I've tae go an' get her masel'.'

'Listen, Frankie,' said Scott, who had chosen to stay with MacDougall, much to Donald's irritation. 'Whit good can ye dae? Think aboot it, man. Think o' yer wife, fir fuck's sake . . . An' stop calling me Scooty.' Scott, a father himself, found it impossible even to contemplate what his childhood neighbour of so many years ago was going through.

'A' these years on the opposite side o' the fence fae each other, an' noo here we are, in this fuckin' awfy place, stalked by that bastard,' said MacDougall.

'Aye, it's been a long time, Frankie. A long time since you used tae kick ma arse up an' doon that playground tae,' Scott said with a grin.

'Seems like a different world, eh?' MacDougall stopped his pacing and looked at a painting of a seascape that hung on the wall. Waves crashing on an empty beach.

'A bonnie painting,' Scott said, struggling for something to say.

'Looks like the way ma life's goin' tae be. Empty, wi' nae cunt left in it.'

'I know it's no' easy, Frankie. Naebody could've imagined anything like this would ever happen. It's just unbelievable,' said Scott, rubbing the old gunshot wound on his shoulder.

'Well, it has. I'm telling you, Scooty, I've never been frightened o' that bastard – no' even when he wiz alive the first time.'

'That's the spirit, buddy. We'll dae everything tae get Sarah back – the cavalry's on its way right noo. Ye know fine oor Jim can sort this oot. Daley's the boy.'

'I know whit he's efter, here,' said MacDougall.

'Who's efter?'

'JayMac,' answered MacDougall. 'He's goin' tae flush me oot using Sarah. He's no' daft. He knows it's the only way he'll get tae me.'

Scott looked away; he knew what was coming. There was no way his superiors would allow MacDougall to be used as bait. They would negotiate with Machie if they could, or even threaten him, but the spectacle of two of Scotland's most feared gangsters – one returned from the dead, the other from obscurity – battling it out on some lonely hillside in Kintyre would not be countenanced.

'Ye'll need tae help me, Scooty-boy.'

There it was. Scott turned to MacDougall.

'How'd ye mean, Frankie?'

'Ye know as well as I dae that that prick Donald and whitever other big shot they bring doon here will never let me get near Machie. I need ye tae help me. Ye know fine ye'd be deid if it wisnae fir me.' He stared at Scott, unblinking.

'It's no' as easy as that, Frank. Ye know whit yer asking?'

'Aye, I dae,' MacDougall replied. 'I'm asking ye tae get yer ain back for him almost blowin' yer heid aff. Aye, dinnae worry, I've seen ye rubbing at that shoulder where he shot ye.'

'So, no' content wi' nearly killing me, the bastard's goin' tae be responsible for losin' me ma job an' goin' tae the slammer. No way, Francis, it's no' happenin".

'So ye'll let ma wee lassie die? Look at ma poor wife in there in yer medical room, dozed up tae the eyeballs with sedatives, so she'll no burst her ain heid wi' grief when she wakes up. I know ye, Brian. Yer the same as me; we're fae the same street. Ye can pit the boy in the polis, but ye can never take him oot the scheme an' away fae his ain people, man. Say whit ye like – yer wan o' us.'

'I'm tellin' ye – it's no' happenin",' Scott replied, looking flustered.

*

Jim Daley was in his glass box; there was going to be little sleep for the police officers in Kinloch tonight. The town had been cleared, everyone ordered inside, and uniformed police were searching for Tommy MacDougall's killer, who seemed to have vanished into thin air.

He had jotted down on a piece of paper the names of the main players in this claustrophobic drama: MacDougall and his two dead sons, his missing daughter and his wretched wife; James Machie – JayMac; and then his own name, along with that of his DS, Brian Scott. But there was something missing.

He had long since banished the conundrum of Machie's resurrection from his thoughts. What he had to do now was to try and treat this case in the same way he would any other; by being thorough and methodical and waiting for that moment of inspiration that would click everything into place.

Something was nagging at the back of his mind; something he'd missed, or simply not thought of at all. He wrote Duncan Fearney's name next to that of Paul Bentham, the latter in brackets – his own method of indicating the deceased in such a document. He recalled the image of Bentham's aggressive finger-pointing at Fearney as the CID car had bumped its way down the farm track. He remembered being shocked at the identity of the man lying dead in Fearney's barn; he would have bet any money on its being that of the farmer but instead it had been the thick-set figure of Bentham, with half of his brains splattered across the whitewashed wall of Fearney's byre.

Was Bentham responsible for trying to blow his car to smithereens, or was it Machie? Certainly, all of the evidence pointed to Bentham placing the bomb; forensic teams had identified the detonators and explosives used as being identical to those found in Bentham's cottage. However, if he was acting on Machie's orders, as some kind of accomplice, why had he been killed? It didn't make sense. And how did Duncan Fearney fit into the puzzle? Here was a man who defied definition: a mild-mannered farmer who apparently masterminded a considerable tobacco smuggling operation in Kintyre. Something wasn't right, but he couldn't put his finger on it. What, if anything, connected these people?

A knock rattled the door of his glass box as, without invitation, a slightly dishevelled John Donald strode in. He was wearing an open-necked shirt, his eyes were bleary, and he was in need of a shave.

'Sir,' said Daley.

'Ah, Jim,' said Donald, giving an empty smile. 'Good to see you're here trying to keep on top of things.'

'You'll recall, sir, that in the last couple of days we've had two murders here, plus a possible abduction, and my wife and I were nearly been blown to pieces.'

'Quite, DCI Daley, quite,' said Donald, taking a seat. 'I'm afraid I have something more to relate to you. I did mention it during the pageant from hell, if you remember . . . Well, we might as well get this out of the way now. Who knows what horrors tomorrow will bring.' He placed a grey file on the desk.

'I sincerely hope this is not some bean-counting exercise, sir,' said Daley, leaning back in his chair.

'No, it isn't, Jim, but I think you'll enjoy it even less, I'm afraid to say.' He pushed the file across the desk towards Daley.

Daley held his gaze for a moment then opened it.

'I was contacted by the Serious Fraud Office a few weeks ago, just before this sorry mess began.' Donald looked strangely uncomfortable, as though being in the guest chair did not suit – or perhaps something else was bothering him. 'Your brother-in-law, Mark Henderson, is under investigation for his business dealings with some very unsavoury individuals indeed. Knowing of his family connection to you, they flagged it up to me as your commanding officer. Of course I told them they need have no cause for concern, and that your relationship with him was, at best, strained. Their reply was this.'

Daley was looking at a set of photographs, typical surveillance images, shot in rapid succession within a short time frame.

'Henderson has been under scrutiny for some time. They hope to use him to snare a big fish; I know I needn't elaborate on the details.'

Daley had a strange feeling in his chest; a flutter that he knew was not medical in origin. A man and a woman were standing in the forecourt of a car dealership. As the images progressed, the two laughed and giggled together, then embraced and kissed, the man's hand buried in the lustrous hair of his female companion. Another figure arrived in the next shot, handed something to the man, and in the following image was pictured shaking his hand.

Daley flipped to the next photo. The man was holding a set of keys in front of the woman's face; both were sporting broad grins.

In the penultimate image, the woman was entering the Mini Countryman; in the final shot only her arm was visible, embracing the back of the man's head as he leaned into the open window of the car to kiss her again.

'I'm sorry, Jim,' Donald said, with what sounded like genuine sympathy. 'I couldn't keep this from you, not in the circumstances.'

In silence, Daley looked from his boss back down to the images, and flicked through them again slowly. He studied the picture of the first kiss, his heart sinking further into his stomach. The man was Mark Henderson, Daley's hated brother-in-law. The woman was Liz.

Donald was getting up to leave when the police radio crackled into life.

'Two one three to all stations – code forty-two. Repeat – code forty-two.' The delivery was rapid and strained. 'Police officers under attack. Shots fired.'

Both Daley and Donald were on their feet as communications control, located in the Kinloch office, replied: 'Two one three, your position please.'

'On Low Mill Road—' The message was interrupted by what could only be the report of a weapon.

Daley grabbed the radio and he and Donald raced down the corridor and into the control room. The constable at the communications desk nodded at his superiors as they rushed in. The control room was purposefully dark; an ethereal blue glow was emitted from lights on the ceiling, which aided personnel as they monitored CCTV screens, computers and radio communications.

'Two one three, I repeat, your position please.' The constable sounded tense, his face a mask of concentration. After an agonising pause, the radio monitors crackled back into life, sounding louder than usual in the communications room.

'Position is Low Mill Road, at the shipyard. Request immediate assistance, repeat, immediate assistance. Assailant is armed, and—' Just as the officer was about to complete this sentence, another shot sounded.

Daley turned to Donald. 'We've got two armed men from the unit guarding the office, and two at the County. I need one from each unit with me. Please authorise it, sir.' Donald nodded his compliance. 'And get the bar officer to break out the arsenal, sir. I want any personnel on duty with valid firearm authority armed now.' Donald nodded again and hurried off. Daley then requested a radio mic and an open channel. 'This is DCI Daley to all sub-divisional units. Attend Low Mill Road at the old shipyard. Officers under fire. I repeat, officers under fire. Use extreme caution. Armed units are on their way.'

He issued some more instructions to the communications officer, then, as he was leaving the comms suite, almost collided with DS Scott.

'What the fuck's going on, Jim? Is it Machie?'

'I don't know, Brian. I thought you were back at the hotel. Quick, get yourself a vest and a sidearm. Come on.'

For a few moments, Brian Scott stood still in the doorway to the comms suite, stroking his chin and looking grim. He sighed, and then with a shake of his head followed his boss to the armoury.

27

The shivering constable was crouched behind a rusted metal tank, left behind in the grounds of the disused shipyard. He was trying not to breathe heavily, lest a cloud of his frozen breath reveal his hiding place. He and his colleague had been sent in search of the murderer of Tommy MacDougall. A few locals had spotted a man running from the scene and into an as yet unidentified pick-up. Even though it had been considered likely that the perpetrator of this most public crime would attempt to make his escape by road or sea, in an effort to get as far away from Kinloch as possible, when the two young constables came across a vehicle matching the description of the pick-up in the car park of a disused shipyard, they had decided to investigate. When a shot rang out in the darkness, both police officers had darted for cover, regretting the fact they had not asked for back-up, as they had been ordered to do in the event of any kind of discovery.

He had heard a yelp from his partner when the second shot echoed around the old sheds which had once housed Kinloch Shipbuilders. Then, for the last few minutes, there had been silence.

At his back, he could hear the dark waters of the loch lapping at an old slipway. He continued to take short breaths, waiting for help to arrive. At least, he reasoned, he had managed to send his message for help.

A sudden noise to his left almost made him yelp in fear. He turned towards its source, only to see a large black rat scurrying down the slipway and along the shore beyond. He had expected to find a man with a gun standing over him, ready to take his life. As he tried to recall the lessons taught him at the police college about how to behave in such situations he found he was struggling to stave off tears.

Where the fuck are you? he thought. Come on, come on. Please!

Then he heard something else, something faint. He held his breath and listened carefully; a groaning noise was coming from somewhere to his right. It must be his colleague, whom he assumed had been hit and was now writhing in pain.

Another noise, clear and quite unmistakable, carried across the cold night air. Someone was walking towards him.

As police officers, both in and out of uniform, jumped into cars and vans, DS Brian Scott tarried, watching Jim Daley drive away with a uniformed constable and a member of the Firearms Unit. He had drawn a weapon on Donald's authority, since he lacked the relevant paperwork, which, he reflected, was probably in the chest of drawers in the spare room of his house in Glasgow.

The backyard of Kinloch's police office was bathed in the orange glow of the powerful outdoor lights; Scott could see the tracks of cars and vans imprinted on the frost that covered the black tarmac.

'Fuck, I need tae go an' check somethin', Norrie,' he said to the bar officer as he walked back down the corridor. 'By the way,' he shouted, stopping and turning for a moment, 'is it OK tae take yer motor? Those bastards have fucked off an' left me stranded.'

'Here,' his colleague shouted as he fumbled in the pocket of his trousers for his car keys, then threw them to Scott. 'An' don't bring it back covered in shite,' he said, as Scott gave him a thumbs-up and continued down the passageway.

He opened the door to the CID office and walked into Daley's glass box where he cast about on his boss's desk for a pen. He jotted down a few words on a discarded envelope, and then walked over to a filing cabinet where he knelt down and opened the bottom drawer. There was nothing in it apart from a bottle of whisky. He placed the note under the bottle and carefully closed the drawer.

The young constable wanted to scream. He berated himself for ever joining the police as he took shallow breaths. His whole body was now trembling with fear and cold. He tensed again as he heard the scraping of a heavy sole on gravel near the slipway, just on the other side of the metal container against which his whole body was pressed, like a climber halfway up a treacherous rock face. Without warning, he felt a strange warmth descend down his leg, then realised, to his horror, that he was pissing himself. Urine exited his left trouser leg and spilled over his ankle and shoe, sending a small cloud of steam into the freezing darkness.

The groaning he had heard a few moments ago began

again, low and intermittent, as his colleague struggled with pain and consciousness.

As he heard the footsteps of his tormentor moving away from his hiding place and towards the stricken man, he felt a surge of horror. He took a deep breath, then crept slowly around the side of the container, a squelching noise issuing from his left shoe. He fumbled in his belt for the pepper spray that he carried as a matter of course, removed the canister slowly from the webbing, and cringed when the Velcro fastening ripped noisily as he slid the little vessel into his hand. It wasn't much, but it was some kind of defence, and it might give him a chance against the man with the gun.

He edged his head round the side of the metal box, his fingertips sticking to the icy metal. He could see a man clad entirely in black, standing with his back to him, a handgun held at his side.

The young constable took a deep, anguished breath.

Scott pushed open the door to the family room to find Frank MacDougall lying on the sofa, his hands cupped behind his head. He looked exhausted, but there was something – a sharpness to his features perhaps – that induced fear in the watcher. Frank MacDougall had been dragged down by tragedy, but he was most certainly not out.

'Scooty, ma boy, whit took you so long?' he asked, remaining in his recumbent position.

'This,' replied the policeman, opening his jacket to reveal the shoulder holster that held his sidearm.

'Did ye make it yersel?'

'I wiz trying tae work oot how much time I'd spend inside,' Scott answered, his expression dark. 'Here.' He threw the car keys to MacDougall. 'The black Astra in the yard. Ye'll need tae get past the bar office, mind.'

'I widnae worry, Brian,' MacDougall answered coolly. 'If every copper that ever helped me had been sent doon, there wid be nae room in the pokie fir honest criminals. I've managed tae break intae plenty places o'er the years, so I dare say I can break oot o' here.'

'Aye, that's as may be,' Scott said, removing the pistol from its holster. 'Come on, ye know whit has tae happen noo.'

MacDougall looked up at the policeman, still not moving. 'It's just as well none o' us know what's in the future, Brian,' he said, his face momentarily sad, then, with an agility that defied his years, he stood up in one fluid motion and took the pistol from Scott's shaking hand.

'Yer no' the only man here wi' weans,' Scott said quietly, then turned his back on the gangster.

'Right enough, Scooty.' MacDougall smiled. 'But yer the only wan wi' a heart.' He raised the gun and slammed the handle into Scott's skull.

There was no sound from his colleague, or his tormentor. In the moonlight, he could make out the line of a path in the low grass bank that bordered the shore. He was a good sprinter; he'd won prizes for it at school, and could outpace any of his teammates in the local football team he turned out for. He would be able to cover the short distance across the gravel yard and onto the path in no time, his flight almost masked by the darkness.

He took a deep, silent breath and eased up from his crouched position, wincing in fear as loose gravel cracked under his shoes. But no noise came to him on the still night air. Above him, stars twinkled in the deep, dark blue of the night sky.

He started to run.

MacDougall moved quietly through the deserted corridors of Kinloch Police Office. He could hear the distant crackle and muffled tones of a police radio, so he turned away from the noise and slipped through a door into the male changing room. He passed his hand up the inside of the wall and located the light switch.

He was faced with an array of grey lockers. The room had the faint smell of dirty socks and damp clothing, sweat and disinfectant. All apart from two of the lockers were closed. He opened the first; it contained a large fluorescent jacket, a pair of black, well-polished boots, a torch with a rubberised casing, an unopened packet of cigarettes and an old newspaper. He picked up the cigarettes and walked to the next open locker. In it hung a complete uniform: trousers, a black shirt, an anti-stab vest and a cap. MacDougall pulled the uniform trousers from the hanger and examined them. They would be slightly big, but they would do; better too big than too small.

The first four strides of his escape bid went well; his fifth didn't. Something caught under his right foot and he stumbled to the ground, the gravel chips stinging his hands as he tried to break his fall.

He lay face down, winded and struggling for breath on the cold ground. From nowhere, a powerful hand grabbed his stab-proof vest and dragged him onto his back. In the moonlight he could see the dark figure of a man, his face hidden by a balaclava.

'Get up. Yer coming wi' me.' The young cop was hauled to his feet, then he felt the touch of cold steel on his cheek as the barrel of a handgun was thrust into his face.

'Please, please don't kill me,' the cop whimpered.

Just as he was losing all hope, he saw flashes to his right and realised that, at last, the cavalry was on its way.

28

Daley was in the third car in the convoy from Kinloch Police Office. He squinted into the darkness as his and the other vehicles sped through the open gate and into the car park of the disused shipyard.

In front, the main Firearms Unit car swung across the road. Daley skidded his car to a stop and rolled out of the vehicle into a crouched position. His passengers followed suit, and all three men crouched behind the Firearms Unit car, as one of the unit's officers gestured to them to stay down.

A van and two other cars raced into the yard behind them, stopping at the barricade of police vehicles. Sirens were silenced, though the night was illuminated by red and blue flashing lights.

Daley crept into the driver's seat of the car and unhooked the radio from the dashboard. 'DCI Daley to the Lima unit at Kinloch shipyard. Your position, please.' The radio hissed without carrying a reply. He was about to ask the same question again, when he heard a shot.

MacDougall decided against wearing the fluorescent jacket, opting instead for a black uniform fleece over a stab-proof vest. The garment was a lot heavier than he had expected it to be, but he guessed that to stop a blade it would have to be robust. Now dressed in full police uniform, replete with cap, he made his way to the door of the changing room, switching off the lights before quietly opening the door. The corridor ahead was empty; on the wall in front of him was an illuminated sign that read Fire Exit. On the wall next to it was something else, printed on official notepaper and signed by the Chief Constable: *This emergency exit is to remain closed at all times, unless in the case of a fire or similar occurrence. Opening this emergency exit will automatically activate the office alarm system.*

MacDougall smiled to himself.

Daley was holding the loudspeaker attached to the Firearms Unit vehicle. 'We are armed police. Put down your weapon, put your hands on your head and walk towards the police vehicles until I tell you to stop.' He sounded considerably more authoritative than he felt.

There was no reply.

'Keep trying the Lima unit on the radio,' he told the uniformed cop standing next to him. 'And where's DS Scott?' He looked behind him at the other police officers present. They shook their heads. 'Fuck's sake.'

Just then, he heard a shout coming from what had been the main building of the shipyard, which loomed in the darkness ahead.

'Police officer, don't shoot! Don't shoot!' The young policeman was standing stock-still now, his hands on his head. 'There's a gun trained at my head,' he shouted, realising that he had their attention now. 'I have a message for DCI Daley. Please listen carefully. He's going to kill me if I get this wrong.'

Daley held the mouthpiece to his chest, breathing heavily. Haunting images of too many dead faces once again flashed before him.

'Go ahead.' His voice sounded loud in the still air. 'What does he want?'

The young policeman half turned his head, listening to someone behind him. 'He wants to swap,' he answered, his voice wavering with fear.

Daley looked at his colleagues. 'OK,' he replied. 'What's the deal?'

'He wants you, sir.' The policeman's voice was thin and pitched higher now. 'He'll give you five minutes before he kills Dawson . . . then another five before he kills me.'

Daley took a deep breath. Red and blue lights shimmered in clouds of freezing breath in the cold night air. He had hoped that only one of the officers had been involved. 'He'll have to give me a couple of minutes.'

'He's saying five minutes until he kills Dawson, sir, no bargains.'

'Fuck it,' said Daley, turning around. 'Get me Donald, right now.'

Superintendent Donald stood in the dark room. The fire alarm was sounding, and a red light flashed on the ceiling of the office. He smiled as he saw the dark Astra pull out of the office car park and down Kinloch's Main Street. As the rear lights of the car disappeared from view, the door to his office burst open and the bar officer rushed in.

'Sir, we've just found DS Scott unconscious in the family room, and MacDougall's gone.'

'What?' Donald exclaimed. 'How? Where's Scott now?'

'In the medical room, sir. The force doctor's on his way. Sir, also, I have DCI Daley on. There's a hostage situation.'

'A what?' Donald blinked, as though he was finding this information much harder to assimilate than the news about MacDougall's flight.

'Here, sir,' said the bar officer, handing the superintendent a phone.

'Go ahead,' Donald said into the receiver.

'The two members of Lima unit have been taken hostage, sir, and he's threatening to shoot them.' The strain in Daley's voice was apparent, but he was concise and focused. 'It's a straight swap – me for them. Get yourself over here and take operational charge.' The last few words were a command, then the line went dead.

'Jim!' Donald shouted. 'Bastard!' he exclaimed, and smashed the handset onto the desk. 'Get me a car!'

'Should we inform headquarters about MacDougall, sir?'

Donald hesitated. 'Yes, yes, do that. Broadcast MacDougall's disappearance too. Go on then,' he shouted, as the bar officer waited to see if he would receive any further instructions.

Donald pulled a mobile phone from his pocket, dialled a number and held it to his ear. 'What the fuck is going on? This is not what we talked about.' He listened for a moment, then rushed from the office.

Brian Scott lay on the trolley bed in the police office's medical room. His thoughts were muddled by the blow he had taken to the head, though the consequences of his actions had become apparent as soon as he had regained consciousness. He could hear the sounds of a commotion in the hall, which he knew was more than likely something to do with MacDougall. His personal radio was sitting on the small table beside his bed. As he leaned over to pick it up, pain surged through his head, his vision shot through with sparks and flashes.

After a second attempt, Scott fumbled the device into his shaking hands and switched it on. Mercifully, as the device lit up, the noise of the office alarm ceased, and he was able to hear the divisional radio traffic. It took him a few moments to work out what was happening.

Donald's voice was booming from the radio: 'Donald to DCI Daley, come in, over.' He sounded brusque, a tone Scott recognised immediately, having so often been on the receiving end of it. 'Donald to all units at Kinloch shipyard, on *no* account is DCI Daley to effect the hostage exchange. I repeat, on *no* account must this go ahead.'

Silence.

Scott held his breath and rubbed his throbbing right eye as he waited for his friend to answer.

When the reply came, it wasn't from Jim Daley. 'DC Waters to Mr Donald – too late, sir. The swap of hostages is taking place now.'

Scott didn't wait to hear Donald's response as he struggled from the bed. He stood, then felt faint and had to lean against the wall for a few moments to regain his balance.

'Fuck's sake, Jim, what're ye doin', man?' he muttered as he made his way from the medical room.

29

Daley walked slowly towards the two young police officers, one of whom was moaning weakly and being supported by the other.

'Get your hands above your head,' a disembodied voice commanded, echoing in the former shipyard outbuildings.

Daley did as he was told. He was almost level with his colleagues, staring past them into the shadows, trying to get a glimpse of the gunman.

'Just Daley, towards me,' said the voice. 'You other two, stay where you are.'

Daley didn't move. 'I won't take another step unless you allow my officers here to get to safety,' he said.

'You're in no position to bargain,' came the terse reply from the darkness.

'On the contrary,' answered Daley. 'If any harm comes to any of the three of us, my officers are under orders from me to shoot.' There was steel in the chief inspector's voice.

After a pause, the gunman ordered the uniformed officers to continue to safety. Daley noted the relief on the face of his young colleague as he struggled to drag his charge behind the barrier of police cars.

'Keep coming, Daley,' the voice echoed, as the detective marched slowly into the darkness.

Daley could barely see anything; he had entered a cavernous three-sided shed, the roof of which blocked the winter moonlight that illuminated the scene outside.

'Stop right there,' a voice, close by, ordered.

Daley couldn't be sure, but the harsh tones were definitely familiar. 'What do you want?' he said. 'You must realise this situation is hopeless. Give up and—' He wasn't given time to finish.

'Shut up and listen.' The voice was closer now. 'I want to tell you something.'

Donald arrived at the shipyard in a squeal of brakes, swerving his car into place behind those already at the scene. Like his DCI a short time earlier, he rolled out of the car and ducked towards the firearms vehicle ahead. A spotlight had been set up, illuminating the narrow pathway that led into the corrugated iron shed.

'Just what the fuck is going on?' Donald demanded.

'DCI Daley has just entered the building, sir,' replied one of the officers on the scene.

'Fucking brilliant. Just what we need, ridiculous heroics, the stupid c—' He stopped, aware that a DC was gaping at him, unused to hearing senior officers describe other senior officers in such a way. 'Give me a sitrep now.'

Daley had often wondered why silence was described as deafening; now he knew. It could have been one minute since his captor had last spoken, or it could have been five; it was hard to be sure under the circumstances. He forced himself to concentrate, to focus on the dynamics of the situation and how best to change them in his favour. He decided to say nothing, to ask no questions. He remembered a lecture on hostage incidents at Tulliallan, the force's training centre; the best thing to do was to hold back, encourage and cajole. It was all he could do to try and save his own life. Just as he was beginning to doubt the effectiveness of his decision to remain silent, the man spoke again.

'You're brave, Mr Daley, I'll gie ye that.' Whoever was speaking was on the move, the scuff of his footsteps echoing around the large empty space.

'If you're referring to me being willing to swap with those for whom I'm directly responsible, it's more to do with duty than bravery,' he replied, almost certain that he could make out movement to his left in the gloom.

'Duty?' the man questioned. 'Duty comes in many forms, Mr Daley.'

'Meaning?' Daley batted the question back.

'Meaning, duty isn't merely the preserve of police officers,' the man said, moving into view.

'I daresay,' replied Daley, less edgy now that he could see his abductor. 'Though if you think shooting police officers and taking them hostage is dutiful, I would think again.'

'A means to an end, nothing more,' the man replied, now only feet away from the detective.

Daley still couldn't place the man's voice, which was muffled behind a black balaclava. But he did know one thing: this was not James Machie.

Donald gave hushed instructions to the two officers from the Firearms Unit. Once he was finished, both armed men

225

darted out from behind the barrier of police cars towards the rusted container that had provided a hiding place for one of their number only a short time ago.

Donald moved next to speak to the young cop who had just regained his freedom and was now shivering in the back of the police van. His injured colleague had been immediately removed from the scene for urgent medical attention.

'You're sure there's access along the shore to the rear of that building?' Donald asked.

'Yes, sir,' he replied, swallowing heavily. 'We've had some bother with local kids since the business closed, so I check that side of the site regularly.' He was doing his best to keep it together in the face of his superior.

'Good,' said Donald, staring into the darkness across the black water of the loch that hissed along the pebbled shore.

Many years of the best criminal education had taught Frank MacDougall to be resourceful. He knew he would have to ditch the Astra, so he drove to the edge of the town and parked in an anonymous side street lined with cars. Many of the vehicles were relatively new, so he discounted them; modern locks and alarm systems were the preserve of the new breed of thieves, who used the latest techniques to breach the enhanced security systems. In his youth, Frank MacDougall had been one such opportunist – an expert with a bent coat hanger, hammer or screwdriver – able to remove a car radio in seconds, then sell it on for a few quid to buy dope or a few pints.

He parked the car next to a decrepit model of a more venerable vintage, then exited his vehicle and flipped open the boot. The low light in the trunk revealed a tartan travelling rug and a number of empty supermarket shopping bags. He fiddled with the carpeting, which lifted easily away to reveal a recess into which was strapped a small toolbox.

MacDougall smiled as he forced the screwdriver into the door lock on the driver's side, then gave it a sharp tap with a small hammer. Instantly, the locking keys sprang up, enabling him to tug the door open. He sat in the car, bent forward, cradling his face against the wheel, while he worked busily underneath the steering column. After a few seconds, the car gave a throaty rattle. He felt a sudden surge of nostalgia as he quietly closed the door, then pulled out into the street. Here's to the good old days, he thought. It would be a few hours before his crime was discovered, by which time he would be ready to face the past in a different way.

Daley's captor grabbed his sleeve and pulled him across the floor to where a steel chest and an upturned cable drum sat side by side, palely illuminated by a beam of moonlight slanting through the gloom from a window high on the side of the building.

'Sit down,' commanded the man, gesturing with the gun.

Daley did as he was bid, taking a seat on the cable drum, which felt cold and damp through his trousers.

The man was silent for a moment, then began to speak, this time in whispered tones. 'It's amazing what coincidences life throws up,' he sighed, sitting down heavily on the metal chest opposite Daley.

'In what way?' asked Daley, watching his breath rise through the blue moonlight.

The man didn't respond. With one hand, he grabbed the balaclava under his chin and pulled it roughly over his head.

Even in the poor light, the face of Duncan Fearney was unmistakable.

Donald tapped his fingers on his knee as he mulled over his many problems. He had tired of the double life he was leading, which had at first so appealed to both his ambition and greed. Now here he was, freezing his bollocks off in a disused shipyard, in the middle of the night, in a town he hated, while his insanely brave DCI performed all kinds of heroics that could well bring the world crashing down around them both.

He felt his phone vibrate, so he removed it from his pocket and stared at the bright screen. *I need more time.* The writing jumped out at him in the darkness of the police car. He threw the phone onto the passenger seat – he couldn't deal with that right now – then brought the police radio to his mouth.

'Donald to unit personnel, report, over.'

The radio hissed into life. 'At the rear of the building now, sir. We're trying to gain access to a window on the wall, stand by.'

Donald didn't bother to reply. He thrust his feet out in front of him and leaned back in the seat, eyes closed, head shaking slowly from side to side.

30

'Duncan,' Daley said, 'what are you doing?'

'I've been asking myself that question for a long time, Mr Daley,' Fearney replied, his voice heavy with regret.

'A man like you, what could possibly have prompted all of this?'

'I've not lived in Kinloch all my life, you know,' said Fearney, seemingly not listening to Daley. 'Married a local lassie, a farmer's daughter. I grew up on a farm as well, up country, just south of Oban.'

'I suppose affairs of the heart will take you anywhere,' said Daley, trying to keep his tone light.

'Aye,' Fearney replied after a pause. 'Some things just eat away at you, Mr Daley – at your soul, I mean.'

'I know that only too well, Duncan.'

'But some things are worse than others.' Fearney was clearly in reflective mood, despite the circumstances. 'There are jeest certain things ye can never get oot o' yer mind, and ye can never tell anyone about. D'ye know what I mean?'

Daley didn't answer. He knew Fearney was confessing, but to what he wasn't sure.

'Are ye no' goin' tae interrogate me?' Fearney asked,

ending the silence. 'No doubt ye found that arrogant bastard, Bentham?'

'Yes. Why did you do it, Duncan?'

'Because he wiz a bully an' a fucking killer, Mr Daley. I couldnae take it any mair,' Fearney said, his voice earnest. 'I cannae take any o' it any mair.' He looked at the policeman. 'I'd nothin' tae dae wi' a' that stuff wi' your car, Mr Daley, honestly. He wiz crazy.'

'How did you even get involved with him, with all of this, in the first place, Duncan?'

'I found something oot, Mr Daley, jeest by chance ye understan', a few years ago.'

'We have plenty time, Duncan. Just tell me what all this is about.'

Fearney bowed his head and let out a sob. His shoulders began to heave as he wept uncontrollably. 'I wiz an only child, Mr Daley,' he managed to say. 'Ma folks lost three weans as infants; I wiz the only wan that survived. Ma mother wanted another child, efter me, but the doc told her she coudnae have any mair.' He took a steadying breath and wiped away his tears. 'She wiz fae the East End of Glasgow, Mr Daley,' he blurted.

'Really? What part?' said Daley, his instinct screaming at him to allow this man to speak.

'Och, some hell o' a place,' Fearney said in disgust. 'I've always hated Glasgow. A' cities, come tae that.' He shook his head. 'She adopted a wee boy. Well, I'm no' entirely sure it was done by the book, but things were different in those days, Mr Daley.'

'They sure were,' said Daley, deliberately keeping his responses brief.

'Aye, well, I wiz nearly four years old when he arrived, so we just grew up the gither, ye ken, like brothers.' He started to cry again.

'What is it, Duncan? You need to let this out, man.'

'He wiz very different fae me, Mr Daley. Good looking, confident.' He laughed harshly. 'I wiz supposed tae be the big brother, but he wiz the one who wid stand up fir me, you know, in fights an' that. Aye, he turned oot tae be as hard as nails.'

'What happened to him, Duncan?'

'Aye, that's the thing,' said Fearney. 'I cannae believe you're the first person I'll tell this.'

'You'd be surprised what people have confided in me,' Daley said honestly.

'When I wiz older . . . in my late teens an' efter.' He began to choke up again. 'I started tae—'

'Please, Duncan, get it off your chest. You'll feel better.'

Duncan Fearney cried like a man who had lost the most precious thing in the world. 'I loved him. I fucking loved him, Mr Daley.' Fearney was shouting at the top of his voice, as the secret he'd held inside for so many years eventually broke free.

'Did he know?' Daley asked.

'Aye, no, I don't know. He tried tae kiss me wance, when he wiz pished, but we never did anything, or said anything. Jeest went on, laughin' an' jokin' – me at least – pretendin' we were the way brothers were supposed tae be.' He held his head in his hands, as though the weight of it was too much to bear. 'Whoot is it they say, Mr Daley? The love that dare not speak its name, is that no' it?'

'Yes,' said Daley, forcing thoughts of Liz from his mind. 'That's right, the love that dare not speak its name.'

The two men fell into silence.

Fearney was the first to speak. 'Eventually, he got himself a girlfriend. Bonnie lassie, a' blonde hair an' big blue eyes. A real stunner.'

'And how did that make you feel?' Daley asked, wincing as he remembered that question being asked so often of him during his anger management sessions.

'I wiz devastated. I knew I had tae get away, away fae him. It wiz breaking ma heart.' Fearney's voice trembled as he relived the emotions of so many years ago.

'So you came to Kinloch?' Daley asked.

Fearney nodded. 'I had an auld uncle doon here who had a sma'holding. Jeest enough tae keep a roof o'er his heid, aye, an' mine tae for a wee while, until I met Sandra. Her faither was dying, an' he had no sons. We got married.'

'And what about your brother, Duncan?' Daley asked. 'And how does that bring us here?' He gestured into the darkness.

Fearney took a few deep breaths, as though trying to collect himself. 'I'm here cos o' ma ain foolishness, nothin' mair. I thought I could find oot whit had happened tae him. I wiz so wrong.' He stopped again. 'Bastards like Bentham and that fucking Tommy.'

'What? You killed Tommy because of all this? I don't understand.'

'I snapped, Mr Daley, plain and simple. I did tae Tommy whit he wiz goin' tae dae tae me. Aye, he thought I wid just stand by an' let him, like some daft wee laddie.' Fearney looked desperate. 'I wiz the weak link. Gettin' caught, I mean. He wiz feart I wid blow the whole thing; turn Queen's evidence, or whootever it is you ca' it. They needed me oot o' the way, Mr Daley, just in case.'

'So you killed him. And then you sent him down the wire to distract everyone while you made your escape.'

'Aye, though as soon as I heard the weans screaming, I regretted it.' He lowered his head. 'I had tae kill him. It wiz either him or me. I knew folk wid come up tae the roof when nothin' happened. He thought I wiz weak. But he found out differently.' Fearney's face was the picture of defiance in the gloom; defiance mixed with shame at the thought of what he had done.

'It wasn't a pleasant spectacle.' Daley answered, in a more censorial manner than he intended. 'But why did you do it? I still don't understand.'

'He was in on it tae, Tommy. The drugs, I mean.'

'Drugs? What did you have to do with that, Duncan?'

'Nah, I stayed away fae a' that, Mr Daley. Well, as much as I could, anyhow.' Fearney looked contrite. 'The drugs – aye, an' the tobacco – wur left on deserted beaches, a' aroon the peninsula. I jeest accepted the deliveries. I stored the fags an' a' that. I selt some o' it tae, jeest cos I know so many folk, Mr Daley. Tommy wiz jeest a fetch-and-carry merchant, though he liked tae think he wiz in charge.'

'So who was in charge, Duncan?'

'Aye, I'll tell you it all, Mr Daley. Just be patient,' Fearney said, standing up. 'Here, ye might as well take this. I'll no' be getting oot o' here.' He handed the gun to Daley.

'What do you mean?' Daley placed the weapon at his side and remained seated.

'My folks both died,' said Fearney, ignoring Daley's question, 'an' I never even went tae their funerals, cos I knew he'd be there. He carried on wi' oor faither's ferm – no' that he wiz very successful, fae whoot I hear; near bankrupted the place. Then he just disappeared – vanished. The police came tae see me, since I wiz his next o' kin. Well, the only one they could find.' The look on Fearney's face was one of disbelief and pain. 'Of course, there wiz nothin' I could dae tae help them, wi' no' seeing him for so long.'

'So he was there one minute and gone the next?' Daley asked. 'Did none of his friends or family know anything? When did this happen?'

'Oh, six years ago, somethin' like that,' said Fearney. 'Turns oot she'd left him years before, an' took his son wi' her, and he kept himself tae himself. They never kept in contact, an' naebody could find her. The polis telt me he'd probably killed himself – no' an uncommon thing fir farmers tae dae these days, Mr Daley.' Fearney broke off as he started to sob again. 'He left a sma' fortune, tae. I'll never understand it – nearly fifty thousand pounds in cash, in bags a' ower the ferm.'

'You've no idea where it came from?'

'Nah. The police reckoned it was the proceeds o' crime, so them an' the tax folk got their hands oan it, an' since there was naebody . . .'

'That's strange, Duncan.'

'Then, a while later, I wiz watching TV . . . I just couldnae believe whoot I saw.'

'What?'

'I saw the news – a trial in Glasgow. I couldnae believe it. There wiz oor Angus, plain as day. Other guys tae. The one who gave the evidence, I saw him later, aye, an' no' on the telly either.'

'What? Where did you see him, Duncan?'

At that second, something caught the detective's eye; a

flash of red light flickered across his vision, then appeared on the other man's shoulder.

Fearney, with his back to the source of the light, didn't see it, and opened his mouth to speak. 'Oh, you know him a'right, Mr D—'

There was a sharp crack, and the farmer's chest erupted. For a moment he stood completely still, before tumbling towards the policeman like a demolished building. Daley managed to catch the falling man and, struggling to hold his weight, laid him on the ground.

'This is DCI Daley. Cease fire!' he shouted, and leaned over Fearney. Even in the gloom it was easy to see that the light had gone from his eyes, his revelation dead on his lips.

31

Sarah MacDougall was lying on a threadbare couch, using a dirty knitted blanket as a cover. Through the window she could see the first grey light of dawn break through the darkness of night. She had dozed fitfully, her mind taken over by her thoughts and fears. When she dreamed, she saw Cisco, her oldest brother, sitting on the bottom step of a stairwell in a dank Glasgow multi-storey, covered in his own blood. She could see the blood seeping from livid slashes all over his body, pooling at his feet in a crimson puddle. Despite this, in her dream he smiled, urging her towards him with his left hand. As she got closer, a suppurating wound ripped open across his face, sending a spray of blood across the white dress she wore. His features transformed from those of the sibling she had loved into those she despised. She had the same dream every night.

In the midst of this brooding, she heard a familiar sound, a distant chime, which drove the dream from her mind. Her mobile phone was ringing.

DS Scott sat in the passenger seat of a police car as his colleagues spread around the derelict shipyard. His head hurt nearly as much as his heart, which pulled at the centre of his chest like an enormous, heavy knot.

He knew his friend was safe, but equally he knew every-thing was wrong. The whole scene, at which he had arrived belatedly on foot, felt unreal. Donald was standing tall beside a police van, talking into a mobile phone, his features stern and unyielding. Scott had arrived just as the superintendent had given the order to shoot the gunman without warning, because of the perceived risk to one of his officers. Though Donald would have to answer for his actions, Scott could think of no man better suited to mealy-mouthed squirming before a disciplinary panel. And going on past form, he would probably get a promotion and commendation for his speed of thought and sangfroid.

Despite this reasoning, Scott still felt ill at ease. He watched as a tall, bulky figure moved towards him in the ethereal light of dawn. Even from a distance, it was clear that Jim Daley was not happy. Scott could see his flushed cheeks and furious expression. His tread was purposeful, leading directly to the car in which Scott was sitting.

'A'right, Jimmy-boy?' Scott enquired with forced bonho-mie. 'A bit too close for comfort, eh?'

'Never mind that, Brian,' Daley said, leaning into the open window on Scott's side of the car. 'Tell me what happened to Frank MacDougall.' His face was devoid of any signs of sympathy, a look Scott had seen on many occasions but never directed at him. He watched as Daley walked round the front of the car and eased his body into the driver's seat.

His face was expressionless as he listened. 'Aye she's here, but wait a minute – nae "How are ye, how ye doing?" or "Yer sounding better than the last time I saw ye?"' He strode, phone in hand, into the small room where Sarah lay on the couch. 'Och, come on, my man. D'ye think I wid dae that tae such a nice wee lassie?' he said. 'Ye know me.' With a smile on his face he handed the phone to Sarah.

'Hi, Daddy,' she said, her voice wavering. 'Don't worry about me. I'll be fine. This monster doesn't—' Her words were cut short as the phone was snatched from her grasp.

'See, my old friend, Daddy's little girl's doin' just fine. Fir now, at any rate.' He smirked as though he was staring into the face of Frank MacDougall himself. He listened to MacDougall's reply, then snorted with derision and clicked the phone off. He turned to smile at the girl who sat on the dilapidated couch, embracing her knees, which were drawn up to her chin. 'There ye are, darlin'. Daddy's on the ba' a'ready. Pity he wisnae so keen on helping the rest o' your family.'

'I don't want to talk about Cisco,' she said.

'Naw, I was referring tae yer brother Tam,' he said, clearly enjoying this.

'What?'

'Yer faither's threatenin' me doon the phone, tellin' me I'll get ma throat cut, the same as Tommy.' He grinned broadly. 'Call me old-fashioned, but tae me, once yer throat's cut, yer prospects at longevity are severely curtailed.'

She looked up at him, noticing the silver sparkle of stubble on his chin picked out in the thin light.

'He caught me unawares,' Scott answered, exasperated by Daley's repetitive questioning.

'So you say.' Daley's face was blank as he stared at the face of his subordinate.

'Whit are ye tryin' tae say?' Scott shouted, loud enough to attract concerned looks from two uniformed cops standing thirty yards away.

'Come on, Brian,' said Daley, a look of disgust on his face. 'Your old neighbour – a buddy from your childhood, not to mention one of Scotland's most dangerous criminals – just happens to pick you to effect his disappearance, just as you've been issued with a firearm and a set of borrowed car keys.'

'Have ye seen the fuckin' lump on the back o' ma heid, Jim? I struggled aff ma sick bed when I heard ye wiz in trouble. An' ye accuse me o' bein' corrupt? I cannae believe this is you speakin', Jim. Whitever happened in that shipyard must've done somethin' tae yer reason.' Though Scott was almost shouting, his eyes spoke of a different emotion as he implored his friend to believe him. 'If ye remember, it wiz me who nabbed MacDougall in the first place.'

'Oh yes,' answered Daley, after a pause. 'And I have to admit, Brian, I wondered about that at the time too.'

'Listen, *sir*,' said Scott. 'I don't fuckin' know whit's wrang wi' ye, but I'm no' sittin' here wi' a banging heid just for the pleasure o' bein' knocked tae bits by you.' He moved to open the car door.

'Stay where you are,' Daley ordered. 'Whatever I may think or not think, Brian, you know as well as I do that that bastard over there will be all over you like a rash as soon as he clears things up here.' Daley's voice was much quieter, as he massaged his temples, feeling the exhaustion of the last few days catch up with him.

'Don't worry aboot him, Jim,' said Scott. 'He'll be tae busy covering his back efter this carry-on.' He nodded towards the mortuary van that had just pulled up in the yard.

'Yes,' Daley replied thoughtfully. 'You would think he would.'

'Whit d'ye mean?' Scott looked sidelong at Daley.

'I don't really know what I mean,' Daley answered. 'There's something going on here, something I'm missing – something that's been gnawing away at me for months, if you must know.'

'Oh,' said Scott, looking out of the car window as the sun spread golden rays over the loch, turning it from dark blue to a light green. 'Right,' he added, rubbing his chin.

32

She struggled to keep up with him as he strode down to the little jetty where the boat was tied up, bobbing in the swell in the clear morning light. She watched as he swung a large holdall aboard with ease, then carefully laid a metal-bound case on the deck of the small craft.

The sea was calm, slate grey, not yet reflecting the cold blue of the sky in which gulls circled, squawking loudly in the still air. The jetty itself was slick with white frost, as were the small windows in the wheelhouse. He grabbed Sarah roughly and bundled her on board. Bulked up with clothes against the chill, he looked even more formidable.

'Take a wee seat, an' we'll set off an' see Daddy,' he said, pointing to a little bench at the side of the tiny cabin. 'Who'd have thought Frankie an' me would take tae life on the ocean waves, eh? What does he fish for, again?'

'Just for pleasure, he's not making a living out of it,' she said. 'You try living in this godforsaken place for years with nothing to do.'

'Oh aye.' He grinned. 'I've been having the time of my life for the last few years, darlin'. Been a blast.'

'Better than being dead, I imagine.'

'Don't know, I wisnae there,' he said, misquoting the philosopher.

'At least you had time to improve your mind,' she said.

'D'ye think so? Mebbe I learned things that I didnae know before, but as far as my mind goes, well, ye cannae improve on perfection. Right, just you hold on tight. It's time tae put things right.' In a puff of blue smoke and mechanical rattling, the diesel engine roared into life.

John Donald hated satnavs. They had taken him up hill and down dale over the years, so he was surprised when the small car park next to the bay appeared in view. He parked facing the ocean, then took the mobile phone from his pocket and looked at it anxiously. He had a signal – as they had promised – though no new messages. He leaned his head back and closed his eyes as the strains of Mendelssohn's 'Scottish Symphony' soared from the speakers, lending even more drama to the scene outside. In the distance, a large sea freighter punctuated the horizon and the white sail of a lonely yacht slanted into the distance.

Donald was almost asleep as his mobile pinged into life. He felt beads of sweat break out on his forehead as he read the message. He forced himself to breathe deeply and focus; the knot in his stomach grew even tighter.

As Daley walked into the hospital, an agitated constable jumped from his chair and ran to his side.

'Sir, Mrs Robertson is awake and asking for her family. I don't know what to say. The doctor's won't sedate her any further, sir.' Betty MacDougall had been taken to the local hospital, the shock of what was happening to her family simply too much for her to cope with.

'OK, son,' said Daley, trying to reassure his subordinate. 'I'll take care of it.' He walked into the private side room where Frank MacDougall's wife was sitting in bed, rocking backwards and forwards, her eyes red with tears: the picture of misery.

'Hello, son,' she said. 'Have you got Frankie with you?'

'No, I'm sorry,' said Daley, taking a chair at the end of her bed. 'I need to talk to you.'

'I want to see Frankie,' she wailed in reply, just as a harassed-looking doctor appeared in the room. Daley smiled, recognising the man who had revealed Liz's pregnancy.

'Mr Daley,' the doctor said, with a weak smile. 'I'm afraid Mrs Robertson is in no condition to be questioned by the police. I take it that's why you're here?'

'Mrs Robertson is not under arrest, doctor,' Daley assured him calmly. 'I'm just here as a visitor. Is that not right, dear?' He smiled at the woman in the bed.

'Aye,' she said. 'I need tae speak to this officer, anyhow.' Daley was pleased that she seemed to have retained at least some reason. The young doctor frowned and left the room shaking his head.

'You said something a couple of days ago,' said Daley, conscious of the fact that their conversation might be cut short when a more senior medic arrived.

'I cannae remember,' she said, already sobbing. 'When?'

This could be a fruitless exercise, but the chief inspector had to try. 'In your house, just recently, the first time we met at the farm.'

Though she had closed her eyes, tears still rolled down her face. She tried to brush them away with a trembling hand.

243

Despite her age and mental plight, the detective could see the ghost of the beautiful woman she had been years before.

She looked him straight in the eye. 'Dae ye never get times in yer life when it's a' too much, son?'

'Yes, I think everyone does, Betty,' said Daley, taking her hand in his.

'The problem is when those are the only times ye have, the only ones ye can remember . . . that's when it a' gets too much. Ye just hide, aye, hide in a corner in yer own heid.'

Daley smiled at her, but said nothing. At times like this he felt like a fraud, representing himself as a caring human being, when in actual fact all he was interested in was extracting as much information as he could from this poor soul, and then abandoning her to fate as the pursuit intensified. She was a means to an end, a tool, nothing else. Not for the first time, Daley was repulsed by his own actions.

'D'ye know the first time I saw him?' she said, a brightness in her eye.

'Who?'

'Jamie Machie. Aye, wee Jamie Machie.' She smiled, as though the memory of the monster in far off days gave her pleasure, something that surprised Daley. 'Bright as a button he wiz, heid an' shoulders above the rest o' the weans. Bonnie tae. Aye, right bonnie. He could charm the birds oot o' the trees, Mr Daley,' she said, looking genuinely happy for the first time since they had met.

'How people change,' Daley commented, then wished he hadn't. He had that gnawing feeling in his head again; the sense that he had the answer but couldn't piece the strands together, couldn't tie the rope tight enough to allow him to pull what he needed from the depths of his mind.

'I wiz three years or so older than him,' Betty said, her voice light and conversational. 'Aye, an' Frankie tae. Though he went tae a different school fae me on account o' him being a Fenian an' a'.'

Daley marvelled at the way casual sectarianism could enter a conversation in the west coast of Scotland. The idea that Roman Catholics and Protestants went to different schools, different churches, led different lives, in a city the size of Glasgow, had bemused him since he was a boy. Children living cheek by jowl in the old tenements who, left to their own devices, would have become playmates and friends. But that was impossible once the veil of bigotry was thrust onto them by their families. Children who shared the same close would grow up as ignorant of each other as though they came from different planets. While Daley had been brought up in the Roman Catholic faith, his father had no time for bigotry, so as a child he had been encouraged to mix with the other boys on his street who went to different schools and wore blue jerseys when they played football on the red blaes pitch at the bottom of the road. It was probably the greatest thing his father had ever done for him.

'But that wiz later on, Mr Daley,' Betty MacDougall said, the smile on her face stripping the years away. 'When I first saw him he was in his christening shawl. I was only wee mysel' but I mind o' it like it was yesterday.' She patted the policeman's hand at the memory.

'He made a big impression on you, Betty.'

'Aye, I suppose he did. There they were, wi' the wee blue shawls an' the wee rattles – they were blue an' white tae. Mind you, in oor street in them days, even the cats an' dugs wiz blue an' white.'

'You said "they", Betty.' Daley's ears had pricked up.

'Aye, of course,' she replied, a puzzled look spreading across her face. 'Ye wid hardly get one christened an' no' the other.'

Just then the door burst open to reveal the junior doctor, a middle-aged nurse and a young man in a suit. Betty MacDougall withdrew her hand from Daley's grasp and pushed herself back into the corner of the bed, her face a mask of fear.

'Mr Daley,' said the nurse, 'you have no right whatsoever to be here. Mrs Robertson is in no condition to be questioned by the police.' She cast a disgusted look at the young doctor, who was biting his lip.

'I'm not here as a police officer,' Daley replied, furious that they had interrupted Betty MacDougall's reminiscences.

'Do yourself a favour, Mr Daley,' the well-groomed young man advised, an arrogant smile on his face. 'Leave now, before I contact your superior. I know your boss is in Kinloch at the moment.'

'All right,' said Daley. He rose and looked down at the stricken woman as tears began again to stream down her face.

'You can tell me about that christening another time,' he said, hoping to elicit one more snippet of information.

Betty MacDougall merely sobbed. Mary Robertson was back and Daley knew he would get nothing more from her.

'Right, officer, on your way, please. You realise that I'll have to make an official complaint about your conduct today.' He looked at Daley haughtily.

The man was tall, but Daley was taller. The policeman walked to within inches of him, smiled and patted the man on the shoulder of his expensive suit. Daley's voice was low and not without menace. 'Don't worry, son, I'll be sure to let the heath board know how much you enjoy a recreational smoke. We arrested your dealer last week and he keeps excellent records. Your name was top of his list.'

The detective walked out of the room.

The car was small and nondescript. Donald was surprised; for some reason he had expected a much grander vehicle. He peered at it, trying to see the occupants, but the sun was too bright and he found it impossible to discern anything other than two shapes occupying the front seats.

Donald recalled the other times he had felt this nervous. He remembered his first day in the shipyard in Govan. He had left school the week before, only the paucity of his parents' expectations exceeding the pitiful list of qualifications he had to show for his many years in education.

He recalled the noise, the heat, the vastness of the yard where some of the world's greatest ever craft had been built. He had been placed under the tutelage of a middle-aged welder, a thin man whose tongue was as sharp as his nose, which was already turning blue due to his addiction to drink. He hardly spoke to his youthful charge, and when he did it was usually in a gruff, expletive-ridden manner.

On Donald's third day in the Glasgow shipyard he and his mentor were detailed to weld a part of the vessel, high up under the prow. To access this, they had to ascend steel scaffolding to an alarming height. As Donald, who had never before been troubled by vertigo, looked at the void beneath him, his stomach lurched and dizziness took hold. The sensation heightened as they neared the top of the scaffolding, which swayed more alarmingly the higher they rose. He

247

remembered the way his chest had constricted, anxiety making his breath short, and how a film of sweat had coated his brow.

Without warning, his mentor had grabbed his arm and pushed him out into the abyss, over the flimsy rail of the scaffold pole. He stared into the emptiness, his heart thumping, as he desperately tried to cling to the scaffold planking with his toes, the only thing, apart from the welder's grip, that kept him from death.

'I want ye tae tell me yer a wanker,' the man had said, as he levered his charge further out over the gap, like a sail on the boom of a yacht. 'An' if ye dinnae, ye fuckin' nancy boy, I'll fuckin' let ye go. And dinnae think anybody gies a fuck aboot whit happens tae ye, ya little runt. There's accidents here a' the time, know whit I mean?'

Donald could see a group of men, far below, laughing and pointing at his plight. He felt his bladder weaken; the humiliation of his own urine running down his leg and spreading a dark stain across his blue boiler suit had been nothing compared to the fear he felt.

'I'm a wanker,' he said quietly, his mouth dry.

'Nae good,' his tormentor sneered, loosening his grip on the young Donald's arm.

'I'm a wanker!' he shouted at the top of his voice.

'Cannae hear ye.' The welder's fingers began to slip on the sleeve of Donald's oily boiler suit.

'I'm a wanker!' Donald roared at the very top of his voice, after which he spewed copiously.

Despite his embarrassment, his relief was palpable as he was pulled back onto the scaffold platform, falling onto the wooden planking with a clatter.

'An' ye pished yersel tae. Yer a clatty bastard, as well as a fuckin' self-abuser.'

Donald remembered how he felt that day: the weight in his chest, the fear of death. Most of all though, he recalled the hatred, the silent need for revenge now focused on the man who had perpetrated such horror upon him. It was the feelings prompted by this incident that became the driving force in his life, the sharp spur that prodded him up the greasy pole. The next day, he resigned his apprenticeship and applied to be a police cadet.

Donald looked across at the other vehicle in the car park, detecting no movement. He closed his eyes, and again the years dropped away. He was on duty on his beat in Glasgow's Townhead. His four years as a cadet were over; he was now a police constable.

There was something familiar about the figure that staggered out of the run-down pub. The man stopped, fumbled in his pocket, and turned away from the breeze, cupping his hand to light his cigarette, before turning in the direction of the young policeman.

Donald watched as the man drew deeply on his cigarette. There was a dark lane two doors along from the pub. The man walked along the pavement and disappeared down this lane, leaving only a trail of cigarette smoke in his wake illuminated by the streetlights. Donald waited for a few heartbeats, then followed him.

'What the fuck?' the man exclaimed as he turned round, one hand against the wall as he urinated in the alleyway, momentarily blinded by the bright torchlight that shone in his face.

Donald said nothing and directed the torch beam to the ground, away from the man's face.

'Aw fuck's sake, the fucking polis,' the man said, as he watched the policeman bend down and pick up something from amongst the detritus in the lane. 'At least gie me a fuckin' chance tae finish before ye huckle me.'

The brick was rough and bulky in Donald's hand. The pitted surface bit into his palm as he smashed it repeatedly into the man's head. Eventually, the man fell into a pool of his own piss and out of existence.

'Who's the fuckin' wanker now, you bastard,' said Donald, as he threw the brick at the shattered skull. He walked from the lane, then slowly down the street, running his fingers along the plate glass windows of shops on one side of the street, and scrutinising those on the other side of the road carefully. The radio in his pocket crackled into life.

'Two one two, your position please. Anything to report?'

'Swan Street at Canal Street. Nothing doing, over,' the young Donald replied.

'Roger, carry on.'

33

Daley stopped at the end of the hospital corridor. Despite himself, he turned into it, then walked past a series of private rooms until he reached the one with a sign that read 'L. Daley'. Without knocking, he turned the handle on the door and walked into the room.

She was fast asleep. He felt his heart leap. Her thick auburn hair spilled across the white pillowcase. Her pallor hinted at her most recent trauma and current condition. He stared at the upward slant of her button nose, which he found so irresistible. Her small mouth was a perfect Cupid's bow, slightly open, revealing the tips of her white teeth; a mouth that drew the eye, gladdened the heart and beckoned to be kissed.

He stood, watching his sleeping wife, his heart breaking. The surveillance footage of her at the garage with Mark Henderson was etched in his mind's eye. The affection between the pair spilled from every frame: his hand in her hair, the way she angled her face up into his. He imagined her pale blue eyes staring up at her sister's husband with the gaze he had hoped was reserved for himself.

Then came even darker thoughts. Her body entwined with another's: her scent; the red-brown of her nipples; her long, graceful neck arching back as she gasped in the ecstasy of release; her fingernails leaving red welts on someone else's back.

For as long as they had been married, Liz had displayed a much more casual attitude to sex, and therefore, he presumed, to fidelity, than he. It was though that apogee of jealousy – the thought of a loved one being taken, possessed by another – somehow didn't mean anything to her; as though she couldn't understand why flesh penetrating flesh could possibly garner a feeling of revulsion and despair.

And now – now everything was worse. Jim Daley was about to become father to a child he could never accept as his own. He had lived with his wife's indiscretions for years – the memories haunted him – but now there would be a living, breathing testament to her dalliance. The sin of adultery made flesh.

He walked from the room and quietly closed the door.

The countryside hotel was a converted two-storey house, standing just off the road. Faded plastic tables and chairs, with puddles of melting ice, were scattered around an untidy beer garden to the front of the property.

Despite the cold weather, the door to the public bar was propped open with a beer keg. As he walked in, his nostrils were assailed by the sharp aroma of newly applied bleach blended with the more sickly sweet bouquet of stale alcohol.

'Aye, we're jeest opened,' shouted a woman from somewhere behind him.

Startled, Donald jumped, then, in an attempt to impose his authority, slowly walked to the small bar and pulled out a stool. 'In that case, I'm sure you won't mind pouring me a large whisky.'

A short, middle-aged woman waddled into view, dressed in a baggy white jumper, grubby black leggings and flip flops. 'Is that your car outside?' she asked, bridling at the tone of her new customer.

'Yes,' Donald replied. 'Is that a problem?'

'No' really,' she said with a shake of the head. 'It's your licence. Remember, the cops often pop in here for a cup of tea. You know, the guys in the big traffic car.'

'Oh, do they now? Well, I'll keep my eye out for them, rest assured. Now, what about that whisky?'

She busied herself placing a small glass under a large optic attached to an outsized bottle of whisky. 'I heard the boss o' the polis doon here got flung oot o' the hospital the day, so you better watch your back.' She placed the drink in front of Donald, who threw a twenty-pound note onto the bar and knocked back the drink in one gulp.

'Oh, don't worry. I'll keep a particular look out for that man, sounds like a thoroughly unpleasant individual,' said Donald, holding up his glass. 'Same again.'

As the woman went about her business, Donald took in his surroundings; the usual collection of tatty bar stools and battered copper tables arranged across a bare wooden floor still damp from its cleaning. At the far end of the room, beside another door, was a sign that read Beer Garden, Toilets, Public Telephone.

Donald fumbled in his pocket for the coins he had collected the previous evening in the hotel and recalled one of his mother's favourite sayings: 'A drinker's never short of loose change.'

'Just going to use your toilet,' he said to the barmaid as he paid for his next drink. Through the door, he was faced by a yellow payphone protected by a Plexiglas canopy. His hand shook as he inserted a coin and dialled the number he knew so well. The voice he used when his call was answered was very unfamiliar to him; he kept the conversation short and hung up without saying goodbye.

MacDougall wrestled with the padlock on the hull of the small cabin cruiser. He had been on it before, as a guest the previous summer, when he and the owner, a local man, had sailed around the island of Gigha.

He had become a reasonably proficient sailor in the last few years, and he enjoyed being at sea. The motion of the vessel, the tang of the salty air and the ever-changing panorama were an assault on the senses. The first time he had sailed alone, he had pondered just how far this experience was from the relentless boredom of his youth, spent in a crumbling tenement in Glasgow's East End. Narrow horizons begat narrow minds; the reasoning was flawless, yet across the generations nothing was done to correct this social dichotomy. It was as though the poor were not only an underclass, but an alternative species, condemned to experience life on a completely different plane. He knew his daughter was living proof that families like the MacDougalls, victims and perpetrators of crime across the generations, could change. He hoped Sarah would take the MacDougall name, at least, to new, greener pastures.

After a few moments, he encouraged the engine into life, released the fore and aft ropes, and eased the craft out into the bay. MacDougall knew this boat was capable of thirty-five knots, at least; he eased out the throttle, all the time looking at the instrument panel. He roughly calculated that it would take him just under an hour to reach the coordinates that had been texted to him from his daughter's phone. It was an easy sail, straightforward, no hidden rocks, sandbanks or submerged wrecks. Getting there wasn't going to be the problem – keeping Sarah alive was.

Machie had chosen the location well. With the infamous Corryvreckan whirlpool so close at hand it was most unlikely that they would be bothered by other shipping. He pictured – not for the first time – James Machie's face, wondered how the years had changed him, honed his animal cunning, ruthless cruelty, his skill of being able to turn almost any situation to his own advantage. Yet, he had an Achilles heel: arrogance. JayMac had always been guilty of overconfidence, and that led to carelessness. Had Machie not been so relaxed about his 'contacts' in the police, and their ability to watch his back, the family empire would have reached new heights and none of them would have been forced into the scurrying retreat of each-man-for-himself self-interest. He would not be on a stolen boat with an assumed name. His sons would still be alive.

He thought again of Sarah. Machie would have no qualms about killing her in front of him. How could he bear to watch the life drain from those intelligent green eyes? Despite being surrounded by death and horror for most of his life, this was one pain that Frank MacDougall was determined not to endure.

A small plate above the console read *Morning Prayer*, the name also displayed along the side of the craft. The irony of this was not lost on the middle-aged man who piloted the vessel out to sea, silently praying for the apple of his eye, his daughter.

34

'The bosses have been on from headquarters, sir,' said DC
Dunn, as she hurried to Daley's side in the yard of Kinloch
Police Office. 'There's been a development.'

Daley followed her through the security door and into
the office. DS Brian Scott was standing in the large CID
office, a fresh bandage around his head, looking like a tennis
player from the seventies. Daley nodded curtly at him. Try
as he might, the chief inspector could not accept that the
disappearance of MacDougall was not, in some way, down
to the collusion of his friend. He had run the circumstances
behind the gangster's flight through his mind over and over
again; it still didn't make sense.

'Aye, right, there you are, sir,' Scott said hesitantly. 'We've
been tryin' tae get ye on the blower.'

'I've been in the hospital, so it was switched off,' said
Daley, without looking at his DS. 'Now, what's been
happening?'

'A few minutes ago, HQ received an anonymous phone
tip-off.' Scott spoke in a businesslike manner that Daley
wasn't used to. 'They've tried tae trace the call, but it was
from a private payphone, and the caller didn't stay on the
line for long.'

'So, what have we got?' Daley said, looking impatient.

'Take a look here.' Scott led his boss over to a large map of the Kintyre peninsula that took up a sizeable part of one wall. Due to its scale, the cartography was detailed, showing the names of farms, historical features and the like. Scott stood beside the map, then, looking every bit the unlikely weather forecaster, began gesturing at details on the map. 'Noo, a' we have tae go on is basically a set o' coordinates,' he said, squinting at the large map. 'DC Dunn, play the audio, please.'

The young officer pressed a few keys on her computer, and a familiar greeting played into the room. 'Good morning, Police Headquarters, Pitt Street. How can I help you?'

There was a pause, then the sound of a breathy voice. 'I have information about Sarah MacDougall.' The man tersely gave a list of map coordinates, then slammed the phone down.

Scott stretched out his hand and landed a thick index finger on a patch of sea just off the coast of the peninsula. 'That's just aboot exactly the location mentioned,' he said, holding his finger at the point for a few moments.

Daley walked up to the map, and looked more closely at where Scott was pointing. 'What does that say?' he said, running his finger along a Gaelic word.

'Corryvreckan, sir,' said DC Dunn. 'It's a whirlpool. Says on Wikipedia that it's the third largest in the world.'

'Whit the fuck's Wikipedia?' asked Scott.

'Who would know of Machie's movements apart from himself?' said Daley. 'And just why would he leak them to us?'

'Beats me, Jim,' Scott replied, some of the tension between them abating. 'Ye never know wi' that bastard. The worst bit

257

is, they want us tae commandeer a boat an' go an' check it oot.'

'They want *what*?'

'Aye, they cannae get the Force boat doon here fir four hours, an' the chopper's busy wi' a search for a missing wean o'er at Motherwell. We're it.'

'And just where are we to find this boat?'

'Oh, that's all sorted. Dae ye mind the guy doon the quay wi' a big RID.'

'RID?'

'Aye, thon big speedboat affair,' said Scott, displaying what he thought to be sound nautical knowledge.

'RIB, Brian. Rigid Inflatable Boat.'

'Is that no' whit I said?'

Despite himself, Daley couldn't hide a smile. 'Here we go again.'

'I've rounded up the firearms boys, but as fir tactics, well, that's your department, gaffer. Whit is it yer man a'ways says?'

'With power comes responsibility.' Daley shook his head, and headed for his glass box.

The small vessel began to yaw as they approached their destination. From nowhere the sea had whipped into white-capped restlessness, out of kilter with the flat calm of the cold, windless day.

'I hope you know what you're doing,' said Sarah, staring out of the small cabin window.

'Whit are ye on aboot? It's no' the sea that ye need tae worry aboot. In any case, this is whit they call the Grey Dugs, no' even the whirlpool proper. We'll just need tae keep an eye oot fir Daddy.'

In the distance, it looked as though the sea had been raised, was higher somehow. Sarah opened the small door to the rear of the cabin. She had felt fine for most of the journey, but the sudden restlessness of the sea was making her feel queasy. Hold on, she told herself. Hold on.

Without warning, the little craft was rocked by a wave and Sarah fell against the side of the cabin, banging her head against the wooden panelling.

'Yee-ha!' Machie roared, holding onto the small ship's wheel, his legs planted firmly apart to aid his balance. 'Makes ye realise yer alive, eh?'

'Do you never tire of being an arsehole?' Sarah spat out the words.

'If nobody did stupid things, nothing intelligent would ever get done,' he replied, having to shout now because of the noise of the sea, and the moaning, cracking and creaking coming from what seemed like every part of their tiny boat.

'Spare me the fucking Wittgenstein,' she shouted. 'You really are as mad as everyone says, aren't you?'

'What makes ye think that?' he shouted in reply, as he stared out of the sea-splattered window, a smile playing across his lips.

'Mr Newell,' Daley shouted as he hurried down the pontoon. DS Scott, DC Dunn and three members of the Firearms Unit jogged in his wake, all dressed in red survival suits, replete with heavy, water-resistant fleeces borrowed from the Lifeboat Station. The straps on Daley's lifejacket were already chafing at his crotch through the thick material of the suit. Even underneath the padded lifejacket, Daley could plainly see the bulge of his stomach, which he patted with grim resignation. Briefly he wondered why the diet his wife had forced him on wasn't working, then banished the thought from his mind, as it brought with it the aching in his stomach that accompanied any reminder of Liz.

'Glad to see you're all kitted out correctly,' Newell answered. He cut a tall, patrician figure in his dark blue survival suit and red life jacket. He held out his hand to help a nervous-looking DC Dunn aboard. 'The sea is cold at the best of times, and at this point in the year it's perishing – incredibly dangerous, in fact. I've got to say, this is not a mission of choice for me.'

'Aye, but the money's no' bad,' retorted Scott, shambling along the pontoon, waiting his turn to get aboard.

'No pockets in a shroud, Sergeant Scott,' Newell replied, without a change of expression.

The low murmur of chatter made Daley turn round; he didn't know why he was surprised that the crowd on the esplanade was so large. This was Kinloch, after all; everyone knew what was about to happen before it actually did.

'I hope yous are of a religious bent,' a grizzled man in a thick jumper and flat cap shouted, the stub of a well-smoked cheroot clasped between his thumb and forefinger. 'Where yous are aff tae, ye'll need the Almighty tae keep ye safe. Is that no' true, Alistair?' He pointed what remained of his cheroot at a man who was standing a few feet away.

'Aye, they do that,' said Alistair. He was a tall, thin man, and as if to exaggerate his long, grey face, he wore a leaden-coloured raincoat. 'They tell me that the Tartan Shroud is at its worst for many a year,' he said mournfully. 'That's her nickname, ye know.' He tried to catch Daley's eye.

'No' it's naw,' called another voice from the crowd, a woman this time, short and fat, wearing a bright yellow fleece. 'She's called the Speckled Lady, every bugger knows that.'

'Yer arse, Ann McCardle,' said a young man wearing a black donkey jacket over his blue bib and braces, the yellow badge on which picked him out as a council employee. 'The Cauldron o' Sorrow – that's what you're looking for.'

'Away,' said an old woman at the front of the crowd, turning her head to disagree with the others. 'It's ca'ed the Widow's Plaid, so many men have been lost there o'er the years. My granny telt me hersel', an' let me tell ye, she wisnae a wummin prone tae exaggeration, no, nor gettin' things wrong, neithers.'

'A bit like yersel, Jessie,' shouted someone. 'Unless ye've had a few too many doon in the Douglas Arms.' This elicited roars of laughter.

The next person to speak did so in a voice so quiet that Daley couldn't make out what was being said. The crowd silenced, and then parted, to reveal the weathered face of Hamish, who was, as usual, puffing on his pipe, sending clouds of pungent blue smoke into the cold, late-morning air.

'No' tae worry, Jessie, yer grandmother wiz a lovely wummin. Aye, just lovely. I mind o' her when I wiz in the school,' he said, much to Jessie's edification, who agreed with silent nods of the head. 'I mind her fine, doon the pier greeting the sailors wi' a wee smile an' a cup o' tea. Aye, she gladdened many a mariner's heart before they were sent tae an uncertain fate oot on the boundless depths o' the broad ocean.'

'Aye, an' no' jeest wi' cups o' tea, neithers,' the man with the cheroot said, turning an alarming shade of red as he burst into laughter and went into a paroxysm of coughing. 'I heard she strapped the mattress fae her bed tae her back, afore she headed doon tae the quay.'

'Aye, Donnie.' Hamish waited until the laughter died down again, and the small crowd had settled. 'You'll be the expert in mattresses, right enough. Every bugger knows yer lazy arse is never off one.'

The crowd, even some of those busy on the RIB, laughed at that.

'At least I'm no' some cod psychic.'

'I widnae have thought you'd know the difference between a cod an' a flounder,' Hamish said quietly, puffing on his pipe. 'Was it no' you who sold that American tourist a' that bream an' telt him it wiz wild Scottish salmon? Or maybes that wiz some other crooked fusherman wi' a great gut who stank o' cheap cigars.' The old man's face broke into its usual grin.

'Ye auld bastard,' the red-faced man growled, throwing down his cheroot and trying to force his way through the crowd towards Hamish.

'Noo, Donnie, think before ye act, man,' Hamish said, as the burly man shouldered his way towards him. 'Daein' me physical herm, in front o' the constabulary wid be even mair stupid than that fling ye had wi' yer wife's sister. Aye, an' only you an' yer ain conscience know jeest whoot a marital flux that must have caused.' At this, the crowd drew in a collective gasp.

Unperturbed by the continued threats of violence from Donnie, Hamish made his way onto the pontoon towards Daley.

'I'm in a bit of a hurry, Hamish. What is it?' the detective said.

'I'll jeest say this, Mr Daley,' said Hamish, leaning his head close to the police officer in a most conspiratorial manner. 'Nothin' is ever quite whoot it seems.' He patted Daley on the shoulder then walked back onto the esplanade, where he was soon lost in the crowd.

35

As the small boat heaved, so too did Sarah MacDougall. She had been at sea many times in the last few years, but this was, by far, the worse she had ever felt. The old tip was to keep one's eyes on the horizon, but here the horizon didn't exist: all that she could see through the cabin window were brief glimpses of the dark, tumultuous sea, as the little craft was hurled to the top of one wave, then cast to the depths in the trough that followed. The contents of her stomach were long gone, deposited over the side into the roiling waters; the acidic bitterness of bile burned her throat as she retched again. Hold on, she mouthed to herself.

'No' long now.' He turned to her, eyeing her plight with a cold sneer. 'C'mon, darlin', we don't want you lookin' a' pale and uninteresting for poor Daddy.'

'Why don't you just fuck off,' she replied weakly.

Frank MacDougall held on tight to the wheel of the cabin cruiser as the boat was buffeted by the angry stretch of water he had just entered. Ahead, the sky glowered, presiding over a seascape that he would have thought impossible only a few short minutes before. The satnav continued to bleep content-edly, indicating that he was holding the right course.

He held a clear picture of his daughter in his mind. She was everything to him. Of course, he told himself, he loved his wife, but her decline had been rapid and his overwhelming emotion towards her was one of pity. Sarah was young, beautiful and confident, the kind of child everyone coveted but was so rarely blessed with. His stomach turned at the thought of what Machie might have in store for her. He had regrets – every parent does – but his had now manifested in a spectacular way.

As he clutched the ship's wheel with white knuckles, he thought of his two dead sons. Was he sorry they were gone? Well, yes, of course he was. Was he proud of either of them? The answer was most definitely in the negative. As human beings, they had both reminded him of his younger self: brash, arrogant, cruel and stupid. Too stupid to realise that while crime could provide all the trappings of a successful life, the essence of success lay in the realisation of achievement. What was a new car, a big house or designer suit without the inner knowledge, the personal satisfaction, that these things were the proceeds of hard work and talent? Not the product of another's misery or, worse still, their demise. He had grown more and more jaundiced by life within the Machie crime family and consequently had given little thought to turning informant when arrested by his old neighbour Scott for drug trafficking. There had been only one way out, one way to stay out of prison and the thirty-year sentence that would have swallowed him up. In the end he had betrayed a monster.

And now that monster had his daughter.

Just when she thought she couldn't take any more, the motion of the vessel seemed to ease. Almost imperceptibly at first, then all of a sudden the waves seemed much less large and intimidating; the sea no longer battered off the cabin window, nor were they cast into shadow by the stomach-churning descent into the depths of the trough.

He loomed over her, smiling, as though reading her thoughts. 'Now then,' he said, bracing himself against the slight swell with one arm against the wall. 'By my calculations, we've got a wee bit o' time before Daddy arrives.'

'So?' She looked up at him defiantly. 'Oh, sorry, shall we have a quick philosophy seminar?'

'I wiz thinking o' somethin' a wee bit mair intimate,' he said, easing over to the young woman.

'Meaning?' She looked up at him.

He grabbed her roughly by the hair, pulling her head towards his crotch with one hand, as, with the other, he undid his zip.

The engines on the powerful RIB throbbed as the ad hoc police squad sailed towards the exit of Kinloch harbour. Skipper James Newell was strapped into a high seat behind a white dashboard displaying the vessel's instrumentation. The police officers were on the open deck, secured into seats on which they sat astride. Newell had explained that as they could reach almost fifty knots, the unusual nature of the seating was essential, enabling them to steady themselves as the RIB careered through the waves.

'Yer man wisnae kiddin' on aboot the cauld,' said Scott, holding onto the handrail which protruded from the seat in front. 'I'm freezing ma bollocks off a'ready.'

'I'm not sure you should even be here after your knock on the head,' Daley replied.

'Aye, well, here I am.'

Daley cursed as the phone in his pocket vibrated. He awkwardly retrieved it from a deep pocket of the survival suit, then scrolled through the email he had just received from the police up in Oban.

'I want you to take a look at this, Brian,' he said.

DS Scott squinted at the phone.

'I'm sick o' seein' that bastard,' he shouted to Daley above the throb of the engines. 'Where the fuck is he now?'

'That's just it, Brian. That's not James Machie. It's Duncan Fearney's adopted brother, who disappeared just about five years ago.' Daley watched Scott as he stared at the phone.

'It cannae be,' Scott spluttered. 'He's Machie's spittin' image.'

'He's Machie's twin brother. Or, *was*, to be more accurate.'

'What?'

'It's what Duncan Fearney told me before he died. Before he was killed, I should say.'

'Fuck me,' said Scott, holding tighter to the handrail in front of him. They were passing the island at the head of the loch and entering the open sea beyond; as the noise increased, so too did the speed of the vessel, its trim changing so that the prow rose into the air, offering less resistance through the waves and making higher speeds possible.

'We've found our ghost, Brian.'

With that, Scott thrust his head forward and spewed between his legs.

36

Frank MacDougall scanned the horizon. He was in more placid waters now, and had almost reached his destination. The heater of the pleasure craft blew a steady stream of hot air into the cabin. MacDougall wasn't sure whether that or fear was responsible for the beads of sweat that he could feel on his brow. He tried to collect his thoughts as the distant roar and crashing of Corryvreckan drowned out the normal maritime soundscape of seabirds. As he eyed the horizon once again and was about to give up, his phone rang.

'I can see ye!'

'Aye, well, I cannae see you,' MacDougall replied.

'Look at yer compass, Frankie. Steer forty-five degrees an' ye'll get tae see yer lovely daughter again.' The phone went dead.

MacDougall turned the boat and eased the throttle forward, desperately trying to think of a way out of his predicament.

Despite the bracing sea wind, the odour of Scott's sickness hung about the open boat. Daley was examining his phone. His frequent calls to Kinloch Police Office in an attempt to find Donald had been completely unproductive; he had not been in contact with the office, nor was he answering calls or messages. Daley thought this typified the man. Here he was heading out to sea to try and bring one of Scotland's most dangerous men to book – for the second time – and his superior was nowhere to be seen. Should the operation be a success, he was in no doubt that Donald would reappear, ready and willing to accept all of the plaudits. But it was true that in the last few days he had seen his boss's mask slip, and more of what he remembered as the real man re-emerge. Why?

So many issues about this case troubled him. He was convinced that an unseen thread ran through everything, yet he couldn't work out what the connection was, and how it could possibly unite individuals as diverse as Machie, Donald, Fearney and the MacDougall family. He had a familiar feeling in his stomach, a feeling that he was so accustomed to he was unable to immediately identify it. After wrestling with the problem as the boat bumped through the waves, it suddenly dawned on him that he was experiencing the same knot in his gut that he had when he knew Liz was being unfaithful; a gnawing, cloying sadness that undermined everything he thought or did. Was it down to his suspicions regarding his wife and Mark Henderson, or was there another, more troubling reason, something he had missed?

'Penny for them, big man,' Scott shouted, almost at the top of his voice in order to be heard above the roar of the huge diesel engine and the rush of wave and wind.

'I wish we could find the boss,' Daley shouted in reply.

'Why? What'll he contribute? We've got orders from on high. Who needs him? Be careful what you wish for, Jim.'

Daley was pleased that the temporary impasse between he and Scott had righted itself, but he was still unhappy at the role his DS might have played in MacDougall's escape. He thought back to Duncan Fearney, and what he had said in the seconds before the red dots found him and his body exploded in a spray of blood and gore.

Who was the individual he *knew* so well?

Daley looked sidelong at Brian Scott. Could he be the man that Fearney was referring to? Daley hoped not, wished it with all of his heart.

He thought of the man who had ordered the shots that killed Fearney. The knot in his stomach got tighter.

Sarah looked at him as he checked the automatic pistol, loaded it, and checked it again. Somehow, it reminded her of watching the glass blowers in Venice. It had been a school trip, just after her fourteenth birthday. Her private school hoped that exposure to the delights of Florence and Venice would inspire their young minds, and they were right. She had watched entranced as these men turned amorphous lumps of molten glass into beautiful bowls or vases, the concentration, the expertise apparent in their every move-ment. She saw that same skill now, as he checked and rechecked the weapon; the end result of his expertise, however, would not be beautiful.

She had a salty taste in her mouth; he had been rough, forcing her against the side of the cabin, pinning her to the thin walls as he thrust deep inside her. Despite the pain, the sickness, the discomfort – perhaps because of it – she had climaxed, her body contracting with pleasure as she felt him come inside her.

'Here's Daddy,' he said, staring out to sea through a pair of expensive binoculars. 'Better tidy yersel up, ye dinnae want him tae see ma cum running doon yer leg, honey.'

'It's obvious you don't have children,' she said defiantly.

'Thank fuck,' he said, removing the binoculars from his eyes. 'They a'ways let you doon, know what I mean, kid?' He began to laugh, then picked up the gun and held it to her head. 'Be a good wee girl, for a change. Yer comin' on deck wi' me. Let's say hello tae yer auld man.'

'Stop it,' she said, brushing the gun away.

MacDougall could see the boat now; it was bobbing gently in calm waters, yet behind the vessel the sky was dark above a tormented sea, as Corryvreckan churned in fury. It was as though James Machie had chosen the geographical feature best suited to his personality as the site for their meeting.

As MacDougall neared the other craft he eased back on the throttle. He could see two figures standing on the aft section of the vessel, behind the square cabin. His heart leapt in his chest as he saw Sarah, and sank almost immediately to the pit of his stomach as he recognised his former partner in crime holding a gun to her head.

Daley's mobile burst into life. He had given instructions that he was to be contacted via the RIB's radio should his phone no longer work, but he was relieved that – from the point of view of contacting Donald, at least – he still had some kind of signal.

'Just had the Coastguard on, sir.' The bar officer at Kinloch Police Office had to shout to be heard.

'And?'

'A diving vessel located to the south of Corryvreckan has spotted two boats in the area, actually heading into the first portion of the whirlpool. They were so worried that they called the Coastguard immediately, in case they were tourists or something.'

'OK. Any sign of the boss?'

'No, sir. We keep trying his mobile, but absolutely nothing. The second I find him, I'll contact you.'

Daley ended the call and signalled to Newell. 'How long to our destination?' he shouted above the tumult.

'We'll enter more unsettled waters in about ten minutes. After that, well, I'll just have to judge how safe it is to proceed.'

'OK,' Daley replied, not liking the doubt he detected in Newell's voice. Surely if the other two vessels could weather the conditions, so could they?

MacDougall came to a halt twenty feet from the vessel on which his daughter and her abductor stood. He walked out of the cabin and onto the deck, and for the first time since JayMac had sworn vengeance upon him from the dock of Glasgow's High Court, they came face to face.

'So it is you,' said MacDougall. 'I'd hoped it wiz a' just a fuckin' bad dream, stories fae a' the sick fucks that wanted ye back. Nae such luck. Ye better no' have touched a hair on her head, ya bastard.'

'Ahoy there, me hearty,' Machie shouted, his mouth open in a wide smile but his eyes cold, exactly the way MacDougall remembered them. 'Yer in nae fuckin' position to threaten me, Frankie-boy. This time, a' the cards are stacked in ma favour.'

'Enough o' the fucking preamble,' said MacDougall. 'I know what ye've come for so spit it oot. This isnae aboot revenge.'

'That's no' very polite raising yer voice like that, Frankie,' Machie shouted in reply. 'Just you ease over here, and come aboard.' He shoved the gun against Sarah's head, making her yelp in pain.

'Take it easy. I'm coming.' MacDougall walked backwards into the cabin, not taking his eyes off Machie, who yanked Sarah's head back by the hair.

MacDougall could feel the pistol tucked into his waistband, the metal cold against his back. He didn't know how he was going to do it, but he was going to kill James Machie.

37

MacDougall eased his craft closer to Machie's. Though the sea was relatively calm, the power of the whirlpool created a kind of restlessness he had never witnessed; tiny pinnacles, each tipped with white foam like small peaks on an iced cake, coated the sea between the vessels. He saw Machie turn to Sarah and for a heart-stopping moment thought he was about to kill her. Fortunately, he let her go. MacDougall watched his daughter bend down to retrieve a long wooden boat hook, then tentatively held it out towards him.

'Here,' Machie shouted, throwing a coil of thick rope across the narrow void onto MacDougall's boat. 'I want ye tae tie us together. This pretty wee thing tells me that that ye can tie a fine knot noo.'

MacDougall caught the end of the heavy rope and tied it around two metal gunwales on the side of his vessel, while on the other, Sarah did the same. Soon, the boats were secured together.

The two middle-aged Glasgow gangsters stood looking at each other, framed by the turbulent waters of Corryvreckan in the background.

'Lost a bit o' weight, Frankie,' Machie shouted.

'Yer no' looking too bad yersel, for a dead man,' answered MacDougall. 'Right, let's get on wi' it.'

Suddenly it was like a different world. The RIB was tossed in the air, then after what seemed like an eternity smacked down into the water with a hard crack. Daley felt his spine jar painfully. To his side, Scott had begun to retch again. The DCI wondered again about the wisdom of bringing his DS along. This thought was banished as the boat was flung into the air once more, this time returning to the sea bow first, soaking everyone aboard with stingingly cold water.

'Tae think I near joined the fuckin' Merchant Navy,' Scott groaned, water dripping from his matted hair and down his green-tinged face.

Newell was staring, grim-faced, out into the tumult. For the first time since his wife had almost died, Daley prayed – this time, for himself.

Machie waved the pistol at MacDougall. 'C'mon, get yersel aboard. This wan'll help ye,' he said, gesturing at Sarah, who held out her hand to help her father bridge the small gap between the two vessels.

'Sarah,' MacDougall gasped as he clambered on board, hugging her close. 'What has he done to you?' he whispered in her ear.

'Nothing, Daddy, I'm fine,' she said, surprising him by pulling free from his embrace.

'Is this no' where ye say, "If ye've touched a hair o' her heid, I'll kill ye?" said Machie.

'We both know it's no' ma daughter you're interested in, you bastard.'

'Dae we noo? Just whit am I interested in, then?'

MacDougall caught a change in Sarah's expression out of the corner of his eye; a quizzical look, directed at Machie, which he couldn't reconcile with the situation, or her predicament.

'Oh here,' said Machie, gauging the body language between father and daughter. 'Did Daddy no' tell ye his big secret? Somethin' naebody knows, apart fae me an' him – an' I only know the maist important part o' it.'

'Leave her oot o' this, JayMac,' said MacDougall, clenching his fists in anger.

'Aye, that'll suit ye just fine, eh, Frankie-boy? A few years' worth o' water under the bridge, but still the same old liar, eh?'

'Daddy, what does he mean?'

'Oor wee agreement – the wan between me an' yer faither. I take the glory – the kudos, if ye like, oh aye, an' all the blame – while he runs the show an' takes the dosh. That's the abbreviated version but I think that about covers it, eh, Frankie?'

'An' whit if it does?' MacDougall shrugged his shoulders. 'I've no' exactly been tripping the light fantastic o'er the last few years. Sarah'll vouch for that.'

Machie stared at the young woman. 'Ye can get enough o' anything: drink, sex, drugs, even power. Efter a while, it a' turns sour – been there, done that kinda shit. The only thing is, in ma game nae cunt gets tae retire, know whit I mean?' Machie was in full flow now, his face growing darker. 'But Daddy here comes up wi' the perfect solution. Just dae whit ye want, he says: travel, shag as many women as ye can get hard fir, stick half o' Colombia up yer nose, it doesnae matter. I'll run the show, call the shots. Aye, an' don't worry, ye'll get a cut – efter a', you're the main man, JayMac.'

'So what, did I break the contract? It wiz hardly fuckin' RBS we wiz running,' MacDougall retorted.

'Naw,' said Machie, 'even we're no' that fucking bent.'

'And just what is the point to all this?' said Sarah.

'The point is, darlin', that yer man here an' his protégé, Gerry Dowie, they get fed up. Here's me, daein' exactly whit I want tae dae, but gettin' bored, so whit dae I dae? Time tae get back in the saddle, says I. Take the reins again, tae continue the equine metaphor. Get a proper cut o' the business – ma business.' He stopped, staring at MacDougall. 'But that wisnae goin' tae happen, wiz it?'

'Even if a' that did happen, so what? You've escaped death, an' I escaped the jail. No' a bad exchange fir the lives we've led.'

'*So what* is a' the dosh ye spirited away when ye did the deal wi' the cops. Aye, leavin' me in the frame, taking the big fa', while you an' Gerry stashed the millions until the heat wiz off an' ye could take a wee jaunt, disappear and spend it,' Machie spat. 'Time tae spill the beans, Frankie-boy.' He held the gun to Sarah's temple.

Daley felt as though he was about to explode. The RIB had been thrown in the air and crashed back to sea more times than he could count. Despite his concern for the officers under his command, all he could do was brace himself against the sea's ferocity and grip the handrail in front of him for dear life as he awaited the next bone-jarring thud.

As the RIB crashed into the waves, Daley's head jerked upwards, his neck arched in the agony of it all. When he opened his eyes, something was wrong. He realised immediately that the seat in front of him was empty; the huddled figure that had been DC Dunn was gone. Frantically, he looked around the boat. The rest of his colleagues had adopted the same position as himself, shoulders down, facing the floor, just trying to endure the trauma the best they could. He was the only one to have noticed that Dunn was missing.

They were in the trough now, the water an enormous wall of water that sucked the daylight from the scene. The grey of the next wave towered above them, the foam visible at the top as they were propelled upwards. Daley, now panicking, managed to lever himself from the seat, straining the safety harness that held him there. In Dunn's seat he could see her harness had been ripped from its housing, and was now stretched across the deck and over the side of the boat.

He craned his neck to see over the side of the boat, and a flash of movement caught his eye. A pale hand gripped what remained of the harness. DC Dunn was alive, but she wouldn't be for much longer.

Daley reached down, releasing the catch on his own harness. As the boat flew through the air, pitching wildly before the headlong plunge, the DCI threw himself to the side of the vessel, his arm outstretched.

38

'Yer aboot tae make the biggest mistake o' yer life,'
MacDougall roared at Machie, who had the pistol rammed
against Sarah's temple while pulling her head back at an
awkward angle.

'The biggest mistake I ever made wiz trustin' a cunt like
you, Frankie.' Machie's face was contorted, eyes flashing with
fury.

MacDougall stared at the scene with horror, desperate to
save his daughter from the man he knew would have no
qualms about killing her. Then a shadow fell across the boat.

From out of nowhere, behind Machie and Sarah, a massive
wall of water was rising. MacDougall tried to keep his face
expressionless; this would likely be his last chance.

'OK, OK,' he shouted. 'She's mair important tae me than
money. Just tell me whit the fuck ye want. Ye can take the
lot, just let her go.'

Machie was about to speak, when he and Sarah were
pitched violently forward. Prepared for the sudden swell,
MacDougall propelled himself towards his daughter's captor.
Machie, caught off balance, tumbled backwards under the
weight of his old lieutenant, his head bouncing off the
wooden decking. MacDougall pressed home his advantage

by straddling his quarry, then aiming a clenched fist into his face. The pistol Machie had been holding spun across the boat, glinting dully in the low winter sun.

The pair wrestled as the boat plunged into the trough left by the rogue wave the whirlpool had created. MacDougall's powerful hands encircled Machie's neck as he battered his head into the decking with sickening thuds. Machie's face turned beetroot and large veins on his temples bulged as MacDougall tried to squeeze the life from his victim.

As he felt Machie's resistance slacken and saw his eyes beginning to glaze, MacDougall redoubled his efforts. He leaned close in to Machie, focused on the moment when he would see the life leave his body; he wasn't prepared for the blow to his head that sent sparks through his vision and flashes of pain through his entire body.

He felt the world slide from under him as he lost his hold on Machie and tumbled sideways onto the deck, the pine planking streaked with rivulets of Machie's blood.

MacDougall struggled to retain consciousness as he tried to work out what had happened. As he attempted to force himself from the deck, a kick to his chest propelled him backwards.

'Stay where you are, Daddy.' As he looked up, through a blur of pain, the vision of his daughter standing over him and pointing a gun at his head was plain enough.

Daley held onto his seat, all the time trying to keep sight of the slender white fingers that grasped the roping on the side of the RIB. He slammed against the inflated sides of the craft and bounced backwards, losing sight of his DC. Frozen water from the deck soaked his face and took his breath away, as he flung his hand over the side of the vessel, blindly searching for Dunn.

As the RIB heaved again, Daley was pitched forward. He knew he had only moments left to save his colleague: there was no way she would survive when the boat crashed into the next trough.

As he was flung forward with the downward momentum, he grabbed a lump in the hard side of the vessel. His heart missed a beat when he felt a hand grasp his; he had her. He gripped Dunn's wrist with all the strength he could muster and attempted to drag the wretched DC from the water. He managed to pull her slightly upwards but she appeared to be entangled in the ropes on the side of the RIB. Despite his strength, Daley couldn't pull her free.

Dunn's desperate expression burned into him, as the darkness caused by their plunge into the next trough engulfed the boat. His grip on her wrist began to loosen, the numbing cold and the slick water making it almost impossible for him to keep a strong hold of her.

A shadow passed in front of his eyes, as he watched Brian Scott propel himself out of his seat and grab Dunn by her shoulders. A split second later, his world went black as the RIB crashed back to the sea and his head hit hard against the metal deck.

39

MacDougall managed to pull himself into a sitting position, his back resting against the side of the vessel. In front of him, James Machie coughed and spluttered on his hands and knees, rubbing his red, finger-marked neck.

'Don't move, Daddy.' Sarah's voice was flat, emotionless.

MacDougall looked up into his daughter's eyes. Her flaxen hair was matted across her forehead and her cheeks flushed by the bitter cold, but she was still beautiful. There was steel there, though, a coldness in her eyes he had never before witnessed. His head sank to his chest as tiredness, pain and a paralysing sadness overcame him.

'No time for a nap, Frankie-boy,' said Machie, dragging himself to his feet. He stood for a few moments, regaining his balance, then staggered over to Sarah MacDougall, who stood over her father, the pistol pointed at his head.

'Please, Sarah. What—' MacDougall wasn't given time to finish the sentence, as Machie's right boot caught him squarely in the mouth. MacDougall retched from the pain, and spat out his two front teeth in a puddle of blood and saliva. As he tried to focus, he looked up at the two shadows looming over him. 'Why, Sarah? If you wanted money, all ye had tae dae was ask' was all he could manage to force through his ruined mouth.

'*Why*, Daddy? That's easy. I don't give a toss about the money. In fact, I knew nothing about your grubby little deal until just now.' Sarah's voice remained calm, seemingly unaffected by the sight of her father lying injured and shivering on the deck of the boat. 'You killed my brother, that's why.'

MacDougall was desperately trying to hold onto consciousness. 'Tommy? I only found out a few hours ago. I—' Again, his protests were cut short.

'Tommy?' Sarah's voice was incredulous. 'Who the fuck cares about Tommy? He was an arsehole. I'm talking about Cisco, my brother Cisco!' She screamed his name at her father, her usual composure replaced by desperate grief.

'I didn't kill him, Sarah. He was a fool,' said MacDougall, blood flowing freely down his chin.

'Oh no, Daddy, of course *you* didn't kill him. You never do your own dirty work, do you? You left that to Gerry Dowie.'

'Aye, yer ain boy. Fuck me, Francis,' Machie said, a cruel smile on his face. 'Ye see, fate is a wonderful thing. Yer wee lassie here stumbled across a guy who knew ma brother.'

'Oh, I wondered when this wid a' blow up,' said MacDougall.

'So ye know,' said Machie.

'I suspected. I hoped it wisnae true, but as soon as I heard there wiz this *ghost* wandering aboot taking revenge on me and mine, well, I knew the polis couldnae fathom it, but they didnae know whit I knew, did they?' He looked up at Machie, still struggling to focus after the blows to his head.

'She's a smart wee girl, ye know.' Machie carried on as though MacDougall hadn't said a word. 'She's been running a great business o'er the last few years – tobacco, drugs – made a small fortune. A real chip off the old block, aren't ye, darlin'?' He enveloped Sarah's shoulders in an embrace.

'I hate you, Daddy.' Her look was poisonous. 'You made my mother's life a misery, and you killed my lovely brother. Gerry's arschole son-in-law told me; all it took was a few bags of heroin.'

'So you believe the word of a hopeless junkie?' said MacDougall, his voice distorted by the loss of his teeth. 'Aye, makes sense, JayMac – turn everyone against me. As though killing ma boy wisnae enough.'

'Aye, you're the man, Frankie.' Machie laughed. 'Pity a' yer family are no' so smart.' His gaze flitted between MacDougall and his daughter.

'What do you mean?' Sarah looked at Machie. 'You told me that Gerry Dowie had Cisco killed, on my father's orders.'

'I've telt ye lots o' things, darlin'.' Machie's stare was blank, suddenly devoid of any emotion and pitiless, like the predator he was.

'Oh, and I suppose you know about what Gerry's son-in-law told Cisco?' Sarah said, looking less confident.

'That's the trouble with people like you,' said Machie, pushing Sarah from his side. 'Yous all think that just cos ye've got a few qualifications, an' somebody telt ye that ye were smart, that other people are a' stupid, and therefore of no consequence.'

'Fuck you,' said MacDougall, blood bubbling from his mouth.

'Oh, don't you worry, we'll come tae the fucking shortly,' Machie replied, leering at Sarah.

'I've only ever cared about two things: Cisco and the truth.'

It was Sarah's turn to shiver as she looked from Machie to her father. 'Cisco told me you didn't care, that you wanted him to leave well alone. He knew something wasn't right.' She stared at Machie. 'He told me that our great-aunt said you had a twin. He knew he was in danger; it was all in his letter.' A tear slipped down her cheek. 'Do any of you ever tell the truth?'

'Listen, Sarah,' said MacDougall, his voice a rough whisper. 'I begged yer brother to leave a' this alone – begged him – ye must believe me. He told me he'd heard that Machie was still alive. Like the arse I am,' he said, staring up at the man who had supposedly come back from the dead, 'I didnae believe him.'

'Aye, more fool you.' Machie laughed. 'Ye've got the same problem as yer daughter, here. Ye a' think yer right a' the time.' He smiled patronisingly at the young woman who still levelled a pistol at her father's head.

'Will somebody tell me the truth,' she repeated, her hand shaking under the weight of the weapon.

'I think I can have a guess,' said MacDougall, spitting blood onto the deck. 'In fact, it's no' just a guess. That useless piece of shit that married Gerry's daughter telt a' who wid listen. I wish I'd listened mair carefully. But ye cannae blame me; I mean, who wid've thought he wid've been stupid enough tae come back.' He continued with a rueful smile. 'Yer new partner here tracked doon his own twin brother and persuaded him to help him with a wee problem; then, instead o' the two o' them living happily ever after in a life o' brotherly love, wi' plenty dosh, drugs an' women, he made sure the stupid cunt would never tell the tale by blowing his heid aff!'

'No!' Sarah shouted, looking at Machie. 'You told me that my father and Gerry Dowie killed the man they thought was you in cold blood, and that you were lucky to survive. You said they had Cisco killed because he found out they were behind the ambulance attack and needed to protect their new identities.'

'I wiz lucky tae survive,' said Machie, his voice patronising. 'Dae ye think dear old Daddy here wouldn't have tried tae have me slotted in the jail? Nah, there wiz no way I wiz rotting in there, watching ma back fir thirty years. Fuck that.' He smiled at MacDougall. 'Ironic thing is, years ago, your auntie Marion wiz the one who gave me the clue. Telt me how I'd had a twin brother, an' my poor dear mother could-nae afford the baith o' us, so wan o' us got sent tae the country tae distant cousins, or some fuckin' thing. Guess I drew the short straw.'

'Aye, an' poor Marion paid the price fir that, ya bastard,' MacDougall shouted, with all the venom he could muster.

'Ye know fine how auld women gossip, Frankie.'

'Aye, so you killed yer ain brother, but that wasn't enough, was it?'

'Come on, did ye really think I wanted yer boy runnin' aboot tellin' a' who wid listen that I was alive an' kickin'?'

'There ye are, darlin'.' MacDougall's voice was quiet again, and there were tears in his eyes. 'James Machie killed yer brother. Oor Cisco.'

When Daley came to, the sound and fury at the heart of the whirlpool had abated. He was lying on his side in the recovery position, shivering despite the silver thermal blanket draped over him. His head was aching, and his right arm felt as though someone had tried to pull it off. He remembered DC Dunn, and forced himself to sit up. 'Dunn, is she OK?'

'Aye, Jim, she's OK.' Scott's familiar voice was reassuring. 'She's a wee bit battered, but alive an' kickin', thanks tae you, pal.'

Daley focused on another silver blanket, which enveloped a pale DC Dunn. She smiled weakly at him. 'Thank you, sir,' she croaked. 'You saved my life.'

'We're through the worst, you'll all be glad to hear,' said Newell. 'Since you were incapacitated, I had to make the decision to carry on through Corryvreckan, then out the other side. There was nothing to be gained by trying to turn back. If I'd known the conditions were going to be as bad as they have been, we'd never have left port. We caught an unexpected flare in the damn thing. It can happen – saw it once in the China Sea. Mind you, I was in a bloody destroyer at the time, not this glorified beach ball.'

'What now?' asked Daley through chattering teeth.

'I've called the Coastguard. They're sending a chopper from Glasgow. It shouldn't be too long. You and DC Dunn will be evacuated to hospital,' said Newell, sounding every bit the Royal Navy captain.

'Dunn, yes,' said Daley, 'but I'm going nowhere. Brian, get me the radio, will you? I need to talk to the Coastguard.'

'Wait a minute, Jim, yer no' in good nick. Ye've lost a bit o' blood, an' it's fuckin' freezin' oot here. Me an' the boys'll chase Machie an' MacDougall.'

Daley eyed his DS. He looked wet, cold and miserable, but there was something in his face he didn't recognise. 'No, no, Brian, I'll carry on. We've got the chance to put this nightmare to bed now, once and for all. I'm not missing this opportunity. Now get me that radio,' he said, forcing himself to his feet.

40

There was an ominous silence as the two boats, tied together, heaved in the heavy swell.

MacDougall, slumped against the side of the vessel, stared from Sarah to Machie. The former appeared genuinely appalled, while his old partner merely looked bored.

'So what, darlin'?' said Machie. 'I telt ye a lie, so fuckin' what?' Knowledge is, in the end, based on acknowledgement. Know whit I mean? C'mon, Sarah, blow this cunt away. The past is the past. We've got a future together with mair money than either o' us will ever need.'

'Fuck you!' she shouted, still pointing the gun at her father.

'That's the fuckin' spirit, doll,' said Machie, curling his lip in anticipation. 'The auld order changeth. Time tae move on. Go for it!'

Sarah MacDougall's face emptied, suddenly devoid of the pain, confusion and revulsion of only moments before. She stepped back, not taking her gaze from her father, and raised the gun with both hands to point it directly at his heart. She stopped, as a sob shook her slender frame.

'Sarah, I love you,' her father pleaded. 'I never stopped loving ye, any of ye.' He looked at his beautiful daughter, the apple of his eye, as she squinted down the barrel of the handgun, ready to take his life. Despite himself, he closed his eyes in a silent prayer.

'I know what you're like, what you're all like. Maybe it's even my true nature, God help me,' she said. 'You go all out to get what you want with your charm, false kindness, generosity, empathy, the works. How is anyone to know the truth? And when there's nothing to be gained, you turn; you turn on friends, family, anyone who's in your way. Even the ones you love. You are a true sociopath.' Her hands began to shake.

'Fuck you,' Sarah shouted. 'And fuck Wittgenstein.' In one fluid motion, she pivoted on her heel then discharged two shots in rapid succession.

Frank MacDougall opened his eyes just in time to see the look of amazement on James Machie's face as he tumbled backwards over the low side of the boat and disappeared, with hardly a splash, into the freezing sea.

'Darlin', thank you. Thank you,' MacDougall croaked, his voice constricted with emotion.

'Believe me, Daddy,' she said, looking over the side of the vessel. 'You have nothing to thank me for.' A wisp of smoke issued from the barrel of the pistol, now held at her side, as she searched the waves for Machie's body.

'Aye, you're my daughter, right enough,' said MacDougall. 'I've seen it mair an' mair o'er the years.' Slowly, he levered himself from the deck, then reached behind his back, as though he was about to scratch it.

'Oh, and you're an angel,' she replied, not taking her eyes from the choppy waves.

'No, you're quite right, pet lamb. An angel, I'm certainly no'. So, drop the gun. It's clear ye've still got a lot tae learn.'

'Don't call me that.' She spun around to see MacDougall slumped against the side of the vessel, pointing a black revolver at her.

'Families, eh, who'd have them?' He smiled.

She was about to reply when MacDougall held his fingers to his lips, a gesture familiar from her childhood, and one that she obeyed. They listened, as from somewhere overhead the powerful blades of a helicopter sounded above the crashing of the nearby whirlpool.

'Quick,' shouted MacDougall. 'Get on the cruiser an' let's get tae fuck. Help me release these ropes.' He straightened up, ignoring the pain, all the time keeping the gun trained on his daughter. 'Think aboot it,' he said when he saw her hesitate. 'Dae ye no' think the polis will work oot whit ye've been up tae? Didnae think I didnae have a good idea whit wiz goin' on? Gie me some credit,' he said. 'Fuck me. Wi' your brains, we can even go legit, but ye've got tae help me. Let's put the past behind us and get away fae here.'

'And what about Mum?'

'Yer mum's what she's goin' tae be; there's nae betterment there. I'll make sure she gets the best treatment. There's things you don't know, lots o' things. She'll be looked efter, I promise ye. Dae ye think she's been happy stayin' at the ferm o'er the last few years?' MacDougall stood with one foot on the side of the vessel, ready to launch himself onto the bigger boat. 'It's obvious the cops are intae yer little business. How long dae ye think it'll be before ye end up in the same shit I've been in a' ma life?'

'So we just carry on, pretend nothing has happened? Leave my poor mother to rot?'

'The way I see it, we've nae choice. Oh, an' by the way, while we're talking aboot loyalty tae yer parents, you were the one aboot tae kill me.'

'I wanted revenge . . . for Cisco,' she replied, scanning the sky for the helicopter.

'Dae ye really think I'd have killed my own son? That's near as stupid as you thinking JayMac wid have let me live. Look whit he did tae Gerald,' MacDougall spat. 'C'mon, Sarah, it's noo or never.'

She hesitated for a moment, then jumped nimbly into the other vessel, bending to untie one of the ropes that bound the cruiser to the small fishing boat she and Machie had arrived on, as MacDougall did the same further down the deck.

'Oor only chance is tae make fir a wee bay or somethin', set the boat adrift and hide oot for a while until they give up. That chopper'll spot us, so we'll head one way, then change direction, an' make for the inlet o'er on that bit o' land o'er there,' he said, gesturing at the low smear of coastline in the distance. It was only mid afternoon, but already the light was leaching from the sky.

MacDougall saw Sarah's nod, and put his gun away. He limped to the cabin, and in moments the powerful engines of the cruiser roared into life.

'The Coastguard report two vessels, less than three miles from here,' shouted Newell. 'One of them is making towards an inlet and the open sea beyond.'

'What about the other?'

'Moving much more slowly, probably drifting.'

'How long will it take us to get there?' asked Daley.

'Minutes. We've got to get Dunn winched aboard the helicopter though,' replied Newell.

'I know, I know. Ah, here they are now.' Daley pointed upwards to the large red-and-white helicopter that was growing steadily bigger as it approached them.

'I'm OK, sir,' shouted DC Dunn, still shivering under the thermal blanket. 'I don't need to go, just get after them.'

'No. You're going to get treatment,' Daley said, making it plain that the conversation was at an end. He thought of James Machie: why did he have that feeling in his chest, the horrible knot that normally presaged some disaster?

MacDougall steered the craft on a bearing of thirty-five degrees until the large helicopter thudded by. He was surprised that the aircraft had not doubled back on itself in order to check them out again but he stuck to his original plan, swinging round the wheel of the cabin cruiser to head for the inlet.

Sarah was at the back of the cabin, sitting forward with her head in her hands. 'I suppose I've been stupid,' she said, after a long silence.

'If ye mean by trusting JayMac, then, aye, ye have.' MacDougall peered into the fading light of the afternoon.

'I promise you, I just wanted to find out the truth. I would never have let him harm you. He listened to me, you know.'

MacDougall faced the young woman who, up until a few minutes ago, he had thought he knew so well. 'Sarah, you can never control people like him, no' if ye live tae be a hunner' an' fifty. I've known that bastard fir maist o' my life; trust me, he'd have killed me, an' then when he got fed up wi' you, he wid've killed you an' all.'

Sarah made to speak, but found she had nothing to say. She suddenly felt dirty, foolish and ashamed. In her heart she knew her father was right and that, subconsciously or not, she had known it from the very beginning. The shock of finding out that the pitiless individual she had been in league with was responsible for the murder of Cisco, the brother she loved so much, was only just beginning to sink in. She realised it was something that she would be forced to wrestle with for the rest of her life.

She looked across at the spare frame of the man piloting the vessel towards the inlet. In that split second, she knew she had made the right decision. In killing James Machie she had avenged her brother's death.

'Listen,' said MacDougall. There was no doubt; above the low purr of the cabin cruiser's engines, the repetitive thud of helicopter blades was unmistakable.

41

Daley watched as DC Dunn was hoisted onto the helicopter, which then, with a huge downdraft that sent the RIB spinning in the water, sped away.

'Secure your belts,' Newell shouted, as the inboard diesel engine burst into life. 'We'll head for the coordinates they gave us.'

'Fuck me,' said Scott. 'I hope ma harness is a bit better than poor wee Dunn's. I thought she wiz a goner there.'

'Me too,' Daley replied, stretching the webbing restraint over his belly. He still had the knot in his stomach, bred from some subconscious instinct that made him most uneasy. He looked at the officers from the Firearms Unit, all strapped into their seats, straight-backed and professional, then at DS Scott, who was swearing at his safety harness as he tried to find the anchor point.

A few minutes later, with everyone strapped in and Newell happy that the vessel was still seaworthy after the trauma of Corryvreckan, they set off. Not much later, however, Newell bent down to shout in Daley's ear: 'I have an update from the Coastguard helicopter. One vessel, a cabin cruiser, has just been spotted heading up an inlet on the coast near Staffay. I know it pretty well, great place to spot otters.'

'OK. How long will it take us to get there?'

'Not long. Even though they're in a fast boat, it's not as fast as this, and they'll have to slow down now they're in shallow waters.'

'Might be slower, but I bet you any fuckin' money it's warmer and drier,' Scott shouted to no one in particular.

Ignoring the irascible DS, Newell continued. 'Strange thing is, no sign whatsoever of the small vessel – the fishing skiff. It seems to have disappeared.'

'What do you think that means?' asked Daley.

'Hard to say. If they've abandoned one vessel to the mercy of the whirlpool, it could quite easily be at the bottom of the sea by now. My guess is they were spooked by the chopper and are trying to make an escape in the faster boat.' Newell seemed confident in his deduction.

'But surely once they go up the inlet they're trapped?'

'No, not really. This inlet is more like a mini channel. It narrows dramatically, but you can proceed along its length in a small craft and out into the open sea. Have to be careful, mind, but it's a good short cut. Whoever is navigating seems to know what they're doing.'

Daley sat back in his seat as the trim of the vessel changed. They bounced across the waves, mercifully in a much more restrained manner than earlier. Despite the cold day, a bead of sweat appeared on Daley's forehead as he battled the uneasy feeling in his stomach.

'Fuck me, here we go again,' Scott moaned, just before he retched.

MacDougall squinted into the distance, along the length of the inlet. He was relieved to see that it was open-ended; he could see the open sea, and the purple shadow that was the island of Islay.

'I think we can get through,' said Sarah. She was sitting at the map table, studying a huge sea chart she had found rolled into a cardboard tube in the cabin. Though her working knowledge of such a document was patchy, she could figure out which figures referred to the clearance between boat and rocks.

'I'm still worried aboot that fuckin' helicopter,' MacDougall said, shaking his head. I'm no' sure if they didnae see us, even though we were in the lee o' the island.'

'So, what are they going to do? How do they know it's us anyway?'

MacDougall paused, then turned to face her. 'Listen, you don't know everything, darlin'.'

Sarah looked confused.

'At first I had nae idea you were behind the drugs and tobacco shit. Though I had my suspicions.' He sighed. 'Oor Tommy wiz helping me oot. You know he couldnae keep his trap shut.' MacDougall's voice caught at the mention of his dead son.

'Yes, I might have known. Helping you out with what, exactly?'

'Listen, ye don't get much on witness protection, I can tell you. I had tae dae somethin'.'

'Were you working with the police? Oh no, you've been helping them investigate me.'

'It wisnae just any cop, it—' MacDougall wasn't given time to explain, as the vessel jolted violently on a reef at the bottom of the inlet, and he was flung to the floor.

'Daddy are you OK?'

'Aye, aye,' MacDougall replied, picking himself off the floor, 'but I think that's the boat fucked!'

John Donald looked around the table. He was used to dominating such meetings, however, in this case, he was not in the chair; in fact, he was very low in the pecking order indeed.

'Our objective is at hand, gentlemen.' The thin man standing beside a projector screen smiled as he spoke. 'We may have had to use, let's say, *unconventional* methods, but here we are, success almost within our grasp.'

'Yes, but is it though?' questioned an older man. 'If it were to emerge that we used one of the most dangerous men this country has ever seen as a lure to catch a true monster, then we've failed.' He paused for effect. 'The consequences for us, as an organisation, could be terminal.'

Donald saw his opportunity. 'May I say, according to the most recent reports, my men are well on the way to bringing resolution to this mess. Some of my best men, you know,' he said, smiling smugly, as though he was in possession of information the others weren't.

'So you say, Donald,' said the thin man, making Donald bridle. 'What, though, will we do if things do go awry?'

'That won't be a problem,' said Donald. 'These same men will take the fall – QED.' He sat back in his chair, savouring the murmur of approval around the table.

'Up ahead,' said Newell. 'We're just about to enter the inlet. We'll have to slow down a bit.' Sure enough, in thirty seconds, the boat settled its nose into the water.

'Whit the fuck,' said Scott pointing into the distance.

A few hundred yards further on, a white cabin cruiser listed to one side, its nose already submerged.

'Hold tight, gentlemen,' said Newell, as the trim of the RIB changed again.

Daley stared at the stricken vessel with mixed emotions. Could this be a stroke of luck, or was it a ruse, put in place to lure them into an ambush? He was on the point of telling Newell to stop when something caught his eye. In the fading light, he could see a small dinghy making its way to the beach.

'Over there!' Daley drew Newell's attention to the craft. As Newell turned the RIB and made for the shore, Daley watched the team leader of the Firearms Unit release his harness and start removing weapons from the large metal cases that had been lashed to the deck on departure, and had thankfully remained in situ throughout the horrors of Corryvreckan.

As the powerful vessel sped towards the beach, Daley could make out two figures struggling through the surf and onto the shingle. The dingy had been abandoned and was already drifting back into the inlet.

'I'll go in as far as I can, but you gentlemen are going to get wet,' said Newell, eliciting a dirty look from Scott. Daley was handed a sidearm and a bulletproof vest by a firearms officer, then looked on in dismay as Scott eschewed the latter with a shake of the head.

'Get that on, Brian,' ordered Daley.

'Whit, an' sink like a fuckin' stone before I get tae the shore? No' likely, gaffer.' Scott replied defiantly, just as the RIB slowed, only a few yards from the beach.

As Daley unstrapped his harness, he squinted at the fleeing couple: a man and a woman. He presumed the woman was Sarah MacDougall, but who was her companion?

Taking his lead from the firearms officers, Daley launched himself over the side of the vessel and into the freezing surf. It was so cold he momentarily lost his breath; however, as he staggered towards the beach, a mixture of exertion and adrenaline banished the chill. He had only one objective: to catch the couple who were already heading over the sand and onto the machair beyond.

MacDougall ploughed through the grass, Sarah following close behind. They had heard the powerful engines of the RIB as it drew into the shore; now they listened to shouts from the officers as they splashed through the waves towards the shore.

'Bastard!' MacDougall exclaimed as he tripped over a boulder and fell onto the sand, the handgun slipping from the waistband of his trousers. As he struggled quickly to his feet, he saw Sarah grab the pistol and turn to face the pursuing police officers, her arm outstretched as she aimed the weapon at them.

'No!' MacDougall cried, reaching out to her just as two red spots flashed across her chest.

A distorted voice roared: 'Armed police! Stop or we will fire!'

Daley watched as one of the police officers, still wearing a red life jacket, knelt to the ground and took aim with a short-barrelled weapon.

'Sir, I need your permission to return fire,' the unit leader shouted to the DCI, just as a shot issued from the machair and whistled over the heads of the diving police officers.

'Go ahead,' Daley roared.

The marksman fired two shots.

For Frank MacDougall everything went into slow motion; even the report of the handgun fired by Sarah failed to register in his hearing. He saw the orange flash from the barrel and a puff of smoke as the gun discharged. Sarah's shoulder shot back with the recoil of the firearm.

In the same instant he realised that the police would return fire, he leapt in front of Sarah, just in time to shield her body from two shots, which hit him squarely in the back.

The chase was over.

42

Superintendent Donald zipped up the dark flight suit as he hurried across the tarmac of the remote airfield to the Chinook helicopter.

As he strapped himself into a bench seat, alongside other similarly clad figures, he tried his best to quell the nausea in the pit of his stomach. Had he done the right thing? Could this mean the end of everything?

He felt his stomach lurch as the powerful aircraft lifted from the ground then, nose down, began its forward momentum.

For no reason he could fathom, he remembered the tenement flat where he had grown up; on the wrong side of the tracks in a Glasgow that no longer existed. The black stained walls, the fungus that sprouted from the shared toilet at the end of the landing, serving the needs of four families, the room he shared with his three siblings, the cracked old sink in the 'kitchenette' – a curtained-off nook, part of the small lounge – and even the black-and-white television his father had staggered home with from the pub at the end of the street, and around which the family had gathered to watch, for the first time in their own home, an episode of *The White Heather Club*. In a word: poverty.

He realised why his subconscious had produced this vision of what he now considered hell: the ends justified the means. No matter the cost, he had left that tenement far behind.

Donald looked across the flight deck of the helicopter, his eyes resting on one of the men who sat, shoulders hunched, looking at the floor. Suddenly, as though he felt Donald's gaze upon him, he raised his head, to reveal a gnarled face. The superintendent's stomach lurched as he saw the cowering figure in a Glasgow alleyway all those years ago.

The ends justify the means.

The young woman held her father in her arms, his pallor almost luminous in the gloaming. The right side of her face was streaked with his blood.

'Daddy' It was a heartfelt plea for him to hold onto the life that was seeping into the sandy grass of the machair.

Scott bent over his old neighbour, tears in his eyes. 'Frankie, my man, c'mon. We'll get help o'er here quick smart.'

'Aye, right, Scooty,' whispered MacDougall, as blood bubbled from the corners of his mouth. 'Dae ye no' think I've seen enough men die tae know when ma time's up?'

'No, no,' Sarah wailed. 'Please, someone do something.'

With the last of his strength, Frank MacDougall held up his right hand and looked at Scott. 'Listen, will ye dae me a favour.'

'Anything, Frankie.'

'Look efter this yin fir me, ye know whit I mean, Brian.' He gripped Scott's hand weakly.

'Aye, of course I will,' said Scott, forcing a smile.

'Whit's so fuckin' funny?' gasped MacDougall.

'That's the first time you've ever called me by my right fuckin' name.'

MacDougall tried to laugh, but pain took hold, making him wince. 'Here. In my left pocket,' he said, his voice barely audible. 'Help me get it oot.'

Scott did as he was asked and, as gently as he could, fished into MacDougall's pocket and retrieved a slim box, about half the size of a mobile phone, with a flashing red light.

'Whit the fuck? Whit's this?'

'Jack Daniels, my friend. Jack Daniels.' MacDougall's eyelids fluttered. His time was running out. He turned to Sarah. 'Naebody could've wished for a better daughter, I mean it.' He smiled, then his eyes rolled upwards, leaving only the whites visible, as his hand fell onto the rough grass.

'Daddy.' Sarah buried her head in the chest of the man who, whatever the rest of the world thought of him, had been her lovely father.

On the far side of the beach, beyond a huge rock almost thirty feet high, a small boat drew into the shore, engines off, on the power of the tide alone. The passenger, dripping wet, waited until the vessel grounded in the sand, then in the gloom splashed over the side and waded heavily onto the beach, slightly weighed down by the heavy bulletproof vest he was wearing under his waterlogged jacket, which displayed two neat holes in the chest.

Daley looked with compassion at the young woman being comforted by Scott. He thought how alike Brian and the man lying dead on the beach looked: the same craggy, lived-in faces and spare yet powerful frames. Nagging doubts about his DS would not go away. He hated the feeling.

'I need to ask you something, Sarah,' said Daley, leaning down so that he could look her in the face. 'Do you know where James Machie is?'

She didn't move, head still buried in Scott's shoulder. Then slowly she raised her gaze and looked straight at the chief inspector.

'I killed him,' she said.

'How? Where?' asked Daley. 'I'm sorry, I have to know. We'll take an official statement later, but I need to know what took place.' Seeing the look of admonishment on Scott's face, he added, 'Just briefly.'

'I shot him twice and he fell into the sea. It was as simple as that.'

'OK.' Daley stood back to his full height. 'I'm sorry I had to ask, and I'm sorry for the loss of your father.'

Sarah stared into the distance, as the purple shade of dusk descended.

'Stand down,' Daley shouted to the armed police officers, who immediately relaxed, no longer cradling their weapons under their arms and scanning the environs for any potential threat.

'Whit dae ye make of this thing?' said Scott, handing Daley the device he had retrieved from MacDougall's pocket.

'Looks like some kind of tracking device,' said Daley. 'Where the fuck did he get it from?'

'Aye, and who the fuck wiz trackin' him?' said Scott, looking at his boss doubtfully.

'What did he say to you before he died?'

'Och, nothin' really.' Scott looked down at the body of Frank MacDougall, now covered by a silver thermal blanket. 'He got me tae take that box oot o' his pocket, then, well, maybe he wiz delirious.'

'Why do you say that?' asked Daley.

'Och, you know, the thing. I asked him aboot it and a' he said wiz "Jack Daniels". Aye, just that, twice, Jack fucking Daniels. Maybe a last request? Ye know fine how much he liked the bevy. I wish I'd had a wee flask o' somethin' on me. I'd have gied him a drop,' Scott said, staring mournfully at the corpse on the ground, regret etched on his face.

An officer approached Daley and murmured something to him.

'Newell says he can't take us back, not with the dark and the bad conditions in Corryvreckan,' said Daley. 'I've told them to radio for a chopper. We'll have to be airlifted out.'

'I cannae say I'm no' pleased aboot that, though I know whit the gaffer'll have tae say aboot a' that expense,' said Scott. 'Eh, while we're on the subject—'

'Hold on, Brian.' Barely visible in the gloaming, a dark figure was making its way down the beach. Daley reasoned that it must be a member of the Firearms Unit, though he couldn't remember any police personnel going beyond the point where MacDougall had fallen.

'Brian, down!' Daley roared, as he dived into the sand. He saw the man kneel with his arms outstretched in front of him, with what could only be a weapon pointed at them.

'Whit the fuck?' Scott spun around as the gun flashed and two shots rent the air.

Daley flinched as his face was splattered with warm blood. Brian Scott fell to the ground.

Calmly the gunman got to his feet and began to walk towards them.

'Jim Daley, my man. Come and get it!' The voice of James Machie was unmistakable as he repeated the words he had shouted at Daley when he was taken down in the High Court in Glasgow all those years before.

Many things seemed to happen at once. One, then two red dots played on Machie's chest as he strode forward. A shot rang out, which stopped Machie in his tracks and sent him stumbling backward. Miraculously though, he regained his balance, and set off again. Daley, aware that his DS was writhing in agony beside him, wrestled the revolver from his shoulder holster and squinted into the darkness. Machie's gun flashed again, and a bullet whined past Daley and into the sand.

Daley focused and took his aim, struggling to find his exact target in the dim light. More in hope than expectation, he squeezed the trigger. Machie stopped dead. His arms fell to his sides, and he toppled face down, blood soaking into the sand from the neat hole in his forehead.

'Brian!' Daley struggled to his feet, as a thudding overhead noise grew louder. In seconds, the beach was illuminated by white light and the sand was whipped up as a Chinook helicopter came in to land.

'Fuck me,' said Scott, his face lit by the searchlights coming from the aircraft. 'Ye'll need tae get me the number o' that helicopter mob.' Daley leaned in closer to hear him. 'That's some service.' He coughed blood, and his eyes closed.

The unit commander ran to Daley's side. 'That bastard! He was wearing a vest, sir.' He stopped, looking down at the DCI who was cradling Scott's limp figure in his arms.

43

Daley stared through the glass wall of the room in Kinloch Hospital. Scott had been too weak for the journey all the way to Glasgow in the Chinook, in which Donald had miraculously appeared with a phalanx of Special Branch personnel; just too late to encounter danger, just in time to take imperious command. Scott's condition would have to stabilise before he could be taken to one of the city's main hospitals in a specially equipped aircraft – if he stabilised.

Daley felt a hand on his shoulder. Liz stood behind him, wrapped in a white hospital gown.

'Oh darling,' she said, smoothing his hair. 'I'm so sorry.'

'He's not dead yet,' Daley spat, turning away from his wife, who instinctively removed her hand.

'What's wrong, Jim?'

Daley stayed silent, motionless, as though mesmerised by the sight of his colleague – his best friend – battling for his life.

'Please, darling, don't shut me out,' she whispered, running her hand down his back.

'Do you call *him* that?'

'Call who what?'

'You know who. Mark Henderson.'

'Mark? What's all this about?'

'It's about the truth.' Daley turned on his heel, his face a blazing mixture of hurt and anger. 'In my job I have to shut my eyes and close my mind to most of the horrors that go on in the world, otherwise I would go insane. But I can never shut my heart to how I really feel. It's impossible.'

There was silence, except for the bleeping and wheezing coming from the equipment that was keeping Brian Scott alive on the other side of the glass.

'I don't know where you get these ideas from, darling. You know the score between him and me. He's my sister's husband. I have to be civil.' She looked up at her husband, her face the picture of innocence.

Daley fished into the inside pocket of his jacket and removed a large black-and-white photograph, which he handed to his wife.

'In your case, very civil,' he said as she looked at her own image, kissing Mark Henderson, his hand buried in her hair.

Daley walked away.

When he returned to the office, he was dismayed to find Superintendent Donald sitting behind his desk.

'Ah, Jim. How are things at the hospital?' Donald looked up at him over a pair of reading glasses.

'What are you doing?'

'Writing my report.' Donald leaned back in Daley's chair, which squeaked in protest. 'I knew I would find all I needed here. Young Miss MacDougall has already provided some interesting information,' he said with a self-satisfied smile. 'Turns out one particular piece of scum – Andy Lafferty, Dowie's son-in-law – was the initial connection between

Sarah and Machie. He assisted in the ambulance "assassination" and confirmed Cisco's suspicions that Machie was still alive. Also provided Machie with the Dowies' new hiding place. All very helpful. Pays to strike while the iron's hot. Sarah was *most* cooperative.'

'You're all heart,' said Daley. 'She's just witnessed her father being killed.'

'Needs must, Jim.' Donald was unrepentant. 'We all have to do our bit to improve performance. Things are changing. Scotland is about to change. Myself and other senior police officers and members of the security service up here have decided to steal a march on the establishment down south – get ahead of the game, so to speak – in preparation for a new independent country. We will have a new agency, united against crime, whether it be large or small.'

'And what if the vote is no?' Daley asked.

'We'll see.' Donald smiled smugly. 'Even in that unlikely event, the genie is out of the bottle. The old order changeth, James, and I for one don't expect to be left behind.'

'Really,' said Daley, his blood starting to boil. The old order had been changing for a long time for Donald, who had been using the phrase for as long as Daley could remember.

'Listen, Jim, today has been a great success. We've ended this awful Machie resurrection; we even know how he did it. Just shows you how much things have changed in the last fifty years. They used to breed like bloody rabbits in the slums of Glasgow. Kids brought up by grannies and aunties, conniving midwives and priests keeping the secret. Nobody knew where they were. We can't blame ourselves for not discovering the long-lost twin theory.

'There will be an investigation into the behaviour of the prison staff who were guarding Machie, of course. The most likely theory is that he swapped with his somewhat naïve twin during the hospital visit. Hence all the cash at the farm. Anyway, we'll soon find out the truth.'

'There are a lot of things that will have to be investigated, sir,' said Daley, remembering Duncan Fearney's last words.

'Meaning?'

'Meaning, get the fuck off my chair and out my office.'

After a few tense moments, Donald stood up. 'I know you're under pressure, Jim. Worried about Brian, oh, and Liz, no doubt, so I will let this little outburst go.' He walked to the door. 'But only this once.' He left the room and closed the door quietly behind him.

Daley sat down heavily in his chair, unpleasantly warm from Donald's backside. He felt profoundly depressed. His marriage to his pregnant wife was probably over. His best friend was hovering on the verge of death. And another traumatic case had clawed at his soul.

He opened the bottom drawer of the filing cabinet. The half-empty bottle of whisky rolled back to reveal the small note that had been tucked underneath it. Daley recognised Scott's scrawl.

If you're reading this, I'm in bother. Donald made me spring MacDougall. An unofficial order, he said. He's up to something. I need help, Jim. B.

It was then that it struck Daley: the convenient death of Duncan Fearney, the tracking device in MacDougall's pocket.

John Donald. JD. The same initials as MacDougall's spirit of choice: Jack Daniels. Were the dying man's words a veiled message, or just a coincidence?

'Oh, you'll know him.' Duncan Fearney's last words sounded in his head.

Daley was well into the whisky, but instead of dispelling his fears the alcohol was having the opposite effect. The faces of his wife, Mark Henderson, Donald, Duncan Fearney, James Machie and Frank MacDougall coalesced in a sickening parade before his mind's eye.

There was a quiet knock at the door.

'Come in,' said Daley, still distracted by his thoughts.

The door opened to reveal DC Dunn, wearing an Arran jumper and tight jeans, hands thrust into the pockets.

'I'm sorry to disturb you, sir,' she said. 'Is it OK to come in for a minute?'

'Of course, in you come.'

'I just wanted to . . . to thank you for saving my life.' She tried to smile, but broke down into tears. 'I'm so sorry about D.S. Scott.' A large purple bruise covered her right cheek and her face bore a number of cuts and scrapes, testament to her ordeal.

'Sit down, sit down,' he said, gesturing to the seat at the other side of his desk. 'Do you drink whisky?'

'I'm in the CID, of course I drink whisky.' She regained her composure and beamed through her tears.

Daley removed another glass from the filing cabinet and filled it with a good measure of the expensive Springbank single malt. 'Here,' he said, handing it to the DC. 'You look like you need it.'

They sat quietly on either side of the desk for a few moments, letting the spirit do its job.

Daley watched Dunn. She closed her eyes every time she sipped her drink. He wondered why he hadn't noticed before: the button nose, the high cheekbones, the sweep of auburn hair. She was the very image of the young woman he had fallen in love with years before. He felt a pang as he remembered the first time he had met Liz.

'Here's to you, sir,' she whispered, raising her glass as her face broke into a shy smile. 'And thank you.'

'A pleasure, my dear. Cheers.' Daley raised his glass and looked straight into her beautiful ice-blue eyes.

Acknowledgements

A huge thank you to Hugh Andrew and all at Polygon for signing me up and ensuring DCI Daley lives on. A special mention for my editors, Alison Rae and Julie Fergusson, who have worked so hard. It's great to be in the hands of such professional and capable people.

I am also very grateful to my wonderful and wise agent, Anne Williams of the Kate Hordern Literary Agency; indeed to Kate herself.

I endlessly appreciate my family, Fiona, Rachel and Sian; without their support in art, as in life, I would be diminished and hapless. I find it sad that my parents, Alan and Elspeth Meyrick, didn't meet Daley, Scott, Hamish et al, but then again, maybe they have. God bless them.

To the good folk of the real Kinloch – Campbeltown in Kintyre. Despite being ignored, ill used, starved of funding and attention and generally placed at the bottom of the list as far as government is concerned, there thrives a community as warm as it is resilient. You will travel far and wide to meet folk as kind, entertaining, funny and unique; here is a place apart. If you find yourself with itchy feet, direct them to 'The Wee Toon', for Campbeltown and its environs are as beautiful as they are unspoilt, a treasure trove of history and culture. I can only strive to do you justice through your fictitious cousins. Thank you all so much for your support and kindness.

D.A.M.
Gartocharn
June 2014

The D.C.I. Daley thriller series

Book 1:
Whisky from Small Glasses
ISBN 978 1 84697 321 5

When the body of a young woman is washed up on an idyllic beach on the west coast of Scotland, D.C.I. Jim Daley is despatched from Glasgow to lead the investigation. Far from home, and his troubled marriage, it seems that Daley's biggest obstacle will be managing the difficult local police chief; but when the prime suspect is gruesomely murdered, the inquiry begins to stall.

As the body count rises, Daley uncovers a network of secrets and corruption in the close-knit community of Kinloch, thrusting him and his loved ones into the centre of a case more deadly than he had ever imagined.

Book 2:
The Last Witness
ISBN 978 1 84697 288 1

James Machie was a man with a genius for violence, his criminal empire spreading beyond Glasgow into the

UK and mainland Europe. Fortunately, James Machie is dead, murdered in the back of a prison ambulance following his trial and conviction. But now, five years later, he is apparently back from the grave, set on avenging himself on those who brought him down. Top of his list is his previous associate, Frank MacDougall, who unbeknownst to D.C.I. Jim Daley, is living under protection on his lochside patch, the small Scottish town of Kinloch. Daley knows that, having been the key to Machie's conviction, his old friend and colleague D.S. Scott is almost as big a target. And nothing, not even death, has ever stood in James Machie's way . . .

Book 3:
Dark Suits and Sad Songs
ISBN 978 1 84697 315 4

After a senior Edinburgh civil servant spectacularly takes his own life in Kinloch harbour, D.C.I. Jim Daley comes face to face with the murky world of politics. To add to his woes, two local drug dealers lie dead, ritually assassinated. It's clear that dark forces are at work in the town, and with his marriage hanging on by a thread, and his sidekick D.S. Scott wrestling with his own demons, Daley's world is in meltdown.

When strange lights appear in the sky over Kinloch, it becomes clear that the townsfolk are not the only people at risk. The fate of nations is at stake.

Read an extract from *Dark Suits and Sad Songs*,
the third D.C.I. Daley thriller.

Prologue

Solemnly, the pontoon bell tolled, roused by the breeze that
blew across Kinloch from the Atlantic beyond, carrying the
promise of a milk-warm beginning to another glorious
midsummer day. The first sepia light of the sun embraced the
sleeping town in its glow.

As though roused by this, the wheelhouse door of *The
Alba* swung open. The sun reflected softly off the varnished
oak door, flashing more keenly from the polished brass of the
porthole, as Walter Cudihey strode out onto the narrow
deck, his face a mask, eyes dark. In his left hand he carried a
petrol can, his right, bunched into a fist, grasped something
small and out of sight.

With a fluidity of motion that belied his age and physique,
he loped over the side of the vessel and onto the pontoon
decking. He cast his gaze across the oily blue waters of the
loch, over the steep side of the harbour wall and on to the
road and beyond, where stood a solid granite structure,
silhouetted in the first light of morning. Atop this monument
to the war dead of Kinloch was a simple cross, black against
the glow of the rising sun. Cudihey turned his back on the
memorial and, facing east, sat neatly cross-legged on the
wooden planking, his pupils pinpricks in the morning light.

He sat for a few moments and then, neither changing his expression, nor removing his gaze from the horizon, lifted the can and poured its contents over himself. The clear liquid splashed over his bald head, soaking the small fringe that was the remnant of his hair and drenching his white T-shirt, Bermuda shorts and the wooden decking as it began to glug deeply from the emptying Gerry can.

Cudihey, eyes now closed against the stinging fuel, blindly laid the can down, flicked the cap off a brass petrol lighter, hesitated for a heartbeat, then with a quick downward flick of his thumb ignited a flame which quickly spread up his arm and consumed his whole body, first in red, then green, fire. The fire crackled deeply as Cudihey's body surrendered to the flames, rendering down like a Sunday roast.

Seabirds cried and distantly a dog barked as a dark pall of putrid smoke spread from the harbour and across Kinloch, souring the early morning air. As the flames spread to the decking, globules of burning fat found their way to the loch and hissed in the still waters. A woman screamed as the whole length of the pontoon began to blaze.

A black mass, momentarily visible through a veil of fire, slowly toppled backwards as the ruined decking collapsed into the water, sending a wave of steam into the fetid air.

1

Jim Daley woke with a start. Squinting at his watch, he noted the time was 5:28. Propping himself up on one elbow, he tried to collect his thoughts, as well as take in his surroundings. His mouth was dry, his head throbbed and he felt slightly squeamish; an undeniable product of the overindulgence of the night before. Like far too many nights recently, he thought.

As the early morning rays poured through the flimsy curtain, he was dismayed to find that he was taking up far too much of a small double bed, which, while it wasn't his own, wasn't exactly unfamiliar. The walls were adorned with modern prints and arty black-and-white pictures; above his head, a straw hat trailing a bright red ribbon was pinned to the wall.

Beside him, the long auburn hair of the woman he had spent the night with cascaded across the white pillow and framed her round face. Her breathing was heavy and her long lashes flickered as she slept and dreamed. He took in her pale beauty for only a moment before darker thoughts began to crowd his mind and the sickness at the pit of his stomach returned, as cloying and insistent as ever.

With as little commotion as his large frame would allow, he levered his legs over the side of the bed, looking at the messy floor for any sign of his own clothes. Alongside a lacy bra, discarded black tights and a pair of knickers – so slight they barely merited the name – lay his shirt; light blue and huge amidst the other garments. On top of it lay a silver foil packet, torn open to reveal a used condom, knotted then tucked neatly back into its former home. He sighed as he rubbed at the stubble on his chin.

As he pulled on his shirt he noted in the wardrobe mirror that his face, despite gaining lines and shadows hitherto absent, was noticeably thinner. Unfortunately, as he breathed in to fasten his trousers, the extent of his persistent gut banished any fleeting joy. He removed his jacket from the back of the room's only chair and winced as coins fell from the inside pocket, jangling noisily in the quiet room; though not enough to wake his sleeping companion, who merely turned her head, rearranging the display of her hair on the white linen. Despite himself, despite the difficult situation he had engineered, despite the habitual deep pangs of Catholic guilt, he smiled. She was so beautiful. He donned his jacket then stepped over the rest of the mess towards the door.

Once in the narrow hallway, he did his best to collect his thoughts. He had always been an early riser, though this was, even for him, a smaller hour than normal to be awake and fully functioning; especially after drinking wine the previous evening, which he could still smell on his breath. As he reached the lounge his mobile phone burst into life, demanding his attention. He picked it up from the coffee table, noted the missed calls, and read the new message, a frown exaggerating the lines on his forehead. He was about to start looking for the house phone when a sound from behind prompted him to turn round.

'Morning, sir . . . Jim,' she said with a smile, raising her eyebrows at her initial mistake. Daley looked into her ice-blue eyes, down to her small, upturned nose and red lips, the lower of which had a slight pout. Even under the folds of her dressing gown her long, graceful limbs were obvious, as was the cleft between her breasts that sent a shaft of desire through him. Not for the first time, he was reminded of a young Liz.

'Morning,' he smiled. 'How are you?'

'Fine. Tired, I guess. Trouble?' She looked at the phone in his large hand.

'If Brian was here, he would say, "a policeman's life is not a happy one". I have to get in ASAP. I was going to give them a quick call – do you know where the phone is?' He looked at her pleadingly, a comic grimace on his face. 'The bloody signal here is a pain in the arse – thanks,' he said as she handed him the phone, retrieved from under a magazine on the couch.

'Coffee?' She yawned.

'Eh, yes,' he replied, looking about for somewhere to sit. 'Just a quick one, then I'll need to get going. You know how it is.'

She smiled at him weakly; she knew all too well exactly *how* it was. He was her boss, more than twenty years her senior and they had been lovers for almost seven months.

'If they ask for DC Dunn, tell them you don't remember exactly who I am.' She looked over her shoulder with a grin as she made her way to the small kitchen.

He watched her pad away. In all honesty, it was difficult, very difficult. In order to keep their relationship secret, he had encouraged her to move from her flat in the town centre to a pretty little rented cottage on the outskirts of the village of Machrie, five miles outside Kinloch, off the road and down a farm track, where even the most determined gossips of the town would find it difficult to uncover their secret – or so they had thought. Within days of her move though, and less than twenty-four hours after his first visit, he was stopped in the street by a local acquaintance, who felt it was 'only right tae let him know jeest whoot everybody was sayin'. After a period of coolness, during which he felt lonelier than ever before in his life, he had returned. Since then, though trying to remain as discreet as possible, they'd carried on their illicit affair, and soon, if anyone had really cared in the first place, the nods and winks stopped – in the main, anyway – and life returned to some sort of normality.

He began by promising himself that he couldn't love her, that it was all part of life's rich experience. Then, when she wasn't there, he felt an emptiness that gnawed at him; unable to sit down, stand up, sleep, or perform any of the other mundane activities of which most of life comprised. He loved to be around her. She was kind, with a quiet determination and dry sense of humour. They made sense together; they had similar tastes, they laughed at each other's jokes, and both understood the demands of a career in the police force.

As he overheard her moving around the kitchen, he could hear she was singing a song to herself. Like him, she loved music but was tone deaf, making it impossible to discern the tune she was murdering. He looked at the ceiling, rubbed his eyes and sighed. He knew he shouldn't have carried on with this relationship. They had kissed on the day he had saved her life, the day he showed Liz the pictures of her in the arms of Mark Henderson – the day his life had changed. He had tried to reason with himself, but to no avail. Liz's absence had left a gaping hole in his life, one that only his young subordinate appeared able to fill.

He was careful to dial 141 before entering the number for Kinloch Police Office; even though gossip, rumour and speculation had died down, he didn't need to rekindle the fire.

'Daley here,' he said, almost yawning. 'What's up?' He listened for a few moments, then began to rub his forehead, muttered a hasty goodbye and clicked the phone off.

'Not good, I take it?' Mary Dunn's face was serious as she passed Daley the steaming mug of coffee.

'No. Not good at all. In fact, I would get dressed if I was you.' He gave her a weak smile, as he tentatively sipped the strong coffee.

She watched him walk to his car and drive away. Certainly, he was not the young, groomed, tanned and moisturised specimen of manhood held up as the ideal to women of the twenty-first century; he was almost twice her age, but it didn't seem to matter. She thought he was fine; confident without being arrogant, brave but also thoughtful. He made her feel special, he made her heart leap.

Dunn brewed another cup of coffee. Soon she would have to put on her mask, pretend that the man in the glass box wasn't the man she loved, but what he had been from the beginning – her boss. She pushed the hurt from her mind, telling herself that this was just the way it had to be right now. She didn't want to analyse it all too closely. She didn't want reality to come up short.

The telephone rang. Someone in Kinloch Police Office was about to tell her something she already knew.

2

As Daley drove down Main Street, he could see that despite the hour a large crowd had gathered near the pontoons. A small number of uniformed officers were struggling to maintain order; it looked as though they were fighting a losing battle. He parked his car as close to the loch as the throng would allow and made his way towards the scene. Black smoke was still visible in the clear air and an acrid smell, carried on the warm breeze, assaulted his senses.

'Excuse me,' Daley shouted as he tried to shoulder his way through the gathered locals.

'Aye, let the officer past,' a member of the crowd called.

'C'mon, let the main man through!' someone else insisted. 'Can you no' see how tired-lookin' he is?' This spread a frisson of mirth amongst the early morning onlookers.

'Nae wonder. I'd be stayin' in my bed a' day wae that wee cracker.' At this, many of the locals – despite the visceral scene before them and the bitter smell – burst into gales of laughter.

Though he was used to the banter, the early hour and something about the locus made him angry; the crowd of people so anxious to see the remains of a fellow human being made him feel suddenly sick. He turned on his heel. 'Right, that's enough! Someone has lost their life here and all you can think to do is laugh and joke. I am treating this as a crime scene until I know otherwise, so I want you all to move back and let us get on with our work, otherwise I will be instructing my officers to make arrests. Constables, if you would.' He beckoned to the uniformed officers, who began to push the now much more pliant gathering away from the pontoons.

Daley ducked under the yellow police tape and felt his trousers strain at the behind. Thankful that they remained intact, a small mercy, he walked to the edge of what was left of one of the buoyant decking piers that made up the yacht moorings. Members of the fire brigade were aboard a small wooden vessel, the front of which was badly burned. It was secured next to what could best be described as a gaping black hole which had turned the far end of the decking into an island. He stepped towards the uniformed sergeant and two suited figures who had their backs to him, all peering into the shallow waters of the loch.

'Good morning, gentlemen. An update please, DS Rainsford.'

A tall young man in a sharply tailored suit walked towards him. His long thin face and angular features lent him a haughty look; he wore his hair short and parted to one side. He was slightly taller than Daley who, faced with such sartorial elegance in his junior, felt the subconscious need to adjust his hastily knotted tie.

'Good morning, sir. As you can see, I thought it best that we try to remove the body from the water as soon as possible.' He gestured towards three men who were waist deep in water, two of whom Daley recognised as members of the local RNLI, the other a fire and rescue officer. The lifeboat men wore orange wetsuits, while the fireman had to make do with a pair of yellow waders, over which water was already lapping. 'The tide's on its way in, sir. I trust you appreciate the need for action – even before SOCO get here.' Rainsford's accent sounded neither Scottish nor English – neutral, Daley always thought.

'What about corruption of the scene?' he asked, anxious that no evidence be lost in the attempt to retrieve the body from the loch.

'If we don't get the body out of there it'll start to degrade rapidly, I'm afraid, Jim.' Daley turned towards the short, fat figure of Dr Richard Spence, one of the local doctors, all of whom, given Kinloch's remoteness, dealt with police matters as and when necessary. Daley liked the man, unlike some of the less police-friendly members of the practice, and respected his opinion.

'That's the trouble with this type of thing,' Spence continued. 'Fry 'em then immerse them in cold water. It's a bit like doing it with a side of beef, bits will start coming off – especially in salt water. Best we get him – or her – out of there as soon as we can, Jim.'

Daley thanked the doctor, then turned back to the DS. 'So what else do we know?'

'I spoke to the pontoon manager on the phone a few minutes ago, sir. The boat's called *The Alba*, she docked here yesterday lunchtime. A man named Walter Cudihey booked the vessel in and paid his berthing fees by credit card; the manager's going to email me the details as soon as he gets into the office. I'm also checking with the RYA to see if he's registered with them.' He smiled confidently. 'Apart from fire and rescue personnel dealing with the fire on board the vessel, nobody has touched it.' Rainsford raised his brows and looked down his nose. 'Thought it best we wait for you before commencing a search, sir.'

Daley nodded curtly. 'Yes, you did the right thing, DS Rainsford.' The young detective sergeant had been in place for nearly four months; he was efficient, knowledgeable and bright, though something about his manner irritated Daley. Perhaps it was his honours degree in sociology, his trim physique, or his somewhat patronising manner – maybe a mixture of all three. He supposed he reminded him vaguely of his hated brother-in-law, Mark Henderson. In any event there was something about Marcus Rainsford that Jim Daley didn't like. And he couldn't ignore the obvious: simply, DS Rainsford, despite his undoubted intelligence and grasp of the minutiae of police procedure, lacked one thing – he wasn't Brian Scott.

It took over an hour for the body, by way of an impromptu hoist, to be removed from the loch, during which time SOCO officers arrived to carry out a forensic assessment of the craft and what was left of the pontoon. The body was being prepared to be taken to Glasgow by helicopter so that a detailed post mortem could take place. Locals lined the street as Daley drove up the hill and in through the gates of Kinloch Police Office.

'Excuse me, sir.' DC Dunn was already at her desk, her open laptop displaying some hazy black-and-white images. 'I thought you might want to see this,' she said, gesturing towards the screen.

Daley leaned over her, placing his hand on the back of her chair to prop himself up as he squinted at the laptop. Her hair smelled of strawberries and he watched, absently fascinated, as she used the keyboard scrolling function with one long thin finger to rewind the on-screen footage.

'Here, sir.' The image froze, bringing to a halt a long array of numbers at the top of the screen which meant little to him; in the bottom right-hand corner, the time was displayed as 04:17:23. 'This is footage from the CCTV camera at the head of the pier, sir. It covers the area quite well, though – well, you'll see for yourself.' She clicked an arrow on the screen and the image began to move.

Though the picture was monochrome it was well defined. There was a flash as the cabin door of *The Alba* swung open, revealing a short, fat bald man, wearing a T-shirt and shorts, carrying a large square container in one hand. Daley watched as he jumped easily onto the pontoon and out of shot.

'What now?' he asked, for some reason looking at the top of Dunn's head.

'Just a second – keep watching, sir.'

There was a flash which momentarily turned the laptop screen white. As the glare faded, the flames that now engulfed the yacht could be seen flickering on the extreme left of the picture.

'There we have it,' said Daley, standing up with a long sigh.

'No, wait a minute, sir, that's not all.' Dunn set the image swirling backwards at high speed as she rewound the footage. Daley, leaning back over her again, looked on as the time on the bottom right of the screen scrolled backwards. 'Once I isolated the actual event, I thought I'd do a quick recap to see what happened in the time prior to the fire.' She looked up at Daley and smiled at him. 'Watch.' She stopped the footage at 02:07:48.

Again the cabin door swung open, though this time no sunlight flashed against the porthole. Two men stepped onto the narrow deck of the vessel, one of whom looked very unsteady on his feet. Daley watched as this man was helped over the deck and towards the pontoon by the man with the bald head and Bermuda shorts. Dunn stopped the image, just as the unsteady figure stood up straight and looked in the general direction of the camera. There was no mistake – even at this distance, Hamish's face was unmistakeable.

'Oh no,' Daley groaned.